DAVID ESSEX

Faded Glory

D0528623

HEAD
of ZEUS

First published in the UK in 2016 by Head of Zeus, Ltd.

This paperback edition first published in 2017 by Head of Zeus, Ltd.

9 7 5 3 1 2 4 6 8

A catalogue record for this book is available from
the British Library.

ISBN (PB): 9781784082529
ISBN (E): 9781784082352

Typeset by Adrian McLaughlin

Printed and bound in Great Britain by
CPI Group (UK) Ltd, Croydon CR0 4YY

Head of Zeus Ltd
First Floor East
5–8 Hardwick Street
London, EC1R 4RG

WWW.HEADOFZEUS.COM

For Mum and Dad

Faded Glory

CHAPTER ONE
1953

FLAMING June. Bloody typical.

Albert Charles Kemp smiled at the bedraggled street party. The flags were soaked, the kids' jelly only just edible. Despite the rain, this was a special day, a new Queen crowned and nothing would stop the celebrations. Nothing apart from the weather could rain on this parade.

East London may have been battered and bombed in the Blitz, but these people were brave, proud and full of love for the Royal Family. They had long memories too, remembering the new Queen Mother's many trips to East London and how she'd helped lift morale through the bad times. Their affection for her and her family was overflowing, filling every street party with *God Save the Queen*, *Rule Britannia* and the exciting sense of a new beginning.

Together with a small crowd of locals, Albert had watched the history-making ceremony on a black-and-white television through a local electrical shop window. Now he watched the families dressed in their Sunday best, kids running here and there, mums and dads talking, singing, dancing; a community united. As he walked through the streets full of bunting, Albert felt a sense of belonging. These rough and ready neighbours were his people, these were his streets and this was his home.

Albert lived in a rented, one-bedroom flat on top of a shop that sold second-hand toot. The owner, Simon, never tired of looking, searching, for that elusive Fabergé egg, or an old master in someone's unsuspecting attic. A lover of Sousa's marching music and with a military, waxed moustache to match, Simon and his merchandise belonged to a bygone age. Whenever he saw Albert, Simon would give his usual military-style salute, delivered in a battered German helmet from the war. It had made Albert smile the first few times, but had now become tedious.

Albert reached his front door.

"Greetings, Kemp," called Simon, a Union Jack flag draped around his shoulders like a greatcoat.

Albert nodded with a smile of recognition, put his hand through the letter box and reached for the key to his flat.

In 1953, a door key hanging down on a piece of string through the letter box or under the door mat was the norm in this part of the world. Most of the time, front doors were just left open. Turning his back on a spirited version of the Hokey Cokey kicking off a few doors down, Albert turned the key and went in.

The stairs to his flat creaked reassuringly underneath the cracked brown linoleum. He had climbed this wooden hill so many times that the familiar worn beige and faded pink wallpaper, the nondescript stairwell, felt like home. For better or worse, it was home.

Trying hard to ignore the smell of boiled cabbage that often seemed to prevail, Albert hummed *Land of Hope and Glory* as he progressed slowly up the stairs. Reaching the worn welcome mat on his threshold, he fumbled through his grey raincoat for a second key to open the half-glazed ill-fitting door to his world.

Not that this world was that important to Albert. Two rooms, a few memories and a roof over his head was good enough. A head that once boasted dark and curly hair had now matured with age to silver. A face still handsome, but battered by almost sixty years of struggle. A tough life of World Wars, hard work and the open wounds of faded glory. Still a fit man, Albert had the face of a boxer and the heart of a lion.

Once inside, he closed the door, took off his wet raincoat and hung up his brown trilby hat: a hat he was very proud of, bought from a milliner in the West End to celebrate the end of World War Two.

Rocky, Albert's pet budgie, cheeped a cheery hello as if sensing the excitement in the air flowing from the streets below, while Albert filled the kettle, put a shilling in the meter and lit the gas. In the corner, a comfortable but worn old armchair sat and waited patiently for its owner. On it, Albert had placed a regal cushion recently bought from Simon at a bargain price, commemorating the Coronation of Queen Elizabeth II. He was proud of that.

The kettle's homely whistle spluttered with a head of steam and competed with Rocky's cheerful chirping and a chorus of *Knees Up Mother Brown* from the street below. Albert washed out the lived-in teapot and spooned tea leaves into it. Tea-making ritual concluded, cup in hand, Albert decided to engage his flatmate in conversation.

"Good bird, Rocky."

Rocky responded with a dance of excitement and some manic chirping as Albert unlatched the cage. With a whisper of wind, the budgie took flight, stopping to perch on the room's plastic cream lampshade. Albert took to his armchair, tea in hand. Alone as usual.

His wife, Vera, had died six years ago. The doctors had said it was cancer, but Albert knew it was really from a broken heart. Losing their only son Tommy at the beginning of the war had been a devastating blow for both of them. They said time was a healer, but time had never really healed the heartbreak of Tommy or the loss of Albert's first and only love. It had left scars. But Albert was not a man to wear his heart on his sleeve and he kept the hurt well hidden.

"Good bird, Rocky," he murmured again.

Just when Albert thought Rocky was actually going to say something back, there was a knock on the door.

"Mr Kemp?"

Albert recognised the voice of Mr Abrahams, his landlord and the local money lender.

"A word, Mr Kemp?"

Albert opened the door and Abrahams came in. He was a pale man in his late sixties, wearing his usual long black coat, pigtails and black hat, the uniform of his orthodox religion. He gave Albert a grudging half smile.

"Mr Kemp, good day. I see your rent is overdue."

"I get paid this week Mr Abrahams, you'll have it by Monday."

"That's good Mr Kemp, that is good." Abrahams sniffed the air. "You should open a window, freshen this place up. It smells like a fish market."

Albert remembered the nice piece of smoked haddock he had treated himself to for yesterday's tea. Advice delivered, Abrahams circumnavigated a low-flying Rocky, avoiding one of Rocky's deposits, and pointing to the window he said, "A lovely day Mr Kemp, people coming together" and left with the same grudging smile.

Albert returned to his tea and armchair, switched on the radio and, with Rocky now on his shoulder, listened to the music of the day. Looking around the room, his mind wandered through the sense memories of his possessions: the trophies, the photographs, the snapshots of his life. A picture of Tommy in uniform sat in pride of place on the mahogany sideboard beside boxing trophies, a champion's belt and a yellowing photograph of Albert in his prime, bruised and battered and holding the same boxing belt proudly above his head. There was much to look back on at his age, but not too much to look forward to.

Lost in his thoughts and memories, the chime of a carriage clock on the mantelpiece brought him back with a jolt to the present.

"Six o'clock, Rocky mate," he told the budgie. "Time for me to get going."

Putting the bird back in the cage, Albert put on his coat and treasured hat and headed back down the stairs.

He knew these cobbled streets like he knew his own skin.

They were the streets where he had grown up, streets which were often cloaked in a yellow-grey fog fuelled by the coal-burning of the Victorian terrace houses, local factories and the close proximity to the River Thames and the London docks. Ocean-going ships towered over everything like high-rise blocks from distant shores, emptying strange foreign sailors in exotic dress into the East End streets.

Albert turned the corner and walked past a derelict space, a living memory of the Blitz, where a German bomb had flattened all below it. A street party and happy celebrations now filled the site, children playing and adults celebrating, their Coronation party still in full swing and set fair to go on till late, or until the drink finally ran out. On Albert walked, under the railway arches and on to his place of work, a Victorian public house called the Live and Let Live.

The Live and Let Live was gearing up for a busy opening time, creatively decked out in bunting by Maurice the land-lord and his wife Maria to celebrate the Coronation. It was a cosy, well lived-in establishment, filled with horse brasses, toby jugs, dark wood and the smell of tobacco and beer. Albert worked in the pub as a pot man, collecting glasses and helping out behind the bar. After years of working in the Royal Docks, where each morning the dockers would line up hoping for work on what was called the "Stones", desperate to be picked out by a charge hand to join a gang to load or unload the waiting ships in dock, the relative security of the part-time pub work suited Albert just fine.

They knew Albert here and respected him, and the job brought Albert a little money, which helped. But most importantly, upstairs was a boxing gym, an important link for Albert to the noble art and his glorious past.

After a quick "Evening all", Albert headed towards the boxing gym. The loud voice of Maria, feisty wife of the landlord, followed him up the stairs.

"Albert, don't you be long! It's getting busy, I'm gonna need some help!"

Upstairs, three or four hopefuls were punching bags, while in the ring itself, two men were sparring under the watchful eye of trainer and gym owner Patsy O'Neill.

"Albert," said Patsy in his usual ferocious bark. "Will you come and teach these girls to punch?"

"Not today Pat, I think that day has long gone," Albert replied.

Patsy pushed his ham-like hands through his receding curly hair and glared at the sparring pair. "Now that's a champ, boys. I'm telling you, that boy could fight."

"Yeah," Albert replied, "before these two were born, when dinosaurs roamed the Hackney Marshes. Any glasses up here from last night?"

Albert went back down to the bar with a few wayward empties. It was filling up, locals drifting in and pints being pulled. The regulars were mainly dockers, local men with stories to tell, decked out in a collective uniform of flat caps, leather jerkins and strong arms. A couple of ladies, a little past their prime, were sipping Guinness and gossiping at a corner table. Over by the door, Dolly played her heart out on the piano. The clientele sang along, not always in the same key, but with gusto. These were Albert's people, salt of the earth, working-class folk, and he moved around the smoke-filled room with the odd smile here and the odd conversation there.

But although most people knew Albert, he had always been a man of few friends. Some old mates had passed on, others had moved away to greener pastures in Essex and Kent: an exodus that would become the norm, as Londoners looked to better themselves and bring up their children in fresher and cleaner air. New towns were being planned to house them, towns like Harlow and Stevenage, but as far as Albert was concerned, he was East End born and bred and that was where he was staying.

At the bar of the busy pub, sat Black Lenny, Albert's closest friend. Lenny had come over from Jamaica actually on a banana boat, landing at Southampton with the first influx of immigrants from the Caribbean, bound for the National Health Service, public transport and a new hopeful beginning. After working initially as a hospital porter, Lenny had scrimped and saved and was now the proud owner of a car repair shop, situated locally under the railway arches.

"Did you get that motor going yet, Len?" asked Albert.

"Yes Albert, the old banger is running sweet now, ticking over."

"A bit like me then Lenny, an old banger ticking over."

The men, although from different worlds, got on like a house on fire. Albert endured endless ribbing from Lenny about the West Indies' recent cricket victories over England, with "Ramadhin should be made the king of the Caribbean" being Lenny's constant observation. Albert enjoyed the stories Lenny would tell him of a distant world that he would never visit, of golden beaches and a sun-drenched Jamaica, while Lenny would love hearing stories and memories from Albert about his glory days and the boxing world. Albert was often reluctant to go down memory lane with its many dark shadows and painful yesterdays, but if Lenny pushed hard enough, the effort was worth it. After all, Albert was a man with an impressive past and stories to tell.

"Last orders!"

The ring of the bar bell finally came, followed again by a more determined "Last orders please!"

Albert rounded up the glasses, helped to wash up, collected his wages and with a "Night all", headed for home. The rain outside seemed to sparkle on the cobblestones, softly lit by street lamps that did their best to penetrate the misty night and the damp air. The remnants of the earlier street parties were now few and far between, just a few folks persevering by the dying embers of a celebratory bonfire, talking and laughing.

Back inside the flat, Albert put another shilling in the hungry meter, lit the blue-flamed gas fire and turned on his precious gramophone. He owned a large collection of classical records (this new "rock 'n' roll jungle music" wasn't for him), and after choosing Elgar's Cello Concerto, he sat down to reflect on the day.

The Coronation celebrations reminded him of the celebrations when the war had ended and Britain danced in the streets. He and Vera hadn't danced. Instead they had looked to the sky as if searching for Tommy, hoping he could see that his sacrifice was not in vain. Tonight, with patriotism on every street corner, Albert thought about his son, killed in action just weeks after joining the fight for freedom. How full of life he looked in the photograph, sitting there on Albert's sideboard. There in his uniform, so proud to fight for King and Country.

Although not a sentimental man, past adventures, good and bad, would sometimes engulf Albert. This was one of those times. Memories of the women and children he had tried to save as part of the home guard – their screams, tears and desperation – still cut like it was yesterday. He had been too old to enlist, turned away by the army, but had done all he could at home in the burning streets of London. Sometimes it hadn't felt like enough.

Broken from his thoughts by the clock striking twelve and Rocky's twittering, Albert decided it was time to clear his head of the dark shadows that often seemed insurmountable in the wee small hours. Covering up the budgie's cage for the night and turning off the gas fire and gramophone, his usual late cup of Ovaltine in hand, Albert went to bed.

The next morning, awoken by the foghorns of the ships gliding through the foggy dockyards, Albert rose, had a cup of tea, a wash and brush-up and then, as usual, set off for what had become his morning ritual: a walk round the park, feed the ducks, then back home for breakfast or, if he had money, to the local cafe for a full English.

Albert cherished this oasis, where the birds of London did their best to sing as the sun broke through the late-morning fog. As he walked his usual path armed with a paper bag filled with stale bread, the dark memories of the night before melted away in the morning light.

Crossing the small bridge that led down to the lake, he saw a gang of five or six likely lads having a kick-about. He smiled to himself as he watched their antics. Their lack of footballing prowess was amusing, a toe punt here and a sliding tackle there and many wayward passes. "Not much of a career in football there," he thought.

As Albert reached the lake, the ducks seemed to recognise him as their friend and, in a quacking frenzy, came swimming to greet him as fast as their webbed feet would carry them. Albert found their attention and reliance on his morning visits something he enjoyed. It felt good to be needed. He had not gone as far as naming each one, but he recognised them individually and did his best to see that each one at least got a share of the bread.

He was lost in his duck duty when a mis-hit shot from the gang of boys flew like a cannon ball, hitting Albert in the back, scattering the ducks and causing the wayward football to land in the lake.

"Oi, Grandad! Can we have our ball back?" cried one of the gang.

"Why don't you watch what you're doing," Albert muttered.

"What's the matter Pop, did we scare your ducks?"

The youths started making quacking noises. From out of nowhere, Albert felt the threat of violence. He could smell it in the air as the boys closed in on him.

"Whoever touched the ball last has to fetch it, Duck Man," one said. "That was you Pops, wasn't it? So in you go," threatened another.

Albert was past his best as a fighter, but giving in to these yobs was something he certainly wasn't going to do. Then he recognised a flashing glint in the morning sun. A flick knife.

Albert's reflexes kicked in. Swiftly knocking the knife from the boy's hand, he followed up with a crashing left hook that not only floored the boy, but caused three or four of the gang to retaliate.

Albert's unexpected fight back had raised the stakes and hostility.

Giving as good as he got, but overpowered by their numbers, Albert lost his footing and was manhandled into the lake, much to the amusement of the gang.

"Push him under!"

"Swim Grandad, go on! swim like a duck!"

As Albert went under, his life flashed before his eyes. He saw his Championship-winning boxing match, his son's face before he went to war and never came back, a bright white light. His body was going limp, the light now fading...

Then, as if to break through the underwater nightmare, two hands lifted him out of the water and pulled him to the lakeside. Coming round, belching and coughing, Albert looked up to see one of the boys standing over him. They looked silently at each other. Somewhere in the boy's eyes, Albert saw a hint of compassion.

"Danny, just leave the old git! We're going!"

With one last look, the boy left Albert on the bank and caught up with the others now waiting at the park gates, still quacking and laughing.

When they had gone, Albert shakily got to his feet. His pride was hurt, but apart from a few aches and bruises, he was in pretty good shape. Soaking wet and smelling like a duck pond, he sat on a park bench, the same one he always sat on, thinking over what had just happened. His thoughts first went to the boy that helped him, then to the other boys and their lack of respect. They had seen him as old, past it. When had that happened? Albert's generation had respected and learned from their elders. Now, it seemed they were just there to ridicule, ignore and take advantage of.

"Things are not changing for the better," Albert thought grimly as he squelched his way back towards home.

Suffering some pretty strange looks from passers-by, bedraggled and damp, he made it home and lit the gas fire. Shakily putting on his bath robe, he washed the pond-soaked clothes in a tin bath usually reserved for bath nights. Putting the wet clothes on a wooden clothes horse by the glowing blue gas fire, his eyes went to the photo of his son. He took the photo from the sideboard and lost himself in it for a while. How different Tommy had been to the yobs in the park. He'd had respect.

Putting the cherished photograph back in its place, Albert picked up his boxing belt and wondered about the vivid pictures he had seen underwater. Had he been drowning? Dying?

One thing was for sure. Come rain or shine, he would not be intimidated. He would be back in the park tomorrow.

"No gang of idiots are going to stop me," he thought. "Besides, the ducks will be hungry."

CHAPTER TWO

RECOVERED from his ordeal and ready for work, Albert made his way to the Live and Let Live. There were a couple of amateur fights that night in Patsy's gym to look forward to, and Albert liked to take an interest. You never know; Patsy and him might one day unearth a contender.

He was looking forward to meeting up with Black Lenny too. Len liked a bit of boxing, perhaps not as much as his passion for cricket, but he enjoyed sharing Albert's passion for the game.

When Len had first moved into the railway arches, Albert had been suspicious. The white working classes had resented this big influx of people that looked so different, with a different culture. Feelings had run high, there were race riots in London and a lot of resentment. But Albert, in time, had come to respect Lenny. He respected the fact that Black Lenny was brave enough to enter and become a regular in a pub, ignoring the hostile looks and misgivings of the white locals, persevering, and finally showing that he was actually just like one of them. Len was now accepted by most and had become part of the East End fabric. He even had his favourite seat next to the stairs to the boxing gym and his favoured tipple was a pint of brown and mild.

Just like clockwork, Lenny came into the public bar for his evening drink. A lean Jamaican, wearing the beret that he always wore, some kind of calypso shirt and a broad smile the moment he saw Albert.

"Did you see the Queen?" he said. "Man, she looked lovely." Although Lenny still had a Jamaican accent which somehow conjured up golden beaches and palm trees, it was now peppered with the occasional Cockney twang. "What time do the fights start, mate?"

"We can go up now, Len. The usual?"

Albert poured Lenny's pint and the two friends made their way upstairs. Inside the sweat-smelling gym sat an audience of twenty or so expectant punters. There were ex-fighters, likely wide boys and the odd painted lady, all mixed up with some of the fighters' friends and families. First on the bill were two lightweights from rival boxing clubs: one from Patsy's West Ham, the other from the Elephant and Castle.

The first of the three-round contests started, amidst a muted vocal reaction from the clientele. The Canning Town boy fighting for West Ham was a lanky ginger lad with quick hands. He seemed to be in charge, and after three scrappy rounds was given the referee's verdict. Two more fights followed, with two wins for West Ham and one for the Elephant and Castle.

In the interval before the final fight, an eagerly anticipated heavyweight contest, Albert and Lenny decided to take a break from a cigar-smoking local businessman sitting too close for comfort. Stepping outside to get a breath of the fresher night air, they gave their verdicts on the future prospects of the fighters they had seen.

"They're good boys Len, but nothing special," said Albert.

Lenny was about to reply when the sound of breaking glass shattered the night air. It was coming from the direction of Lenny's garage.

"What was that?" Albert exclaimed.

They both ran to see what was happening. In the distance, they could see a group of young men, some running, a couple on bikes, laughing and making themselves scarce outside Lenny's archway garage.

"Go back to Africa!"

"Black bastard!"

It was the same gang that had attacked Albert in the park. Amongst them, Albert saw the boy that helped him out of the water. Danny. That had been his name.

"Bastards," said Albert. "Bloody idiots!"

Daubed over Lenny's garage doors was "Wogs Out" and "Nigger". Two windows were also broken.

"Scum, Lenny! Scum!" said Albert angrily.

There was a strange quietness in the empty street as Lenny and Albert surveyed the damage. Albert lent down to pick up the broken glass.

"I can sort it out in the morning Albert," said Lenny quietly. "Leave it now, it's OK. Leave it."

Albert felt ashamed that a bunch of yobs had done this to his friend. He somehow felt responsible that boys born and bred in his country, the country he loved, could do this.

"All right Len," he said, seeing Lenny was hurt and needing some time on his own. "I'll drop by in the morning. Sorry about this."

Subdued and angry, with a goodnight pat on Lenny's shoulder, Albert made the short walk back to his flat. Once inside with his usual cup of Ovaltine – a habit from when he was a little boy and an enthusiastic "Ovaltiney" – Albert sat down in his chair, his thoughts roving through the night's events. The lack of respect worried him. It was the nineteen fifties and times were changing, youth was rebelling, modern music was everywhere. This music of the young meant nothing to Albert's generation but everything, it seemed, to these "teenagers": the new word for kids these days. Some of these "teenagers" seemed intent on causing disruption and change with their hob-nail boots and attitude. Nothing good could come of this. Nothing at all.

In the morning, Albert decided to leave the ducks till later and see how Lenny was doing.

At the arches, Len was replacing the glass in one window and had nailed some plywood to the other.

"Almost as good as new, Albert," said Lenny with a wry smile.

"Lovely," said Albert. "I'll make a start on the writing they did."

"Yeah," said Lenny. He scratched his head. "I thought 'Wog' was short for 'Western Oriental Gentleman' and here I am from Jamaica. 'Go back to Africa'? I ain't ever been."

"Don't worry about it, Len," said Albert. "We can get you a loin-cloth and a couple of spears and you can sort 'em out."

Len smiled. "Yeah man, put me down for some poison darts and a big cooking pot!"

The two men set about getting rid of the offensive graffiti with brushes, soap and water. As they scrubbed, a bicycle flew by, ridden by a boy with a girl perched on the crossbar. It was the boy that had pulled Albert from the water in the park. Danny.

"Oi son, can I have a word?" Albert shouted.

The boy ignored him and rode on by, as the girl on the crossbar giggled in defiance.

"You know that kid?" said Lenny with an enquiring look.

Albert pictured the boy the night before, under the arches with the rest of the gang at the scene of the crime.

"I just thought he might know the idiots who did this," he said aloud.

Why wasn't he telling Lenny the boy had been part of the gang? Part of Albert hoped the boy was an outsider who had just fallen in with bad company. Perhaps he deserved a second chance. After all, he had helped Albert when he was dumped in the lake, and Albert had seen compassion in his eyes.

He straightened up from the clean and dripping wall. "Job done clean as a whistle, Len," he said. "I'm off to the park."

"Them ducks must be getting fat," said Lenny. "Thanks for your help, Albert. I'll see you later."

★

As Albert walked home, he felt in two minds. Maybe he shouldn't have protected this boy Danny, but he felt there was good in him somehow. He only looked about sixteen, younger than the others. No doubt the older yobs were a bad influence.

Getting back to his flat, he picked up some old bread and headed out to the park. If the yobs were there again, he would confront them and give them a piece of his mind. Straighten them up. And feed the ducks of course.

It was good to get some fresher air and exercise. Albert loved to hear the birds sing in the welcome oasis of the park, a sanctuary away from the busy and dirty streets. He enjoyed monitoring the growth and progress of the flowers and trees. He knew the names of some of the flowers and a few of the trees: his favourites were a stately weeping willow that seemed to reach down and almost touch the lakes and a scented rose garden, full of colour and sweet-smelling scent. He felt closer to nature and its wonder in this place where worries and trials floated away, where Mother Nature reassured and healed.

Today, thankfully, was much less eventful than yesterday. The ducks and their ducklings were either pleased to see Albert, or pleased to have an easy lunch. Albert was their friend and they would regularly take bread from his hand, as if they knew he was on their side. Pigeons and sparrows would come and join in the feast too. Albert had a special liking for a brave robin with his red breast, pride and impressive courage.

Things felt more normal after Albert had fed his feathered

friends. But he still didn't know why he hadn't let on to Lenny that the boy Danny was a part of the crew that damaged his garage, and he felt a little guilty that he had not been honest.

"The boy must have some good in him," he reassured himself as he walked back home for a late breakfast. "Just in with the wrong crowd."

After a swift bowl of porridge, Albert fed the hungry Rocky with a stick of millet. He'd named his budgie Rocky in honour of the legendary boxer Rocky Marciano; only to find out later from his military neighbour Simon, a bird fancier (with and without feathers), that Rocky was actually a girl.

"A lady," Lenny had chuckled when he found out. "I'll call her Marion, just to annoy you, Albert."

It was time to get to work for the early shift workers and lunch-time drinkers. As Albert walked across the wasteland that had once been a terrace of Victorian houses now flattened by the Blitz, he saw a boy with his bike turned upside-down, trying to fix it. Albert stopped. It was Danny.

The boy's head was bent over the bicycle chain as Albert walked up behind him and whispered a little menacingly: "Hello son. Remember me?"

Danny looked startled and wary, but said nothing.

"What's the problem?"

Albert let the question hang in the air. Danny stared at him with wide eyes.

"I don't think what they did last night was right," Danny blurted.

Maybe there really was some good in the boy after all, thought Albert. There was something in the boy's eyes too, something that reminded him of Tommy. Although he had been intending to give the boy what for, he softened.

"So," he said. "Looks like your bike's broke."

The boy nodded. "The chain's broke or something."

"Yeah, well I know who can fix it," said Albert. "Follow me."

And not waiting for an answer, he put the bike on his shoulder and marched off.

Danny followed reluctantly, weighing up the pros and cons. It was important to get the bike fixed because he cherished the freedom it gave him. Perhaps this old fella could actually fix it.

Albert walked on like the Pied Piper with Danny following behind. But when they arrived at Lenny's garage, Danny stopped in his tracks.

"Where we going?" he said uneasily. "Give me my bike back."

"He won't eat you, son," said Albert. "He hasn't got a big enough cooking pot."

Danny froze like a statue. But a persuasive arm round the shoulder and a gentle nudge from Albert moved them both into Lenny's archway workshop.

Underneath a white Triumph Mayflower car, amidst grunts and groans, protruded two legs clad in Lenny's usual dark blue and greasy overalls. Lenny slid out.

"Nice motor," he said. "Running sweet as a nut." He clocked Danny standing nervously behind Albert. "Albert man, who's your friend?"

"This is Danny, Len," said Albert. "His chain's broke."

Lenny made that noise he always made when confronted with a job, a kind of hissing noise through his teeth. "Let me take a look," he said.

"I ain't got any money," Danny said, feeling very uncomfortable.

"Well, maybe if you're a friend of Albert, we can do you a favour."

Lenny was one of those people that seemed to have everything somewhere: nuts, bolts, bits of engines. If he didn't have exactly what he needed, he could adapt something to fix the problem.

"I need to find a link," he said after studying the broken chain, and made off into the vast amount of precious clutter hoarded in the back room.

Through the open door, Danny could see some of Lenny's prized personal possessions: a signed cricket bat, photos of family back in Jamaica. One photograph in particular caught Danny's eye, a photo of a younger Lenny proudly posing in an army uniform with medals shining on his chest.

Danny couldn't fight back his surprise.

"I never knew that black people fought in the war," he said as Lenny returned from the back room. "Were you a soldier? Like, in the war?"

"Yeah, for all the good it did me," Lenny replied with a

grunt and a hiss as he attempted to fix the chain back on the bike.

"My dad was a soldier too, but he got killed," said Danny. "He never came home."

There was a silence, broken only by the sound of a train rumbling overhead.

"I'm sorry, son," said Albert. "A lot of 'em never came back."

"Got you!" Lenny exclaimed as the chain slid sweetly back into position. Danny couldn't help a smile of relief.

"Do you think your dad would approve of you hanging out with those troublemakers?" Albert asked.

Danny shook his head in a moment of remorse. "But there's nothing to do round here," he added, back on the offensive.

"What about sport or something? Football, or boxing?" Albert suggested. "There's a boxing gym at the Live and Let Live."

"Yes," said Lenny. "Back in his day Albert here was a champion boxer – you don't wanna mess with him boy. Or try cricket, a proper game, that's the way to go."

"Not for me," said Danny, taking his bike, and with a nod of thanks he rode away.

Riding slowly through the streets, Danny thought about Lenny and Albert. Sure, they were still a pair of old tossers, but he respected the things they had done in their lives. Lenny could fix things and had been a soldier. Albert was a champion boxer. That was pretty impressive.

Danny regretted being a part of the gang that had attacked Albert and vandalised Lenny's garage. Albert's advice began to resonate the closer he got to home. Maybe that boxing suggestion could be a goer. A way to earn both money and respect, a purpose.

Many of the streets round here had been flattened in the war, leaving wasteland to serve as an adventure playground for the local kids. A bomb crater here, a derelict half-house there, an awful reminder of the not-too-distant past; thankfully now filled with laughter and games.

One large piece of wasteland doubled as a street market. Blankets were laid out with stuff to sell by folks trying to make a few bob, alongside stalls full of fruit and veg and all manner of things. The market was well patronised by the locals and the sailors off the berthed ships waiting dormant in the docks; ships unloaded with goods from faraway places and reloaded with goods "Made in England". Chinamen, Indians and men from all corners of the world mingled with the locals without any resentment or strange looks. It was as if they all knew that this part of London had a history of welcoming people and immigrants from far-off shores.

Danny and his mum had been evacuated in the war to escape the bombing, like many of the city's women and children, and sent to live with a nice lady called Mrs Packham and her grumpy husband in Burton on Trent. Danny could not remember much about the adventure except for the train journey, which he'd loved. There'd been something magical about the steam-belching engine clickety-clacking through pastures new. He remembered an annoying little girl, the Packhams' daughter, who always tried to mimic Danny's London accent. Most of the local people who lost their homes after the war had been housed in pre-fabs that resembled Nissen huts, or in hasty, half-built blocks of flats. Danny's mum, as a single parent and wife of a lost soldier, had been housed in a Victorian terrace house, two up, two down, which had miraculously survived the bombs.

The door was open as usual. Danny could hear his mum's favourite record of the moment, Nat King Cole's *Unforgettable*, drifting down the street. It certainly was unforgettable, Rosie had played it so many times lately. It never seemed to be off the prized radiogram, bought cut-price as it had apparently "fallen off the back of a lorry".

Pushing his bike into the passage, Danny looked through the half-open door to the living room. His mother was locked in a romantic shuffle with her latest beau, thin, tattooed Ricky with his fashionable Tony Curtis haircut. Ricky wore a string vest, braces, navy-blue socks with bed fluff on them and ill-fitting brown trousers. His real name was Derek, but he preferred Ricky.

"Derek ain't rock 'n' roll," he had explained.

Unnoticed, Danny pushed on to the kitchen and into the back yard and parked his bike by the almost derelict garden shed. Going back into the kitchen, he grabbed a glass of water, downed a couple of gulps, took a deep breath and went into his mum's smoochy parlour.

Rosie Watson had a bit of a reputation. After a brief spell of mourning, when she had received the letter and visit to impart the sad news that her husband, Danny's father, wouldn't be coming home, she had soon become the local good-time gal. Ricky was the latest companion in what was a pretty long and less than impressive list.

"You're late, sugar plum," Rosie said. "Dinner's in the oven."

Danny ignored the invitation of burned offerings. "I got held up," he said. "My bike broke, and I met this old bloke who took me to that black fella with the garage under the arches. He fixed it."

"They shouldn't be over here," said Ricky, waving a half-full bottle of brown ale to make his point.

"He was all right," Danny said, feeling that he ought to defend Lenny. "He fought in the war. Like Dad."

"No mate," said Ricky, shaking his head. "There wasn't any spear chuckers in the war."

Danny wanted to set the record straight and put Ricky in his place, but decided it was probably a waste of energy.

"Where's Dad's war stuff, Mum?" he asked instead. The meeting with Albert and the photo of Lenny as a soldier had made him want to make contact with his lost father.

"Ooh I don't know, Dan," said Rosie, her eyes half-closed on Ricky's skinny shoulder. "Might be in the cupboard under the stairs. Why d'ya want it?"

"Just wanted to see it, that's all."

"All right darling. Have a look, your dad's stuff is in a tin box under the stairs."

Danny looked through the clutter that filled the cupboard. Right at the back, underneath a stinking old mop, he found a battered red and silver tin box. He reverently held the box in both hands, went upstairs to his room and sat on his bed.

Danny's dad had been killed very early on in the war,

before Danny had been born. He had never met his father, which was something he truly regretted. With his father's box, Danny felt closer to him, less alone. Looking at the photograph of his proud dad in uniform, Danny thought back to his empty childhood. He'd missed the trips they would have had to his dad's workplace, the Royal Docks: the massive ships, the cranes, the smell of spices. Not even his mother had come to watch his performance in the school nativity play. He wished he was in the photo, the way he'd seen other children, sitting high on their dads' shoulders. He would have felt like the king of the world.

Danny had always felt empty without a father, but looking now at his dad's photo, his war medals and some letters to Rosie, it felt more like a deep-seated ache. He missed his father so much. And he hated the stream of "uncles" and "dads" his mum had entertained over the years. He loved his mum, but not her philandering.

Danny had tried to ask his mum questions about his dad many times, but Rosie gave him very few answers. Maybe she felt too much pain talking about her late husband and preferred to put the past behind her, trying to forget. And forget she did. Within two months of the death of her husband and childhood sweetheart, she had married Danny's stepfather, Bill Watson. This had outraged her parents-in-law, who saw Rosie's actions as a serious lack of respect for the memory of their dead son. They'd broken off all ties with Rosie and young Danny, and the deep family rift still remained.

The whirlwind marriage to Bill Watson didn't last long, probably due to Rosie's wandering eye. After the war finished, Rosie and Bill went their separate ways and Rosie and Danny moved from Canning Town to Poplar, a couple of miles away.

"Bloody stupid war," Danny muttered as he closed the tin box.

The clock in the hall struck seven o'clock.

"Wendy," Danny said aloud.

Putting the tin box safely under his bed, he headed downstairs and grabbed his bike. With a quick look in the hall mirror to check his dark brown hair, he was out the door. Wendy was Danny's first and only girlfriend. Their friendship had begun when they were just eight years old at primary school. As a redhead, Wendy suffered many anti-ginger antics from the other pupils, despite maintaining that she was not ginger but strawberry blonde. Wendy now worked in a local sugar factory: a pretty girl, petite but strong, with twinkling green eyes and a freckled face like sunshine.

As soon as he left school, Danny had put his name down for the Royal Docks. Working at the docks was a family affair. You had to have a family member working there to get a look in, and as Danny's late father had been a docker before he joined the army, Danny was hopeful. In the meantime, waiting to be accepted, he did casual work on building sites.

Danny and Wendy would meet up after work, sometimes staying in at Wendy's house. Wendy's parents were part of a privileged few that owned a television: a modern black-and-white miracle in an oversized cabinet that would flicker away in the sitting-room corner to be watched in wonderment. Sometimes, Danny and Wendy would take a trip to the local flea-pit cinema the Imperial, if and when they had the money. But most times, just being together was enough.

Riding past Lenny's garage now, Danny thought of his recent encounter with Albert and Lenny. He decided to mention Albert's suggestion of taking up boxing at the Live and Let Live gym to Wendy and gauge her reaction.

Wendy's smart semi-detached house backed on to a cemetery, which had always worried Danny a little.

"I met that black bloke," he said, kissing her as he entered the warmth of the house. "You know the one with the garage that the others smashed up? He's friends with an old bloke that my mates pushed into the duck pond at the park."

Wendy looked shocked. "Why did they do that?"

"They shouldn't have done it," Danny agreed. "I helped him out."

"I should think so," said Wendy.

"Anyway," Danny went on, "they're all right. Lenny the black bloke fixed my bike and the other bloke, Albert, used to be a boxer. He reckons I should take up boxing, you know, to get off the streets and away from bad company."

Wendy's face filled with concern. "Boxing? What if you get hurt?"

"I'm only thinking about it," Danny said.

The truth was, Danny was starting to think seriously about Albert's suggestion. He was sixteen now and searching for something to break the same old scenario of hanging round street corners with his wayward friends, looking for trouble.

To clear the air and get back into Wendy's good books, he suggested they go out.

"Where to?"

"We could go to a pub," said Danny. "There's a good one in Canning Town called the Live and Let Live, we could go there. I'll buy you a Babycham," he added hopefully.

On the bus, Wendy told Danny about her day at the sugar factory, and something about a married foreman asking one of the girls out. Danny tried to seem interested, but was thinking about change, the possibility of getting something new in his life to break the old routine.

As the trolley bus turned the corner, Danny could see the coloured light bulbs that hung outside the Live and Let Live.

"This is us," he said.

Wendy looked at the pub doubtfully as they stood on the street.

"It's supposed to be all right in there," Danny reassured her.

"I don't know, Danny."

"Come on," Danny said. "We'll go in, shall we?"

They found a table in one of the quieter corners. Danny went to the bar to order. As he made his way through the busy clientele, he felt a hand on his shoulder.

"How's that bike of yours going?" asked Lenny.

"Yeah, going good," Danny replied. "Listen Lenny, have you seen Albert?"

Lenny thought for a moment. "I think he's upstairs in the gym. Anything to skip working. Who you here with?"

"My girlfriend."

"Nice," said Lenny, registering Wendy, who looked younger than her years, "but I reckon you're both underage.

I'll buy her a drink, save you breaking the law. Go take a look upstairs, I reckon that Albert's up there."

Danny tried to look indifferent. Deep down, that was why he was here.

"Sure thing, Lenny," he said. "I'll just let Wendy know where I'm going."

"Danny!" Wendy exclaimed. "Look who I bumped into."

Danny recognised the two girls sitting at their table. Wendy worked with them at the sugar factory. He felt a rush of relief.

"You'll be all right for a bit then?" he asked Wendy.

Wendy was already sipping the Babycham bought for her by Lenny and chewing over the latest gossip with her workmates. From the sound of it, the romantic antics of the foreman were high on the agenda. Leaving Wendy happily engrossed, Danny followed Lenny upstairs.

He could hear new sounds coming from above him. Punch bags being hit, ropes skipped, and orders being barked by a raucous Irishman. Danny felt a rush of adrenaline laced with apprehension.

The gym was heavy with the smell of leather and sweat, and full of shadowy figures dedicated to the noble art. Something about the place lit a spark in Danny. He was struck by the dedication, the fitness, the power.

Watching two likely lads from the corner of a well-used ring stood Albert.

"Hey Albert," shouted Lenny. "I've found your boy."

Albert turned. "Hello son," he said with a smile. "You made it. What do you think?"

Danny gave an impressed kind of nod.

"Come and meet the boss, Patsy, he's the trainer here," said Albert.

Patsy, huge and blond and hairy, assessed Danny. "If you can punch like this old champ, Albert," he said, "you could be a contender."

"I'm just looking," said Danny uneasily, well out of his comfort zone. "You know, out of interest. My girl's downstairs so I'd better go."

"Fair enough," said Albert. "Maybe come back some other time."

"Yeah maybe," said Danny.

He went back downstairs. Wendy was still chatting away to the girls from the factory, something about so and so and someone getting engaged because they were pregnant. Danny's thoughts were all of the boxing gym. Perhaps it was a way out.

But first there was work to do. He knew Wendy would not be keen on him taking up a sport that could damage him, or dedicating himself to something that would mean they would spend less time together. But something about this new horizon, this different world, was attracting him like a bee to honey.

Walking Wendy home, he gently brought up the subject of the boxing gym and how interesting it had been.

"It might be something to do," he said. "Somewhere to belong."

Wendy looked straight ahead. "If it's something you want to do, then I can't stop you can I?"

Her icy reaction came across like an Arctic wind.

"Nah, listen," Danny said. "I'm only thinking about it."

Wendy shrugged. "If you want to get your face smashed in, and you don't want to see me much 'cos you'll be busy bloody boxing, then great."

Danny kept quiet. He'd sampled Wendy's temper before, and it wasn't pleasant.

After a rather frosty kiss goodnight, he rode home full of mixed feelings. Up to now, Wendy had been his world. Now there was another world, and the door to it was open.

Despite Wendy's reaction, Danny felt excited about this new challenge. If he became a fighter, he could protect Wendy like he always had done, but even better. There was the question of respect too. He'd been respected at school by both his peers and the teachers, not because he was a good scholar, but because he was a good footballer. He missed that respect, had stupidly tried to get it back by hanging out with the wide boys in the park. It was time for that to change.

Back home, Rosie was half cut and Ricky was snoring on the sofa. As a means to escape Danny's fractured world, the gym seemed even more attractive.

"I might take up boxing, Mum," he said cautiously.

"What do you wanna do that for?" Rosie slurred, planting an alcohol-laced kiss on his reluctant lips. "Messing up your handsome face."

Danny escaped upstairs. He felt the need to reach underneath his bed and open the red and silver tin box again, to look at his father's photo.

"Do you think this boxing lark is a way to go, Dad?" he asked, looking into the eyes on the faded black-and-white photo. "What d'ya reckon?"

"Sure, son," the photo whispered in Danny's mind. "You go ahead. Show them what you're made of."

With no prospect of dock work in sight and to fill the long boring days, Danny decided to start training as soon as possible. It would be good for him to get fit. So the next morning he got up early. He even heard the cockerel crow from a nearby back yard.

"A bloody nuisance, that chicken," Rosie would often say, especially when she was woken after one of her many late nights.

Jogging to the park gates, Danny felt the sweet smell of fresher air inside him and power in his legs. This felt good. He ran and ran, finally taking a breather on a park bench. He had a purpose now. This was a new start.

Someone whistled at him from across the park. He looked up to see Vince and the other Canning Town boys watching him.

"Look at the state of you, Dan," said Vince, shaking his Brylcreemed head.

Danny was a fairly easy target, dressed in ill-fitting navy-coloured shorts, a vest, thick grey socks and hob-nail boots. He wasn't exactly an arbiter of fashion, or the cutting edge of a sportsman.

"What you doing Dan?" Vince sneered. "You look a right tosser."

"I've started training," Danny replied.

"Training? What for, to be a wanker?"

Derisive laughter followed. Danny decided not to rise to the bait. He began running again.

"He's scared," crowed one of the other boys. "He's running away."

Danny ran on through the park, his ears ringing with their jibes and laughter. If anything, they made him even more determined to make a fresh start. Being part of that gang of idiots was yesterday's news. He was looking to tomorrow.

Running towards the duck pond, he recognised Albert in the distance, feeding the ducks. The old man turned as he heard Danny's hob-nail boots pounding the path towards him.

"Blimey son," he remarked. "You training for the Olympics?"

"No," wheezed Danny. "Boxing."

A broad smile crossed Albert's face. "Seven o'clock at the gym?" he said.

Danny smiled back. "Seven it is," he said.

Albert was alone again with the ducks. He watched Danny run into the distance and smiled. Maybe. Just maybe.

The boy's enthusiasm was a positive thing. At least it would get him out of bad company. But only time would tell if he could last the course. If Danny was to make a new start, it would take dedication. Albert hoped for the best, but whispered to the ducks a few words of caution.

"Time will tell. We'll see."

CHAPTER THREE

THE clock in Danny's hall struck six-thirty. Tea finished, Danny was ready to go.

He still had not made peace with Wendy. He had tried saying that he wouldn't do too much boxing and just wanted to go to the gym to get fit, that was all, simple as that. But as yet, his reassurances had not worked. Hoping that Wendy would in time come round, Danny grabbed his bike and pedalled the streets to the Live and Let Live.

Albert was working the bar.

"Good to see you, Danny," he said. "Let's go on up, introduce you to Patsy properly."

Patsy O'Neill wore the scars of both life and the fight world. He'd come over as a fighter from Ireland and settled in the East End, a stocky, fit man in his fifties with bushy eyebrows, impressive sideburns and twinkling blue eyes.

Patsy had respect for Albert, but little respect for his flock of wannabe fighters. He'd seen too many of them fall by the wayside, unprepared for the realities of the boxing life.

"Right then," growled Patsy, hardly looking at Danny. "Let's get cracking. Put these on and take those bloody boots off."

Danny obeyed, putting on the boxing gloves and taking off his hob-nail training boots. He climbed into the ring with Patsy as Albert watched from the corner.

"Now hit these pads I'm holding," barked Patsy.

Much to both Albert and Patsy's surprise, Danny was good, his hands fast and pretty accurate.

"Not bad eh?" said Danny, feeling more confident.

"It ain't all about punching, lad," said Patsy.

The old trainer now put Danny through his paces. Exercise followed exercise until Danny was on the verge of exhaustion and green in the gills. As he lay panting in the centre of the ring, Patsy cheerfully dropped a medicine ball smack dab on Danny's exhausted stomach. Danny heaved and threw up.

"That'll be it for tonight then," said Patsy with a flinty nod.

Any wind of confidence knocked out of him, Danny dragged himself to his feet. He felt embarrassed for letting himself and his dad down. Part of the motivation for this adventure was to make his late father proud, and here he was throwing up.

"That wasn't a bad start," said Patsy, to Danny's surprise.

"Well done son," echoed Albert. "That kind of thing can happen when you push yourself too hard, but just keep pushing. Don't worry about the mess, I'll get a bucket and mop."

Danny felt a little better.

"See ya tomorrow, son." There seemed to be a hint of a threat in Patsy's words, a challenge to see if Danny was big enough for what lay ahead.

Danny, reasonably reassured, nodded back. "Sure Patsy," he said. "Tomorrow."

Back in his room that night, Danny took out his dad's photo.

"I'm going to be a fighter just like you, Dad," he said. "You were a fighter in the war and I'll be a fighter in the ring. I'll make you proud."

Now Danny was on a mission. He trained the hardest, and his progress was impressive. As the months passed, Patsy had to admit that he could have a future.

Meanwhile, at home, Rosie's frolicking was getting worse. Ricky was still in the picture, but coming up on the rails was a new bloke called Ted, a chubby train driver, whose rants whilst lovemaking were chilling. The training was a welcome release for Danny, and he threw himself into it, pushing and pushing as Albert had said.

But his personal life was becoming a bit rocky. Although the spark was still there, the distance between him and Wendy felt to Danny as if it was growing.

"It's always bloody boxing with you," Wendy seethed every time Danny cancelled any arrangements, or ran in the park, or trained at the Live and Let Live gym. "I'm taking second place here, and I tell you what. I don't bloody like it."

"It's for us," Danny tried to tell her. "For our future. I can do this, I can be good."

"Graham says..." Wendy stopped.

Danny's heart thumped. "Who's Graham then? What's he been saying?"

"Just a bloke I work with, for all you care." Wendy applied her lipstick with vigour. "He's a dead ringer for that singer

Dickie Valentine, and a really good laugh. Which is more than you are these days, Danny Watson."

"You seeing much of this Graham bloke at work, then?"

This seemed to touch a nerve with Wendy. "What are you saying?"

"You mention him a lot."

Wendy sniffed. "Yeah well, I do see him more than I see you, don't I? I see you now for a couple of hours now and then, but I'm in work for eight hours a day, aren't I?"

"So would you rather be with this Graham then?" Danny challenged. "It sounds like you would." Wendy's eyes showed how hurt she was by Danny's accusation. "Get out of my house, Danny Watson," she said. "Go on, get out."

Danny left, black thoughts floating in his mind. Deep down he didn't think that Wendy would ever cheat on him, but the training and their lack of time together was creating tension. He loved Wendy and saw his boxing career as something that would benefit both of them. Why couldn't she understand that he was doing it for them both? It was frustrating. He couldn't give up, not now.

Feeling troubled by the argument, Danny decided to telephone Wendy as soon as he got home from his evening run. Going to a local phone box armed with four pennies, he called the Bristows' house.

Mr Bristow answered the phone. "Hello?"

"Hello Mr Bristow, it's Danny here," said Danny. "Is Wendy there please? Sorry I'm calling a bit late."

Mr Bristow sounded irritable. "I think she's gone to bed, Danny. Is it important?"

Danny twisted the telephone wire round his finger. "No it's all right," he said reluctantly.

It wasn't really. He had started building things up in his mind about this Graham bloke, and the thought of losing Wendy was tearing him up.

"I'll tell her you called," said Mr Bristow.

"Thank you." Danny felt a sudden rush of emotion. "Will you tell her I love her, Mr Bristow? Will you tell her that?"

Mr Bristow laughed. "Will do, Danny. Bye now."

Danny hung up, feeling frustrated and worried. He hoped Wendy's father would pass on the message, and Wendy would be able to forget that he had doubted her. He couldn't let go of his dream, not now, but he couldn't lose Wendy either. It was a juggling act that he would have to address.

The following morning, Danny decided to try to explain the importance of his budding boxing career to Wendy. As he rode his bike over to the Bristows' house, he went through the points he wanted to make.

Getting to the Bristows, and ringing the front-door bell didn't help Danny's nerves. The thought of either losing Wendy or losing his new-found boxing mission was too painful to even consider.

Wendy opened the door.

"Nice of you to fit me in," was her spiky greeting.

Danny smiled hopefully. "Can we talk?"

"I think we need to," Wendy said. She jerked her head. "Come in then."

Danny followed her to the kitchen. "Look," he said, "I know you don't like me doing the boxing and it takes up some of my time, but Wend, I'm doing it for both of us. If I work hard and make it, we'll have money, a future."

"You reckon?" was Wendy's non-committal response.

"I love you," said Danny in desperation. "I want to spend as much time as I can with you, honest. I am doing this for both of us, can you understand that? I don't want to end up like my so-called friends. They're destined for a dead end, a life of crime. I want more than that, Wend, more than that for both of us."

Wendy's expression softened a little. Sensing a thaw, Danny took his reluctant girlfriend in his arms.

"I promise we'll spend as much time together as we can," he said.

Wendy looked into Danny's eyes. "Promise?" she pleaded.

"I promise." Danny gave Wendy a gentle kiss. "I need you behind me, Wend, if I'm gonna make a go of this."

"But what if you get hurt?"

"I've got a good team behind me. It ain't gonna happen."

Holding each other felt good. Both of them feeling secure, together and close again felt right.

Wendy broke the warm silence.

"I suppose I will still love you with a broken nose," she said.

Danny laughed.

Wendy struck a boxing-like pose. "And at least you can take care of me with those flying fists," she said.

"Always," said Danny.

And suddenly, the threat of Graham the Dickie Valentine lookalike seemed less of a worry.

★

Time passed under the watchful eyes of Patsy and Albert. With encouragement from Lenny, Danny was becoming, as Patsy put it, a contender. The trio, for Danny, had become like his family. Rosie knew of course that Danny went training, but was more interested in her own social life. And although there was still love between Danny and Wendy, his single-minded focus sometimes still brought the occasional chill to the relationship. Danny did his best to manage the balancing act and went on following his dream.

Three months after joining the team at the Live and Let Live, Danny was summoned by Albert.

"Patsy has some news for you, son."

"Good or bad?" asked Danny.

Albert just shrugged his shoulders. As he had not been able to pay his club subscription through lack of funds, Danny wondered uneasily whether Patsy had finally lost patience and would tell him to leave.

Going upstairs to the boxing gym, which now felt like a second home, Danny could hear the familiar sound of Patsy's voice barking pearls of wisdom to another hopeful.

"Albert said you wanted to talk to me, Pat?"

Patsy gave an intriguing wink. "Pop into the office, son, be with you in a minute."

Patsy's office was full of boxing trophies, posters and photos of legendary fighters. Danny waited tensely, staring at the photos. He wanted to be one of those fighters on Patsy's wall, holding belts and trophies. He wanted it more than anything he'd ever wanted in his life.

Patsy eventually came in.

"Sit down, Dan."

Danny sat on Patsy's well-worn sofa while Patsy took a seat behind his well-worn desk.

"You've made good progress here, Danny boy," said Patsy. "To be honest, I'm surprised how far you've come."

"It's all down to you and Albert," said Danny.

Patsy shook his head. "It's down to you and your commitment, Danny. And now I think you're ready to represent the club."

Danny's heart leaped. The news was exactly what he wanted to hear.

"If you're up for it," Patsy continued, "you could be part of the team to take on the boys from the Bermondsey Club in a month's time, at the amateur contest scheduled at West Ham Baths."

Danny's face lit up with a smile from ear to ear. "I'm up for it," he said.

"Good boy."

Patsy shook Danny's hand, placing a West Ham Boxing Club vest ceremoniously into Danny's grateful arms. Danny thought of his dad. This was his chance to make his father proud. He cherished the faith his new boxing family had shown in him and he was certainly not going to let them down. This was the first step and he was not intending to trip over it.

"Is it all right if I use the phone?" he stammered, hardly able to speak for excitement. "I want to tell Wendy."

Patsy laughed and slapped him on the back. "Don't make it a long one, or I'll get you to pay the bill."

The Bristows' number seemed to ring for ever.

"Wend!" Danny shouted the moment Wendy picked up. "Patsy has put me in the club team. It's brilliant ain't it!"

Wendy sounded cautious. "Is it?"

Danny was taken back by Wendy's lack of enthusiasm. "Yeah," he said after a moment. "It is."

"So what does it mean? That I'll see even less of you?"

Danny's excitement leaked out of him like air from a balloon. "I'd thought you would be pleased," he said. "It's an achievement. You can come and watch and that."

"What, watch you get your face punched in? I don't think so."

"Look, I'll come round tomorrow and we can talk about it."

"Not much to talk about, is there Danny?"

There was an awkward silence. Danny hadn't been expecting Wendy to be so down on his news.

"I love you," he said.

Again Wendy was silent.

"So I'll see you tomorrow?" said Danny, still trying to sound upbeat.

"See you," Wendy replied and put down the phone.

Danny slowly put the phone down. From being full of elation, he now felt deflated. This breakthrough had been what he had been training for, but the most important person in his life still seemed against it.

"Good on ya, Danny!"

"You're ready, champ!"

Leaving Patsy's office, Danny was cheered and congratulated for his achievement by all the boys at the gym.

He couldn't help feeling the irony as handshakes and con-gratulations showered down on him. All their good wishes and congratulations felt somehow empty without the girl he loved feeling the same.

CHAPTER FOUR

THE next few weeks were spent in jogging round the park under Albert's watchful eye, intense training at the gym with Patsy, and attention to diet.

Danny had knocked the fags on the head and was trying to eat decent food.

He was in good shape and felt ready for his debut.

He'd told Wendy about the upcoming fight the night after he'd been selected. Things had thawed a little with Wendy as Danny explained how proud he was to be representing the much-respected West Ham boxing team, and how it could be the first step on the ladder to a successful career. Although there'd been a glimmer of respect in Wendy's eyes, Danny had also felt her indifference.

"You will come, won't you?" Danny asked. "I want you to be there supporting me, Wendy. There at the ringside. Will you do that?"

"I don't like you boxing, Danny," she said quietly.

"But will you be there?" Danny persisted.

She didn't say yes, but at the same time she didn't say no. Danny was hopeful.

A week before the contest, Danny, now registered as a welterweight at ten stone and ten pounds, was called into Patsy's office.

"I've just heard that you'll be fighting a dangerous Bermondsey southpaw called Michael Doherty," said Patsy, coming straight to the point like he always did. "How do you feel about that?"

Danny felt apprehensive. "A southpaw is a bit tricky, ain't it?"

"The boy has a reputation. He is experienced, and was on the threshold of turning professional but didn't quite make it," said Patsy. "He's holding a strong record of sixteen wins to his name and just three defeats. This is going to be a challenge, Danny, and you need to be up for it."

The reality of the forthcoming battle was now dawning on Danny with force. "I'm up for it, Patsy," he said after a moment. "You know I am."

Danny couldn't deny that the southpaw conundrum was daunting. He began sparring with the two left-handers at the gym, but found the unorthodox style a bit of a mystery. Time and time again he was getting caught by big shots, but kept going. After all, he wanted to win this battle, to repay Patsy, Albert and Lenny, to make Wendy and his late father proud of him. Albert was impressed by his dedication, and Lenny, a betting man, was intent on putting some money on Danny.

"Now all you have to do is actually win, man," Lenny chuckled.

★

Fight night was imminent.

Danny had told his mum about the fight, but she wasn't coming.

"I ain't gonna watch my lovely son get bruised and battered," she'd said. "I'm going down the pub with Ricky instead."

Danny wasn't surprised. He was familiar with taking second place to Rosie's liaisons. And Wendy hadn't yet said if she would actually come.

Danny decided to go to bed early, to get a good night's sleep for the big day ahead. However, Rosie and Ted the train driver's noisy bedroom antics (not unlike a train coming out of a tunnel) meant not too much sleep was actually had. The tunnel of love wasn't a good combination with Danny's nervous anxiety. Tossing and turning till the early hours, long after Rosie and Ted were spent and with a head full of Albert's and Patsy's tactics for his big fight, sleep proved elusive.

With dawn peeping through the window, Danny reached underneath his bed for his treasured tin box, looking for solace, comfort and resolve. As he looked at his father's photo, his dad's war medal for bravery seemed to strengthen his own courage. At that moment, there in his small familiar bedroom, he felt invincible. Reassured and tired, he fell back into a restless sleep.

By the time Danny awoke at about ten, Rosie had already left for work at a shop in Stepney that sold electrical appliances. Ted had scarpered in the early hours, keen to avoid Ricky, who had a bit of a reputation.

It felt right to be alone this morning. Danny had a job to do, a point to prove. Any distraction would be a negative.

Albert had kindly bought Danny a steak, a luxury in those post-war days, and had told him to make himself steak and eggs for breakfast. "Give you strength for the fight on the day," he'd said. Danny cooked up the suggested menu in a frying pan and tucked in, not feeling that hungry, but following orders.

Leaving the house and taking a gentle jog to the park, Danny felt amazed at the way the world seemed to carry on as usual. The cranes in the docks loaded and unloaded in the near distance, people went about their business, a postman rode by on his red Royal Mail-issue bicycle. Strange, Danny thought, when it was such a big day for him personally. Strange that life carried on just as usual. Didn't they realise that today he had a date with destiny?

As Danny ran past the pond, he saw Albert busily feeding the ducks.

"Hello champ!" Albert shouted. "How ya doing?"

Danny breathlessly joined Albert on his favourite bench.

"Nervous, you know," he admitted. "Full of butterflies about the fight."

Albert nodded. "That's a good thing," he said. "If you was complacent or over-confident, you'd be an easy target."

Danny looked curiously at Albert. "How did you used to feel?" he asked. "Did you feel nervous when you was in the army?"

"I was too old to join up and fight in the last war," Albert replied. "But I saw the suffering of the Docklands first hand. These people suffered, Danny. Me, and others like me, we worked night and day to put out the fires and try and rescue the innocent civilians from the endless bombardment. I was terrified. They were tough times."

Danny saw the hint of a tear in Albert's blue eyes. There was something very moving, seeing this powerful man show such emotion.

"When I was boxing," Albert continued, "deep down inside I was always scared. But the trick was, not to show it. Although you must respect your opponents, never let them see that you're quaking in your boots."

They were quiet for some time. Just the sound of a horse-drawn milk cart in the distance, floating across the park, the clip-clopping on the cobbles and the clinking of bottles, broke the silence.

"Do you think my dad was scared when he was a fighting soldier?" Danny asked quietly. It was a question that had troubled him for a while. "What do you think he was thinking about before he was killed? Was he scared? Was he thinking of Mum back in England?"

Albert sighed. "I'm sure your dad was a brave man," he said. "A lionheart. He gave his life for your freedom, Danny. I'm sure he would've thought the world of you."

Danny reached into his pocket and brought out his father's medal for bravery. He showed it to Albert. "I'm taking this with me tonight, you know, to give me courage," he confided.

"You do that, Danny boy," said Albert, smiling. "You'll be invincible."

★

There was a real sense of togetherness as Albert and Danny walked side by side through the park. The smell of newly mown grass always reminded Albert of school and the playing field, and the birds were singing in the summer trees. All was calm in a battle-scarred London. The calm before the storm, that physical storm of fighter against fighter.

When they reached the park gates to go their separate ways, Albert and Danny instinctively hugged each other. Men seldom hugged, but now, at this moment, it felt right.

Looking into Danny's child-like eyes, Albert said: "You will make that dad of yours proud, Danny. I know that. Meet me and Lenny about six at the Baths, champ."

Danny answered with a nod. A nod that said, there was a job to do and he was going to do it.

The afternoon seemed to last for ever. Danny kept an eye on the hall clock, which at times seemed like it was going backwards.

At five o'clock, it was time to make tracks. A wave of apprehension coupled with excitement filled Danny's mind. This was it. The forthcoming battle was for real.

He made his way through the streets to West Ham Baths. On his shoulder, he carried his carefully packed sports bag, which he had checked over and over again to be sure he had all he needed for the forthcoming fray. Everything was present and correct: gloves, gum shield, shorts, boots, head guard, West Ham boxing vest. And, most importantly, his prized father's medal.

Albert and Lenny were already waiting for him outside at the Baths. Silently they walked in together. Part of Danny felt like he was walking into a lion's den. Part of him felt like the lion itself.

Inside the hall, chairs were being put out. The ring was already set up and overhead lights shone down on the scene, highlighting the centrepiece for the event.

Danny surveyed the scene, nerves raw and jangling. The canvas-covered floor of the ring, the ropes, the red and blue corners. The arena where dreams could become reality and nightmares waited in the shadows.

He turned to Albert. "Why do they call it a ring when it's actually square?" he asked.

Albert scratched his head. "You got me there, Danny. I don't know. But I'll tell you what I do know. You're gonna do well tonight. Just believe, that's all."

Danny, Albert and Lenny made their way to the shabby changing rooms. Patsy nodded at them as they came in.

"All right, son?" he said. "I've seen many a young fighter make his debut, and know how insecure and nervous you can feel."

Seeing Patsy made Danny feel better, more confident. A couple of the other fighters were in the corner warming up, punching pads and skipping ropes. Danny felt stronger being part of the team, surrounded by young fighters like himself. Boys feeling the feelings he was experiencing.

"Listen up," said Patsy. "Your contest is the second one on the bill. You gotta forget about nerves and concentrate on the job at hand. Can you do that?"

Danny could hear the crowd arriving in the hall: the sound of chairs scraping on the wooden floor, voices from a mixture of ex-fighters, family, friends, small-time crooks and boxing fans filtering through. There was no turning back.

"I can do that, Pat," he said. "Yeah, reckon I can."

After hitting a few pads, Danny went to a quiet corner to compose himself. He felt focused and ready, an inner strength welling up inside him.

"I am the lion," he said to himself.

Inside the hall the level of excitement was rising. The first three-round fight was about to start. An upbeat Patsy left the changing room to monitor his red corner and the progress of the first West Ham boy: a kid from a Traveller family called Elijah Cooper. Elijah had a strong punch and a brave heart, but lacked the necessary boxing skill to overcome his Bermondsey rival. One nil on points to Bermondsey.

The disappointed Elijah came back to the changing room with Patsy's arm round his shoulder and his dad by his side. Danny watched enviously. How great it would be if his own dad were here. He convinced himself that he could feel his father's spirit. It was here in the building, he was sure it was.

Patsy delivered a short post-mortem to Elijah and did his best to soothe the boy's hurting pride. Then he turned to Danny.

"You next, Danny. I believe in you, son."

Patsy's words meant a lot. The big Irishman's belief was not easily earned.

Albert gave Danny a man hug, followed by a mock punch.

"You've got this, son," he said, as Lenny gave him a pat on the back and ruffled Danny's hair.

Patsy's words filled Danny's head. *I believe in you, son.* He was ready.

Things seemed to be in slow motion as Danny made his way to the waiting ring. The chatter of the expectant crowd sounded like it was almost under water. Climbing through the ropes and into the lights, Danny heard a ripple of applause for him, followed by a big cheer for the boy from Bermondsey as their fighter made his entrance: shorter, more muscular, and older, oozing confidence.

Danny did his best to not be intimidated, but it wasn't easy. Albert grasped his face, turning him away from the swaggering gladiator making his way towards the ring.

"Just three two-minute rounds, Danny," he said, looking into Danny's eyes. "Six minutes to show what you're made of."

The words were going in, but not really registering. Danny felt like a rabbit in a searchlight. Everything felt surreal, like a dream.

Patsy checked Danny's gloves and head guard. Danny became aware of an announcement, clouded in echo, coming from the stick-thin, bow-tied announcer standing in the centre of the ring.

"Ladies and gentlemen!" the announcer began. "In the blue corner representing Bermondsey Boxing Club... Michael Doherty!"

Doherty acknowledged the cheers and applause that accompanied his introduction with a wave to the partisan crowd and a spot of nifty shadow-boxing. There was a cockiness and confidence about him, and he certainly had his followers.

"And in the red corner, making his welterweight debut, representing West Ham Boxing Club... Danny Watson!"

Muted, respectful applause from the hosts greeted Danny, easily eclipsed by Lenny's raucous cheers.

The referee called the fighters together to remind them of the Queensberry rules and request a good clean fight. He could have been speaking Chinese as far as Danny was concerned. Not much was registering. It was almost an out-of-body experience. Danny felt he was looking down on himself, watching the scene, but not really a part of it at all. He looked into the eyes of his opponent. The sheer hostility he saw there both fazed him and jolted him back to the reality and the gravity of the situation.

This was real.

Back to their respective corners, Patsy thrust a gum shield into Danny's mouth, coupled with a splash of cold water to Danny's face.

Albert could see that Danny was overwhelmed by the proceedings. The boy needed now to focus and focus quickly if he was to have any chance against the seasoned Bermondsey boy.

"Do it for your dad, Danny," Albert whispered urgently. "Come on son, make him proud!"

★

Danny struggled to focus as the fighters were summoned to the centre of the ring by the referee, a portly man with an enormous moustache and a bow tie to match.

"Touch gloves now," the referee instructed them. "Remember – we want a clean fight."

Danny took another look at his opponent. Doherty smiled mockingly.

"Seconds out!" shouted the referee with a chain-smoking voice.

The bell rang, indicating the start of the match. With one last supportive look to Danny, Patsy left the ring.

"Round one!"

The level of noise from the crowd lifted considerably as the two fighters squared up to each other. Used to the training bubble of the gym, Danny found the shouts and noise distracting. His own breathing inside his protective head guard sounded even louder than the crowd. His legs felt weak, his arms heavy.

He heard Albert's voice shout from his corner.

"Get your guard up Dan, use the ring!"

Danny was lost and finding it difficult to focus. Blow after blow landed from the Bermondsey southpaw. Danny felt bemused, lost, as the points against him registered and the punches kept coming.

He could smell the leather as Doherty's gloves made contact, he could taste the blood from his own nose. With just ten seconds to go before the end of round one, he had failed to connect with a single punch. He hadn't even thrown one.

More by luck than judgement, Danny managed to duck

an enormous left hook just a second before the bell. Patsy jumped into the ring and led him back to his corner, amid the derisory boos of the partisan crowd.

Danny felt cold water on his face as Patsy's fighting tactics flowed over him. Albert was nowhere to be seen. Danny tried to listen to Patsy's instructions, but wondered where Albert was. Perhaps he had left. Given up on him.

Danny was trying to clear his head for round two when he got a tap on his shoulder. Albert was back. In his hand, he held Danny's father's medal.

"For courage, Danny, for courage," Albert whispered. "Do this for your father."

The bell sounded for round two.

Something big had changed, Danny was back in the hall, and back in the fight. No more back-pedalling. Now he was the aggressor.

"Yes Danny, jab jab!" Albert cried.

"Keep moving, son!" rang out from Patsy.

Danny was boxing. Motivation, concentration and courage accompanied his every punch and move. With quick footwork and fast hands, Danny won the second round convincingly on points. The Bermondsey boy had met his match.

Danny's corner was now more confident.

"Keep moving, son," Patsy barked, sponging Danny's face. "Keep going, you're doing good."

"You can win this," Albert said simply.

"Seconds out, third and final round!" coughed the referee.

Patsy wiped the blood from Danny's nose and put the gum shield back into his mouth as the bell for the decisive third round rang out. A slightly stunned but vocal crowd roared the fighters on.

The Bermondsey boy knew this was the round that would decide the winner. It was clear as he sprang away from his corner that he wanted to turn the fight into a brawl and not a boxing match, and he came at Danny in search of a knock-out. But Danny kept to the plan, jab and move, as Doherty's wild flaying arms missed Danny's elusive chin.

Danny was ahead on points when a straight left from Doherty made contact, followed by a vicious right hook. Danny literally saw stars as his knees buckled. He should have gone down, but spinning in his head were Albert's words.

For courage, Danny, for courage. Do this for your father.

A power seemed to come over Danny as he fought back. Having almost been down and out, now he was winning. Punch after punch, blow upon blow rained down on Doherty, a barrage of aggression that brought the crowd to their feet.

Who was this boy, Danny Watson?

In the dying seconds of the round, Doherty was caught by a glorious straight right from Danny that signalled a convincing end to the contest. Doherty, a worthy opponent, crumpled to the canvas.

Albert, Lenny and Patsy were cheering like they'd won the football pools. Lenny was even doing a sort of celebration calypso dance.

"The winner in the red corner, Danny Watson, West Ham Boxing Club!"

Bruised, battered, but elated, Danny and his new family left the ring.

"Get up on my shoulders, man!" Lenny yelled.

"Steady on, Len," said Patsy, smiling. "That's a bridge too far."

Back to the changing room, Danny was walking on air. Handshakes and pats on the back rained down on him.

"Well done, Danny!"

"You beat him, mate! You got him!"

This was respect. This was it.

"Keep calm for the losers, boys," Patsy reminded them. "They was good fights, all of 'em." But his words fell on deaf ears.

Albert was taking off Danny's gloves when a happy Lenny came back in through the door after picking up his winnings from a very suspicious bookie.

"There's a visitor for you, champ," Lenny said, grinning.

Just as Danny thought the night could not get any better, he saw Wendy standing in the doorway.

"I wouldn't like to meet you down a dark alley," she said with a smile.

"Wendy, you came!" was Danny's joyful reply as he picked Wendy up in his arms. "Thank you!"

CHAPTER FIVE

WITH Wendy now on board and cautiously behind him in his quest for glory, Danny was feeling invincible. He started slacking off on the training, coasting through gym sessions. The world was his for the taking.

"Don't let it go to your head, lad," Patsy warned. "Your next fight's against a boy from Dagenham, a lad called Trevor Grey. He's never fought in an amateur contest, so it's going to be tough to judge his form or work out tactics for the fight."

"No problem," Danny said with a shrug. "I'm gonna teach him a lesson."

Patsy looked concerned as Danny shadow-boxed around him.

"I know what I'm doing, Patsy," Danny insisted. "This kid don't stand a chance. You worry too much."

On the night of the fight, the venue in Dagenham was packed. Danny started showboating when the referee introduced him, to boos and catcalls from the local crowd. The kid he was fighting, Trevor Grey, looked nervous.

"Be careful out there," Albert warned as Patsy shoved the

gum shield into Danny's mouth. "Don't take this boy for granted. We don't know nothing about him."

Danny felt irritated. Did his last fight count for nothing? "Ain't you seen the kid's face? He's scared," he said. "This is gonna be over quick."

He leaped up, bouncing on the balls of his feet.

"Wait," said Albert, fumbling in his pocket. "I've got the medal."

"Don't need it, Albert. Not for this one."

Danny touched gloves with Trevor Grey. Winked.

"Seconds out!" cried the referee as the crowd roared.

Ding ding!

Danny came out, his guard held low. He wanted to laugh at his new opponent as he moved around the ring. He could have done this in his sleep.

"Come on then," he challenged, grinning. "Ain't you gonna hit me?"

Hit him Trevor Grey did. A massive right hand almost lifted Danny's dancing feet into mid-air. Danny saw stars, felt the rough canvas on his cheek. Then nothing.

"... nine, TEN!"

Danny became dimly aware of cheering and the stink of smelling salts under his nose. His voice sounded groggy, like it didn't belong to him.

"What happened?"

"You lost the fight," growled Patsy. "And it was bloody embarrassing. Albert? Get this Wonder Boy out of my sight."

Albert led Danny silently through the yelling crowd to the changing room. Danny could barely put one foot in front of the other. He winced as Albert slammed the changing-room door behind them.

"I thought you were serious, Danny." The disappointment in Albert's voice filled Danny with deep regret. "I thought you wanted to be a fighter. You lost that fight because you thought you were too good, you thought it would be easy. You need to take a good look at yourself."

Danny sank on to the bench. "Leave it, will you?"

"Remember I told you to always respect your opponent? Well, you didn't. You took the piss and you paid for it. Listen to me. If you want to keep working with me and Patsy, you need to change your attitude. You've done well up until tonight, but you've got too big for your boots. Think about it."

Albert left Danny by himself. His head felt full of cotton wool and his heart ached. It wasn't just himself he'd let down. It was Albert and Patsy too. The knowledge hurt worse than his jaw.

What would his dad have thought of his performance tonight?

Not much. That was for sure.

Patsy and Albert came back into the changing room. They stood side by side, arms folded.

"I'm sorry," Danny croaked. "It won't happen again."

Training continued. Albert and Patsy monitored Danny closely, making sure that the boy's training regime was up to scratch and Danny's commitment was restored. Danny worked hard to build himself up. He was determined not to let down his team again.

Months wore on, and then years. Danny fought in amateur contests all over London, building his experience, and often maintaining his winning form. Albert was especially pleased with the fights where Danny won with a knockout, as he had spent considerable time teaching Danny to use the power of his shoulders as well as his arms in his punches.

Danny's reputation grew with the passing of time. He was often stopped now for a handshake and a respectful "Hello" from the locals. Wendy and her rather snobby parents were impressed and beginning to enjoy the reflected fame.

"My daughter's boyfriend is making waves as an amateur boxer," Mr Bristow was fond of telling his workmates, in a bid to enhance his manliness at the factory and prove to them all that he wasn't just some distant supervisor, detached and out of touch. "The boy's future looks bright."

For all his increasing fame, Danny was still working parttime as a hod carrier on one of the many building sites in London sprouting out of the bombed ground. Because of the job's physicality, it was almost like training, and of course it brought in some much-needed money. There were times though, when the alarm clock shook and rang on those dark damp mornings, when Danny wished that his boxing path would move up a gear, bringing glory and a more secure financial future for him and Wendy.

They sometimes talked of getting engaged.

"You could be my fiancé," Wendy would sigh, and Danny would choke and laugh and warn her off ever calling him something so poofy.

Mr and Mrs Bristow, together with Rosie, were both of the opinion that Danny and Wendy were too young. But it didn't stop the young couple from dreaming. They talked about weddings, and a family in the future maybe, and where they would like to live. Chigwell seemed top of Wendy's list.

The riches, fame and glory that his new career could bring him shone like a light at the end of a long dark tunnel. Danny wanted it all and more. But at the same time, he had a true passion for the sport, and an even stronger wish to be remembered as a good fighter, just as Albert was.

On the evening before any contest, Danny had now developed a sensible regime. He would spend a quiet night in, collect his thoughts and try to relax. Tonight he had a fight in Peckham. Thankfully Rosie had gone away for the weekend, for a short break in Southend. Danny wasn't really sure who she was with. Ricky or Ted, most likely. He felt the usual nervous anxiety, but there was a different feeling tonight. A feeling of wanting to prove his commitment, take the next step up the career ladder. After a good night's sleep, he set off on his daily run along the road to the park. These days he had proper running shoes, kindly donated by Lenny. As he pounded the streets, he went through the instructions and tactics for the fight, making meticulous preparations over and over in his head.

Albert was on his way out of the park after his morning duck feed.

The two friends met by the park's red and green band-stand.

"All right, son?" said Albert.

Things were indeed all right, thanks in many ways to his unlikely friend and mentor. Danny felt the need to thank Albert for all he had done, and reassure him that he was serious about his boxing career. But Danny wasn't sure how to put his gratitude into words. He didn't want to sound like a softy. Knowing Albert and his dislike of sentimentality, he settled for a less potentially embarrassing, more general conversation.

"So, how do you think I'm doing?" he asked as they sat side by side on the park bench.

"You're doing good."

There followed the kind of comfortable silence that is perfectly fine between friends. After a few minutes, Albert broke it.

"You're a special fighter, Danny. All right, you let yourself down on your second fight, but I've seen hundreds of would-be champions, boys who never had the skill and the attitude needed to make it. You have the skill and the attitude. You just gotta believe, that's all."

Danny felt indescribably moved by Albert's words. They meant a lot to him. "Right," said Albert, standing up. "I'd better get going."

Danny called as Albert walked off. "See you later."

Albert bent down to pick up a piece of stray litter and put it in a nearby bin. Danny smiled at Albert's love and care of his park. He'd wanted to say so much more to thank Albert for guiding him to this new horizon, but when they'd been sat side by side, the words hadn't come out.

"Thank you, Albert," Danny whispered now as his mentor moved on across the park, dead-heading dying roses as he went. "Thank you."

As the sun went down behind the ships and dormant cranes in the early evening, Danny made his way to the battleground, alone as usual. It was the best way to do it. With just himself for company, he could focus more on the job in hand. The distraction of small talk, or indeed any talk, would be a nuisance.

On top of the bus to Peckham, he visualised the fight, the tactics. Patsy had been on at him to keep his guard up as lately, in training, he had started to let his hands drop. The burly Irishman had also reminded him to concentrate on moving; to box, not brawl.

"Show your natural gift as a boxer," he'd said. "And make sure you avoid getting drawn into a toe-to-toe slogging match."

Reaching the hall, Danny found his way to the changing rooms. Most of the West Ham boys were already there.

"All right, Danny?"

"How's it going?"

Danny felt strengthened by their presence, like he always did. They were a strong and close unit. Being part of a winning team and training side by side brought them all closer. It was almost a brotherhood.

Patsy was nowhere to be seen.

"He's not too happy with the way the temporary ring has been erected," Elijah told Danny when he asked. "He reckons it's loose or something."

"A bit like your arse Elijah!" said someone else, to a burst of laughter.

The door burst open and an irate Patsy came storming in.

"Bloody amateurs," he snarled. "What a piss hole. Everyone here? Danny? Good lads, listen up. Peckham has some dangerous fighters, but there's none more dangerous than our Danny's opponent tonight, the toast of South London, Billy Anderson."

The West Ham boys hissed. Anderson had an enthusiastic following and a really impressive record of twenty-six wins, including eight knock-outs and just one loss. And this was only the beginning of his career.

"The boy is a scrapper, not a boxer," Patsy continued, fixing Danny with his gaze. "If he catches you, you will know it."

Danny knew all about Billy Anderson. He listened carefully as Patsy outlined the tactics for the fight once again.

Wendy wasn't coming tonight, as over the last few days she'd been feeling sick. Danny had told her to stay at home and not to worry, he would be fine. But it was still good to see Albert and Lenny arrive to support him. They felt like family these days.

"Looking good tonight, Danny!" Lenny said cheerfully. "That Peckham lad ain't got a hope!"

Danny's bout was second on the bill. With Lenny's words of encouragement ringing in his ears, he made his way to the ring with Patsy and Albert at his side.

"Jab and move, Danny," was Albert's advice as the crowd cheered and crowded around. "Out-box him, don't get involved in a street fight."

"Yeah, out-box him, son," Patsy agreed. "You're the better boxer, keep your distance."

Danny could still hear Albert's stinging rebuke from all those years ago, when he'd lost to the Dagenham first-timer through stupidity and over-confidence. *Don't you ever take for granted that you're gonna win a fight. You must always, always respect your opponent.* It had been a humiliating defeat that had hurt Danny badly, and one he was determined never to repeat.

When Anderson arrived in the ring, it was clear that he was the local crowd's Big White Hope. There had been a lot of talk in recent weeks about him turning professional. He was the hot shot, and Danny, for all his growing reputation, was the underdog.

Anderson seemed to have muscles on his muscles, and Danny could sense his aggression. Tonight, Danny was far from over-confident, and his nerves were raw.

"Seconds out! Round one!"

Just as Patsy had warned, Anderson came out with a vengeance. Danny tried to box, to keep his distance, but the fury of his opponent was intense. He managed to avoid some of the more telegraphed, windmill-type punches, but was caught by a body shot that winded him badly and brought home the vicious power of Anderson's punch.

Round one went to Anderson, the Peckham boy.

"Keep out of trouble, lad," Patsy barked, back in Danny's corner.

"You're doing OK," Albert encouraged. "Keep moving, jab and move!"

The bell went for round two. Anderson, buoyed by the winning first round, came out like a Tasmanian devil, aiming for the kill, spurred on by a partisan crowd baying for blood.

Danny tried hard to follow his corner's advice, but when three vicious blows landed on his head guard and chin, his knees started to buckle.

Dimly he heard Patsy yelling.

"Get your guard up, Danny!" Patsy yelled as a right to the ribs winded Danny again. The referee was looking anxious and on the verge of stopping the fight. If the fight stopped, the contest would be awarded to his opponent. Danny felt a slow, burning anger as he lifted his gloves. He'd had enough of being a punch bag. It was now or never.

With a power he had not shown before, he summoned all his energy and began to fight back.

"Box him, Danny!" Patsy shouted. "Box him!"

But Danny wasn't listening. If Anderson wanted a street fight, he was going to get one.

From back-pedalling, he now moved forward on the offensive. Toe to toe with his opponent, sweat and blood covering his face, his fast hands started to push Anderson back. The crowd sensed the battle was on. In a way, the gloves were off.

The two men fought as if their lives depended on it. Blow after blow, both boxers giving as good as they got. Danny fought on grimly. His punches were landing more accurately than Anderson's manic onslaught.

The mood in the hall began to change. Before Danny started bringing the fight to Anderson, the local crowd had thought that their boy was going to be the easy winner. But Danny had other ideas, and they could sense it.

"Box!" Patsy screamed. "Don't brawl!"

"Keep going, Danny!" shouted Lenny. "Keep landing them punches!"

Danny was matching Anderson's aggression punch for punch. Patsy threw his hands in the air. This was a power-house of a fight rarely seen in the amateur boxing world, and the crowd loved it.

Anderson was in retreat, backing off for safety, when a right hook from Danny caught him like a hammer blow, smack on the chin, visibly shaking him. Sensing his moment, with a left and a powerful right Danny sent Anderson crashing through the ropes and into the crowd.

Anderson wasn't the only thing giving up the fight. The ring was collapsing too. Danny grabbed for the ropes as the structure fell apart beneath his feet. Anderson was out cold, sprawled across the laps of two front-row punters, as chaos descended. The referee gave up trying to call for order and went to consult with the judges. After a brief and confused conversation, the referee waved his arms.

"Draw!" he yelled. "In the circumstances, we call a draw!"

Albert, Patsy and Lenny went ballistic. Even the local crowd were booing the decision. Danny had clearly won, well before the ring had collapsed. After giving his all, fighting the kind of fight Anderson had wanted and beating him, Danny had been cheated.

The travesty of justice left a bad taste in his mouth.

"We should demand a return match," Albert said, angrily pacing in the changing rooms as the officials did their best to reassemble the ring for the rest of the bill.

"Cheating bastards," said Lenny.

"Told you this was a piss hole," Patsy said.

"Next time you'll beat him," Albert swore, lifting Danny's chin up to look the dejected boy in the eye. "Don't worry, son, you'll get your revenge."

As a semblance of calm began to settle, the door was suddenly pushed open and the smell of aftershave lotion wafted in. Albert narrowed his eyes at the two well-groomed newcomers in mohair suits who had waltzed in unannounced.

"Who the bloody 'ell are you?" he said.

The men looked around the changing room like they owned the place.

"The name's Costa," said the taller of the two, producing a business card. No one moved to take it. "Tommy Costa. And this here is my business partner Jack Cohen."

"No one asked you in here," said Albert.

"Steady, old fella," Costa replied. "You don't want to have a heart attack. Who are you anyway?"

"This man is the ex-army middleweight champion, Albert Kemp," Lenny bit out, "and you need to show some bloody respect."

"What do you two want?" Albert said bluntly.

Cohen looked at Albert with a slightly patronising smile.

"Nice fighter you have there Albie boy," he said.

"Good-looking boy too," said Costa, his eyes lingering on Danny. "We've been keeping an eye on him."

Cohen smiled, showing sharp little teeth. "Now, I'm sure you want the best for the boy," he said.

"The best for the boy," echoed Costa.

"He needs proper management," Cohen continued.

"Someone to nurture, to care," added Costa.

Albert was reminded of a comedy double act, but not a very funny one.

"Someone to open doors," Cohen went on.

"Get him the right fights," Costa put in.

Costa's eyes glinted. "Perhaps get him a shot at a professional title."

"And is that you, Albert?" said Cohen, a little too close to Albert's face for comfort.

Cohen was wearing a grey well-tailored suit, pink tie, striped shirt and what seemed to be a gold ring on every finger. The straight man, serious, perpetually glum, with very black hair, greased and swept severely back.

He spoke quickly and sharply with an almost middle-class accent. Tommy Costa looked like a Greek Cypriot, with a five o'clock shadow, long curly brown hair, bushy eyebrows and big brown eyes. His black mohair suit would have fitted fine, if Tommy had not put on a few pounds living the good life. More casual than Cohen, he wore an open-neck white shirt and a pair of very shiny Cuban-heel boots.

"Why don't you call him over," suggested Costa now, his eyes flicking towards Danny. "So we can have a little chat?"

"Go get changed, Danny," said Albert, not taking his eyes off Costa and Cohen. "Len? Patsy? Look after the boy."

"It's all about you, ain't it Albie?" said Costa.

"Standing in the way of a young man's dream," said Cohen.

The men pushed past Albert and headed for Danny. Lenny and Patsy hovered uncertainly.

"Danny boy," said Cohen. "Allow me to present my card."

Albert gritted his teeth as a bewildered Danny took the business card from Cohen's fingers.

"He did well Tony, didn't he?" said Cohen. "Came back strong."

"Yes Jack, a brave boy," confirmed Costa.

"We have been watching you, Danny," said Cohen.

"Like a hawk," Costa put in. "We think, if you have the right people around you, you could have a future."

Danny glanced at Albert. "Thank you," he said. "But I've already got the right people around me."

Patsy stepped up to Cohen, nose to nose.

"I think you should leave now," he said. "The boy's tired. Leave it to another day."

"We can open doors for you, Danny," said Cohen, ignoring Patsy.

Albert didn't like what he was seeing and hearing.

"There's a door over there you can open," he said. "Just close it after you piss off."

Cohen smiled. "Steady there, Albie," he said.

"Just saying hello, that's all," said Costa, with a smile that revealed a prominent gold tooth.

Cohen hadn't taken his eyes off Danny. "I'm sure you think you're in good hands, Danny," he said, "but if you need a little help, give us a call."

As the door closed, everyone breathed again.

"You wanna stay away from people like that, Danny," said Patsy, shaking his head.

"Like I said, I've got a good team," Danny said, and he smiled at Albert as he spoke. "You don't have to worry about me."

The tension in Albert's shoulders eased a little. "I've heard their names, Pat, but I've never seen 'em," he said, turning to the stocky Irishman. "They've got a bit of a reputation, ain't they?"

"Dangerous, the pair of 'em," Patsy confirmed. "And I've heard that Costa fella is one of those sausage jockeys."

"Blimey," was all that Albert could think of as a reply.

He sat down on the slatted bench in the changing room. Jack Cohen had come across as a shifty chancer. Costa seemed more gregarious, more outgoing than his partner, but his overpowering personality and buckets full of smarm, in some ways, made him that bit more worrying.

Not that Albert was worried. He'd seen their type before. They took kindness for weakness, used lies for truth and bullying for strength. Danny wouldn't go near them. He was too bright for that.

★

Danny had planned to stick around and watch the rest of the fights. However, his own traumatic fight and decision, plus the downbeat mood in the changing room, saw him heading off to Wendy's instead to try and lift his mood.

At the bus stop, Danny thought about the meeting with Cohen and Costa. He had kept their card, and for the first time, he now took it out of his pocket and read it.

Cohen & Costa Boxing Promotions and Management. Promoters that Pack a Punch!

"Promoters that Pack a Punch," Danny repeated to himself. It had a certain ring.

His first thought was to deposit the card in a nearby rubbish bin. After all, he already had his team, his boxing family. Why would he need this pair? But, something stopped him. Not really knowing why, he put the card back in his pocket.

There was now a growing queue at the bus stop. Several men clustered round him.

"Well done, son," said one.

"You was robbed," said another. "You won that fight."

The memory of the injustice still hurt. "Yeah," said Danny, shaking the hands that were offered. "Nothing I can do about it though, is there?"

The trolley bus arrived, its two long pole-like arms sparking and clinging to the electric cables overhead. Too often, the arms of the buses became unattached, and a man would have to come to the rescue with a very long pole to re-attach them. The first time it happened, Danny had been a boy travelling on the bus with his mum.

"Is he called a pole vaulter?" he'd wanted to know.

Rosie hadn't bothered to answer.

This bus seemed to be behaving itself. Danny went upstairs and found a seat by the window. Watching the streets, shops and houses pass slowly by, he reflected on the night's events. It was seven years since he'd first taken up boxing. Seven long years. It was crazy still to be fighting at an amateur level. Maybe these Costa and Cohen characters could help him get paid, become a professional. It wouldn't be a bad thing.

His body was still aching from the brutal fight, but all of a sudden Danny felt elated and couldn't wait to tell Wendy about the evening. He had won that fight after all, albeit with one eye bruised and practically closed. He might not look like the victor, but he was. And maybe in more ways than one.

By the time he got to Wendy's, her mother and father had gone to bed. He could see Wendy through the net curtains, sitting up waiting for him. He tapped three times on the stained-glass window in the front door, an attractive piece of glass with the figure of a sail boat etched in it.

"I won Wend," Danny said, grinning, as his girlfriend opened the door. "Although it was given as a draw. What a night. Wait till you hear about it."

"Oh my God Danny, look at your face!" Wendy's eyes were wide as she took in Danny's bruises. She grabbed his hand. "Come in. We need to talk."

For women, "talking" meant emotion and feelings. Words that spelled terror to most men, Danny among them. His gut lurched as Wendy ushered him into the living room and closed the door.

"Sit down, Danny," she said.

Danny sat nervously on the sofa. "What's the matter, what is it?" he asked, feeling like he'd been summoned by the headmistress.

That's when the bombshell landed.

"I'm pregnant," Wendy said.

"What?" said Danny.

"I am pregnant," Wendy repeated with a touch more volume. "Having a baby. *With child.*"

"Oh, pregnant," said Danny, stunned. "Right."

A strange mixture of emotions flooded through him. Shock, pride and fear, all at the very same time.

"Right," he repeated.

"I've not told Mum and Dad yet," said Wendy anxiously.

"Right," Danny repeated.

He was beginning to sound like a broken record stuck in a groove. His head was bursting with thoughts. Searching, thinking of options, thinking of consequences.

"What shall we do?" Wendy said, her voice small and scared.

Suddenly for Danny, everything was clear. This baby was a confirmation of their love for each other from way back when they were just children, when Danny had defended Wendy from the ginger jibes. The beautiful crowning glory for two childhood sweethearts who had turned into adults and were still deeply in love. Soulmates, as Wendy often said.

Danny put his arms around Wendy and held her close. He felt her relax against him. They were having a child of their own. That very special bond of parenthood was going to be theirs now. It was time to jump into the unknown.

"It's going to be fine," he said. "I love you, Wend."

They talked well into the night about all the changes they would need to make. They discussed a few names for the baby, both girls' and boys'. They talked about money, and how they would cope.

"I met these two fellas tonight," Danny said as Wendy rested her head on his shoulder. "They reckon I could turn professional with their help, maybe make some money. I'll meet them, talk to them."

They were both aware that the most immediate hurdle was to tell Wendy's parents. Danny was no coward, but the thought of confronting Wendy's strait-laced folks with the news of a baby conceived out of wedlock was nerve-racking. But he realised that if they were going to have this baby, goodwill from Wendy's folks was an important factor.

"So you'll come over tomorrow?" said Wendy as Danny kissed her good night. "We can tell Mum and Dad together."

He was twenty-three, but Danny had always felt like a boy. For the first time tonight, he truly felt like a man, facing all the responsibility that a baby would bring. He felt ready for it, ready to take it on, whatever the outcome, whatever Wendy's parents thought.

"Of course I will," he said, holding Wendy tightly. "I'll be here at six."

★

Danny spent most of the next day thinking about how Wendy's folks might react. He practised little speeches, tried to imagine the questions they would be asked and what answers he would give. He guessed Wendy was doing more or less the same on her shift at the sugar factory. It seemed a longer day than usual, as Danny longed to get everything over with and out in the open.

On the dot of six, Danny arrived at the Bristows' looking as smart and responsible as he could. He knew that his shiner of a left eye might take the edge off his carefully thought-out presentation, but it couldn't be helped.

Wendy greeted him with a reassuring hug and kiss.

Danny patted her back. "Don't worry Wend," he said. "It'll be all right."

Mr Bristow had not made it home from work yet. Wendy and Danny waited tensely in the living room as Mrs Bristow bustled around the kitchen peeling potatoes for the evening meal.

"That's quite a bruise you've got there, Danny," she said. "Did you win the fight?"

"Yes, Mrs Bristow," said Danny. His throat felt dry with nervousness. "Although the ring collapsed so they called it a draw."

"That sounds dangerous," said Mrs Bristow. "Wendy love, can you lay the table?"

Danny watched the clock on the mantelpiece as Wendy laid out the cutlery. What if he couldn't actually speak when the moment came? What if he failed to make his point and prove himself as a responsible future father of the Bristows' grandchild? He'd decided to call it "the forthcoming baby". It sounded better than "Wendy's pregnant".

"Are you all right for a drink, Danny?" asked Mrs Bristow.

Danny and Wendy had agreed they would tell her parents together, although part of Danny thought that if the news was broken to Mrs Bristow first and she was positive about it, they could get her on side to convince Mr Bristow.

"I'm fine, Mrs Bristow," he said, with as much charm as he could muster.

He hadn't got round to telling his own mother the news as yet, but he knew it wouldn't be a problem. Rosie was so wrapped up in her own world that as long as the newborn didn't clip her wings in any way, she would be fine. Telling Mr Bristow was going to be something else entirely.

A key sounded in the door.

"I'm home," said Mr Bristow cheerfully. "What's for dinner?"

Danny jumped to his feet, but Wendy grabbed his arm and dragged him back to the sofa. They looked at each other. This was it.

"Come into the living room, Dad," Wendy said. "Mum? Leave the dinner for a moment. I – we've got something to tell you."

"Something good?" said Mr Bristow, taking off his shiny black shoes and putting on his tartan slippers as Mrs Bristow appeared from the kitchen with a questioning look on her face.

"Danny and I have an announcement," said Wendy. She paused and took a breath. "We're having a baby."

Danny smiled as brightly and hopefully as he could, stretching out for Wendy's hand. "And we're really happy," he added.

"Right," said Mr Bristow.

Danny was reminded of his own reaction to Wendy's news, except Mr Bristow's "Right" had a different undercurrent.

There followed a strange silence. Danny felt like he was in the dark, without a clue whether the news was going down well or badly.

Mr Bristow paced across the room, stopping by the fireplace to tap and empty his pipe into the grate. Danny watched, holding his breath.

"Do you intend to have this baby?" Mr Bristow asked at last.

Wendy's face showed a determination to keep the situation calm.

"Yes Dad," she said. "We want to have it. We're happy about it."

"We do love each other," Danny put in.

"And we will love the baby," said Wendy.

Mr Bristow reached for his tobacco pouch, filled his pipe meticulously with tobacco and lit it, resulting in a cloud of blue, sweet-smelling smoke. As the first cloud of smoke evaporated into the tense air, he looked Danny in the eye.

"You'll be getting married, of course," he said.

"Of course," said Danny hurriedly. The thought of a wedding was not really on the top of his list, and a shotgun wedding had never entered his mind.

"Good," said Mr Bristow. "That's good."

The awkwardness was broken unexpectedly by Mrs Bristow.

"Well!" she said, giving her daughter a loving hug. She extended her arms to Danny. "I'm pleased for both of you! My goodness, so many plans to make!"

Mr Bristow's expression softened a little. "This will change your lives, you know that," he said.

Danny nodded. "For the better, sir."

"I hope so, son," he said, shaking his head. "I'll go and get washed and changed for tea."

When he had gone upstairs, Mrs Bristow smiled encouragingly at Danny.

"Mr B's a little old-fashioned," she said. "Don't get me wrong, it's not right that you're not married and having a little one, but I know how much you care about each other and I know this baby will be well loved. And you, my little girl," she said, turning to Wendy, "you will be a good mother."

Wendy gave her mother a big hug, dragging Danny into the embrace. Danny closed his eyes in relief as warmth and love filled the room.

Over sausage and mash, there were many happy logistics from Mrs Bristow about wedding plans and baby plans. It was as if she had been waiting for this news her whole life. Mr Bristow had a more considered response, bringing practicalities to the table such as: "When will the wedding be? When is the baby due? Where will the money come from? Where will you live?"

Danny tried to make the point that he would be a good

dad and support his wife and baby, even if it meant working long hours on building sites.

"And there's the promoters you told me about last night," Wendy reminded him, and Danny explained about Costa and Cohen too, and how maybe there was money there if he made the professional fight circuit. He was confident in his boxing family and his ability, although he was fully aware that a baby was a lifestyle changer. If it meant working all hours as a hod carrier to give the little one the start it deserved, he was ready, willing and able.

Wedding plans were the urgent priority.

"You should tie the knot as soon as possible," advised Mrs Bristow.

"I won't have a daughter of mine walking down the aisle six months pregnant," cautioned Mr Bristow.

"What would people think if you were showing under your wedding dress?" agreed Mrs Bristow.

"You could live here," Mr Bristow offered over dessert.

"That would be great, Dad," Wendy said, glancing at Danny. "But we'll put our names down for a council place too."

This pleased Danny. He got on all right with his future in-laws, but having their own place would certainly feel more comfortable.

His head was spinning after all the talk at dinner as he left Wendy with a goodnight kiss on the front porch.

"I said it would be all right, didn't I Wend?" he said.

"It's gonna be wonderful," said Wendy happily. "Night. I love you Danny."

"I love you too."

Riding his bike home, Danny felt very grown up, ready to tackle all the trials and tribulations of being a father. His child would be brought up properly, unlike the fractured childhood that he had endured.

He wondered how his mum was going to react to the happy news. His instinct told him that the chance for Rosie to buy a new hat for the wedding would definitely go down well. He couldn't imagine his mum would ever make the perfect grandmother, but he suspected having the house to herself when he eventually moved out was going to be something she would enjoy.

Rosie and Ricky were just finishing a Chinese take-away when Danny wheeled his bike through to the back and returned to the kitchen to break the news.

"Mum," he said at the kitchen door. "Me and Wendy are gonna get married."

"What d'ya want to do that for?" Ricky grunted, his mouth full of food.

Rosie looked worried. "Don't you think you're too young, love?" she said.

"I'm twenty-three, Mum," said Danny. His eyes uncharacteristically filled with tears. "I love her, she loves me, and we are going to have a baby."

Ricky dropped a prawn ball. Rosie jumped up and away from her chicken chow mein, almost choking in shock. Finally, through the coughs and splutters, she managed to speak.

"My little boy, are you sure?" Emotionally fuelled with alcohol, Rosie dramatically threw her arms round him. "Danny, listen to me, are you sure?"

Danny attempted to calm his mother down with a few friendly pats on her back. "Yes Mum, I'm sure," he said.

"My little boy, a father!" Rosie cried, like a player in a Greek tragedy. "Oh Danny!"

Ricky seemed more interested in some prawn crackers than Wendy and Danny's nuptials. After a reluctant glass of sweet German wine to celebrate, Danny said his goodnights and escaped to his room.

Reaching under his bed for the tin box, he took out the photo of his father.

"Hello Dad," he said proudly. "You're going to be a gran-dad."

Looking at his father's picture, Danny felt sure that his dad would look down and make sure the little one would grow up safe and sound.

It had been a landmark night to remember.

Each morning, Albert tried to feed as many ducks as he could before his bread ran out. It was hard keeping the pigeons off and the odd seagull was a nightmare, but he did his best.

"Albert! I've got something to tell you!"

Albert looked up to see Danny running towards him. The boy was glowing about something.

"Albert, guess what? I'm gonna be a dad! Wendy's pregnant and we're gonna get married!"

"A dad? Marriage?" Albert repeated. "Blimey, son, you sure this is the right time? What about the boxing?"

Danny wiped the sweat from his forehead. "I'll work something out. Great, ain't it though?"

Albert felt concerned. Danny's promising boxing career would come to a halt or suffer, taking second place to a family and wife. Not to mention the financial commitment of bringing up a child.

"Kids cost money," he said. "How are you gonna afford it? Wendy can't work with a bun in the oven."

"I know she can't," Danny agreed. "I need to work harder at the boxing, maybe turn professional to make money."

Uneasiness spread through Albert. He could sense where this was going.

"Maybe those Cohen and Costa blokes could help, you know?" Danny said casually. "So I can make some money."

Albert was only too aware of Cohen and Costa's shady reputation. The thought of Danny being involved with them in any way was worrying. The thought of Danny turning professional was worrying too. But at the same time, he was respectful of Danny's up-and-coming commitments. For the moment, it would be best to keep his powder dry and stay quiet on Costa and Cohen.

"So you're gonna be a dad," he said. "I'm pleased for you, Danny."

"Yeah it's great! But keep it quiet, yeah? Till we're married?"

"My lips are sealed," said Albert. "She's a nice girl too, your Wendy. I wish you both every happiness."

"Thanks, Albert, I appreciate it," Danny said with a smile. "We've already started planning the wedding. I'll give you your invite when they're printed up." He smiled shyly. "And I would like you to be my best man."

Albert was touched. "Lovely," he said. "Look forward to it. Seems like you've got a lot of future coming your way."

"Yeah," Danny agreed. "And I'm going to grab it with both hands. I want my kid to be proud of me."

"You do that," said Albert. "Just keep pushing."

Danny shook Albert's slightly bemused hand. "And it starts now," he promised, with a mock punch to Albert's shoulder.

Albert sat on the bench and thought about Danny's revelations as Danny headed off on the rest of his circuit training, his quest to climb the mountain of success. A change was coming, and Albert wasn't sure it was going to be for the best.

Walking back to his flat, he puzzled over Danny and his boxing future. He prayed the boy would circumnavigate Cohen and Costa. He didn't trust them. There were too many rumours, too many shadowy dealings.

He decided to talk to Patsy about it when he got to work.

"You just missed a couple of visitors," Patsy informed Albert when he arrived at the Live and Let Live. "Them two clowns, Costa and Costalotmore."

"What did they want?" Albert asked with trepidation.

"They seem to believe in your Danny. They were interested in representing the boy and helping him turn professional."

Albert went quiet. The thought of those two wide boys being involved in Danny's future was a chilling prospect. But if they could help Danny secure his financial future for his new family, who was he to stand in his way?

"What did you tell 'em?"

"To come back this evening when Danny's in. They can speak to him directly then."

Albert sat down. "We need to be here, Patsy," he said. "We don't know what tricks they might want to pull."

"Yes indeed," agreed Patsy.

The two men exchanged grim glances.

Tonight was going to be tough.

Danny had spent most of the day with Wendy and her busy mother, making plans for the wedding. He'd never realised how complex it was. Invites, caterers, menus, venues... His head was spinning.

Mr Bristow had shot off earlier in his Hillman Minx to secure the local Conservative Club for the reception. He maintained that the venue had class, and he also knew of a three-piece band that played there on a Saturday night.

"Perfect," he had said. "Not too noisy."

By early evening, Danny was weddinged out, and ready for the physical and mental relief of training.

When he got to the Live and Let Live and climbed the stairs to the gym, there was an unfamiliar smell of aftershave wafting from Patsy's office. Through the window, Danny could see Albert, Patsy and two sharp dressers in conversation. Danny recognised them at once as Patsy beckoned him into the office.

"Danny!" said Costa, jumping up from a chair and giving Danny an overly affectionate hug. Over Costa's shoulder, Danny could see distaste and contempt radiating from Albert.

"Sit down, champ, sit down," Cohen said.

There was a mixed atmosphere as Danny did as he was told. Warmth from the visitors, and a definite chill from Albert and Patsy.

"Danny, we believe in you," said Cohen, with his usual serious face.

"A bit more than some others do," chimed in Costa.

"We think you're ready for the big time, son," said Cohen.

"We know you are," added Costa, his English peppered with the touch of a Greek accent.

"We've been watching you," said Cohen.

Costa grinned. "Like a hawk with a telescope."

"You need representation, Danny," Cohen continued. "People that can guide you to the top, where the pickings are rich. A professional career, with fame and a considerable fortune."

"Considerable, like he says," agreed Costa, stroking his chin with a gold-ringed hand.

Cohen laid a hand on Danny's shoulder. "If we take you under our wing, Danny, the sky is the limit."

"You will fly like an eagle," Costa added.

Albert snorted. "That's beautiful," he said. "Fly like an eagle, you'd like that, Danny, wouldn't you? Just think, you wouldn't have to use public transport no more."

Danny felt worried. Costa and Cohen's exciting proposition looked like it might be a dangerous path, to judge from Albert's reaction.

"Let me spell it out for you, Danny."

As Cohen launched into plans for Danny's future boxing career, Albert left the office without a word.

"He's got work downstairs," said Patsy, looking at Danny. "And I got training. I'll leave you fellas alone. You know, to talk."

"Shut the door on your way out," said Cohen as Patsy left, not taking his eyes off Danny. "We want to propel you into the world of professional boxing, Danny. We can line up a top fight, with a name fighter that'll put you on the map."

"And what do you take in return?"

"Fifty per cent of your earnings."

Danny frowned. "That sounds a lot."

"Fifty per cent of something is better than a hundred per cent of nothing," Costa pointed out.

Danny wasn't too sure what that meant. "I'll think about it," he said. "Have a chat with Albert and Patsy and let you know."

Costa sucked his teeth. "Albert and Patsy are nice blokes but they are yesterday's men, Danny. Faded glory."

"This is your career, Danny," Cohen said, almost with sympathy. "Not theirs."

Danny found himself shaking hands with Cohen and being on the receiving end of another hug from Costa.

"Call us," Costa murmured in his ear. "You won't regret it."

Danny weighed up his feelings as the men left. This could be the answer with a baby on the way. It could offer him security for the family. If what Cohen and Costa were offering was for real, his worries could be over.

But he was troubled by Albert and Patsy's reactions. It was plain to see they didn't share his enthusiasm. "We believe in you," Cohen had said. Did Albert and Patsy feel the same way?

Training was already halfway through by the time Danny joined in. He watched Patsy for some kind of reaction as he punched the pads, but Patsy didn't say a word. Danny sensed that Patsy didn't want to talk about Cohen and Costa's proposal. Was he jealous? Danny couldn't see why. As far as he was concerned, Patsy and Albert would benefit from Cohen's promised "rich pickings".

With training over, Danny said his goodnights and went downstairs to find Albert collecting glasses.

"All right?" he said, in an attempt to test the water.

"Quite a night," said Albert.

He seemed upbeat. Danny relaxed a little.

"What do you reckon about Cohen and Costa then?" he asked.

Albert's lips thinned. "That's for you to decide," he said. "It's your life."

Albert's answer didn't help Danny at all. Deciding that perhaps the discussion was best left for another day, Danny said goodnight and collected his bike from the back of the pub.

Outside, the rain was pouring down. Even so, as Danny rode through the streets drenched from head to toe, there was a fire in his belly. He couldn't wait to tell Wendy that the future was looking bright. Albert and Patsy would come round in time. They only wanted what was best for him.

Wendy was confronted by a drowned rat with a broad smile on his face at the front door.

"I've got some good news," said Danny, dripping on the door step.

"Look at you, you're drenched!" Wendy exclaimed. "Come inside. I'll fetch you a towel."

Danny dried himself quickly.

"What is it then?" Wendy said as he laid the towel down. "Have you heard from the council about a flat? Is there work at the docks, are you starting there soon?"

Danny grinned. "I've had an offer to turn pro," he said.

"What does that mean?"

"It means when I fight, I get paid."

Wendy sat forward and listened as Danny told her all about Cohen and Costa and the earlier meeting.

"It could mean security for us and the baby," he said. "I could buy a car and everything."

Wendy clapped with excitement. "Danny, really?" Then her face fell. "You won't get badly hurt, will you? If you turn pro?"

"I'll do my best not to," Danny said. "Come on Wend. This could be the start of great things!"

And he kissed Wendy's bump to prove it.

By the time he left for home at around midnight, the rain had stopped and the streets smelt clean and fresh. The house was quiet as he wheeled his bike through to the yard. Rosie had clearly gone to bed. Danny suspected she was alone for once, as there was just the clock to be heard, ticking in the hall, not the raucous sounds of intimacy that he had heard so often.

Upstairs in his room, he peeled off his damp clothes and put on a pair of tracksuit bottoms. He could hear the dripping drainpipe outside his room. As he lay on his bed and looked at the damp and mildewed ceiling, he thought about how he was living, with just a few quid to his name and not much else. The work on the building sites was hard and the pay poor. He had witnessed older manual workers struggling, and did not want that to be his life. Not now.

The proposal from Costa and Cohen could be the answer. Looking out of his bedroom window, Danny gazed up to the night sky.

"A new beginning, Dad," he whispered, and smiled, closing the bedroom window's brown faded curtains and switching off the bedroom light. He turned in, his head full of good dreams.

CHAPTER SIX

THE next morning, Danny woke happy and got ready for his morning run.

He was hoping to see Albert at the park, to put him straight on how his boxing family would be a part of his future, and talk the Cohen and Costa business through.

Running through the cobbled streets, he practised in his head the words he would say to Albert. He wanted to reassure him, to let him know that whatever happened with Cohen and Costa, he wanted Albert and Patsy right there by his side.

Turning into the park, he could see the familiar figure of Albert by the bandstand, with a less familiar companion on a lead beside him.

"Monty," Albert said when Danny raised his eyebrows at the Jack Russell sniffing his feet. "He belongs to Simon, my neighbour. I take him out sometimes, when Simon's doing a house clearance."

"Nice," said Danny.

Albert looked glum. "He's a nuisance and the ducks can't stand 'im."

Danny got the feeling that Albert wasn't wanting a deep discussion this morning. He sensed that as far as Albert was concerned, the meeting with Cohen and Costa had never happened. But Danny was determined to talk about it. He wanted to clear the air.

"You know I'm not leaving you out in the cold, don't you?" Danny said. "With Cohen and Costa? I want you and Patsy with me, Albert. But I need to know what you think."

Albert shrugged. "I believe in keeping out of other people's business. It's your life and your decision, son."

"You and Patsy'd get a cut of the money I make," Danny said.

A cold look came across Albert's face. "I didn't get involved because of the money. I got involved to give you a purpose, son, to help you and to get you out of bad company. Make you and your late dad proud. That's all." He bent down to give Monty a treat and a pat. "See ya later, Danny."

Danny felt forlorn. "Yeah," he said. "See you later."

He sat on the bandstand for a while after Albert and Monty left. He hoped he had persuaded Albert that a liaison with Cohen and Costa would be good for all, but he was not convinced. If Patsy and Albert were really against it at this point, Danny wasn't sure what he would do. Should he give up the chance of financial security for his forthcoming wife and baby? Should loyalty to Albert and Patsy be above his material needs? It was times like this that he wished he could turn to his father for advice. How helpful that would be.

He decided to pay Lenny a visit. Maybe Lenny would be more objective, more even-handed. After all, he was always brutally honest. "Call a spade a spade," Lenny was fond of saying. "But don't call me one." The thought made Danny smile. Yes. He'd talk to Lenny.

When he got to the arches, he saw Lenny in his usual position, underneath a car. Lenny was making the sounds he always made when working: a grunt here, a sigh there and that trademark hiss through the teeth.

"Lenny, how you doing?" he said.

"This motor is a bastard," growled Lenny in response.

Danny leaned against the garage doors. "Can we have a chat?"

"Not now, man. Too busy."

"It's about Albert," said Danny, hoping for a more positive response.

Lenny unfolded himself from under the car. "What about Albert?"

Danny relayed the story, and Lenny nodded.

"I already heard from Albert that Cohen and Costa had been to the gym," he said. "Hadn't been told the ins and outs though. So what's your decision?"

"Nothing has been agreed yet," Danny admitted. "But if it means a secure future, some fame and some fortune, I reckon it's something I should do. Albert and Patsy will still be my team. What do you reckon?"

Lenny settled himself on an old beer crate in the corner and rolled a cigarette. "You gotta decide for yourself," he said after a moment. "But before you do, remember this. Albert may not show it, but he thinks the world of you. I think he sees a bit of himself in you, back when he was a contender. Patsy believes in you too. Just remember that." He picked up a spanner and got back to his feet. "I better get on, Danny. OK?"

Danny left Lenny to it. The conversation did not totally solve his dilemma, but he did feel better. His thoughts were out in the open now. He was sure Lenny would speak to Albert, and fill him in on how Danny felt.

After a difficult few weeks, Danny went round to Wendy's as usual. The baby bump now was beginning to show, and Mr and Mrs Bristow were getting more and more anxious to get the wedding over and done. With only two weeks to go till the big day, they couldn't will the time away fast enough.

The thought of their daughter walking down the aisle obviously with child was too terrible to even contemplate.

Danny had told Mr Bristow about the offer to turn professional.

"You could make some serious money, Danny," had been his future father-in-law's positive response. "Be good for your wife and baby, eh?"

It felt good to be in Mr Bristow's good books for a change, an unusual occurrence, and Danny tried to enjoy the feeling. But the black cloud of Albert's reaction still hovered in his mind.

The evening was spent going over the invites, trying to keep the attendance as low as possible for financial reasons, but trying not to leave anyone out. On Danny's side there weren't too many guests: Rosie plus one, an Aunt Ellen, an Uncle Bill, two cousins he hardly knew, Albert, Lenny and Patsy. Wendy's side numbered twenty-two.

"We ought to invite Cohen and Costa," Wendy suggested. "For business reasons. Don't you think?"

Danny could see the sense in that, but he wasn't sure how Albert would react. It was important to try to rebuild burnt bridges without fanning any new flames, but under pressure from Wendy and Mrs Bristow and with an eye to his future, he agreed – as long as they were seated as far from Albert, Patsy and Lenny as possible. Checking the address on their business card, the invites to Cohen and Costa were duly written and added to the pile.

"Fingers crossed," said Danny, more brightly than he felt.

Considerable progress was made in the logistics and arrangements for the big day. The wedding dress was chosen and the matching bridesmaid dresses, a little less spectacular than the bride's of course, were fitted and ordered. Mr Bristow had funded most of Wendy's wishes, even agreeing to an ornate carriage and two white horses to ferry his princess to the church in regal style. Lenny had offered to procure an Austin Princess from one of his richer clients, but Wendy had felt it would be too funereal.

"Thank Gawd I've only got one daughter," was Mr Bristow's answer to the mounting cost.

Wendy had made an appointment for Danny to be fitted for his wedding suit. An uncomfortable event as far as Danny was concerned, but he knew it would incur the wrath of his new in-laws if he turned up at the church in his customary tracksuit. So dressing up like a Victorian gent was agreed to keep the peace. However, no matter how much he loved Wendy, Danny had drawn the line at a top hat. Enough was enough.

Before the Cohen and Costa business, Danny had asked Albert to be his best man. So Wendy had made a joint appointment for the two of them that afternoon.

"To see both of you dressed up in smart tailcoats, waistcoats and cravats will certainly be a one-off," Wendy said as she sent Danny to the hire shop. "And promise to *think* about the top hat?"

Danny dutifully made his way to his three o'clock appointment.

"Can I help you?" asked the rather effeminate man at the counter.

Danny cleared his throat. "I have an appointment with someone named Cyril?"

The man eyed him. "I'm Cyril," he said. "Where is the second member of your party?"

"Not here yet," said Danny, feeling like he was stating the obvious.

After ten minutes, there was still no sign of Albert. This worried Danny. Maybe their recent cooling relationship had led Albert to pull out. But just as Cyril was taking an uncomfortably long time over the measurement of Danny's inside leg, Albert walked through the door.

"Looks like your luck has changed, son," Albert remarked.

Danny was delighted to see his best man. He smiled with relief. "All right, Albert?" he said.

Cyril swept disapproving eyes over Albert's tramp-like appearance. He became a touch frosty and less effeminate.

"Take a seat, sir," he said. "I'll be with you in a minute."

Albert waited as Danny was wrestled into various outfits. Every now and again he gave an approving wolf whistle.

"So the black tailcoat, striped trousers and grey waistcoat?" said Cyril after Albert and Danny had debated the options.

"Works for me," said Albert.

Albert proved to be a rather more difficult project than Danny. He had the habit of stretching out his arms, so that the sleeves of the tailcoats he tried climbed halfway up his forearms.

"Please sir," said Cyril irritably. "You won't be walking around with your arms outstretched."

Albert shrugged his shoulders. "Monkey arms," he said.

At long last, a reasonable fit was found, identical to Danny's. It had to be said, Albert looked transformed and rather dapper. Mission accomplished, Danny put a deposit down. The now giggling pair left a bemused Cyril in his top-hat-and-tails world.

"So Danny," said Albert. "You want a stag night? It's only right. Last night of freedom and all that."

Danny, with a little trepidation, agreed.

"You leave the arrangements in the almost safe hands of me and Lenny," Albert said soothingly. "Next Friday night? Seven o'clock kick-off at the Live and Let Live." And he mock-punched Danny's jaw.

Walking to work at the pub that evening, Albert started to think about the entertainment for Danny's stag night. A traditional stripper, maybe a night up the West End, perhaps a flutter in a casino.

At the bar of the Live and Let Live, Lenny was knocking back a Guinness laced with a dash of Jamaican rum.

"How about we organise a Caribbean night?" he suggested when Albert asked him for ideas. "You know, with straw hats, colourful shirts and plenty of rum chasers. We can have a limbo contest, you know: how low can you go. I'm a natural, years of practice, man."

"Yeah," agreed Albert. "We could get one of those steel bands." Ironically – Lenny hated steel bands: "They sound like a scrap yard."

Several others joined in the discussion. Ideas bounced off each other with a fury, some ridiculous like a bouncy castle in the pub, others quite inspired, like rum punch on tap. In the end, Albert suggested that they should give Danny a wedding present of fifty pounds and a trip to a casino in the West End.

"Danny can have a little flutter," he said. "And so can we."

So it was settled. Calypso, cash and a casino it would be.

"Did the outfit look nice then, was everything all right?" asked Wendy.

"I think we looked the part," Danny replied. "Even Albert looked dapper."

"Good," said Wendy. "Now Dad's checked and almost all of the invites have been answered and everyone's coming."

"Cohen and Costa?"

"Yes, they're coming too."

As Wendy rattled on about bouquets, chicken or lamb and wedding gifts, Danny was silent. The realisation that Cohen and Costa were actually coming filled him with nervous misgivings. Only a short time ago, he'd been with his best man, laughing and joking at poor Cyril's expense. Danny was now concerned that having Cohen and Costa at his wedding would upset Albert again, just when things had warmed up between them.

"Are you listening, Danny? It's like talking to myself sometimes."

Danny did his best to seem interested.

"It will be a day to remember," Wendy went on, full of optimism. "The best wedding of nineteen sixty. Probably in the *whole* of the nineteen sixties."

And maybe it would, thought Danny. Maybe it would.

CHAPTER SEVEN

DANNY wondered what lay in store that evening as he put on his best white shirt and navy-blue suit. The last time he'd worn it was for his Aunt Olive's funeral three years ago, and since then, the bulking up that came with his training had made the suit just a little too tight for comfort.

Combing his hair in the mirror downstairs, he heard a key in the lock. It was his mum, home from her usual after-work trip to the pub.

"Ooh, don't you look smart!" said Rosie. "Where you off to, somewhere nice?"

Danny was used to Rosie's lack of interest in his affairs.

"It's my stag night Mum, remember? I'm getting married."

Rosie advanced and took Danny's face in her hands. "Ah, my little boy, married," she cooed, as tears filled her eyes with tipsy sentimentality.

This was not what Danny needed. He did a quick swerve and a half-kiss and escaped into the evening air.

It was September, and even the docklands had an autumnal smell, with the coloured leaves and the last remnants of flowers all now looking to winter. Whether it was the balmy atmosphere, or being on the brink of one of the biggest days of his life, Danny started to think about growing up as a child in this colourful and emotive area. He thought about his schooldays, when all he'd looked forward to was football practice on Fridays and matches on Saturday mornings. He thought about meeting Wendy and playing kiss chase, sticking up for her when the kids were calling her strawberry-blonde hair ginger. He thought about what was to come: a wife and baby. He wished his dad could have been there, standing shoulder to shoulder with him, to witness the wedding and to see and hold his grandchild when it arrived.

At the Live and Let Live, all seemed strangely quiet. Filled with apprehension, Danny opened the public bar door.

Nobody was inside.

Danny was confused. Had they forgotten?

After some hesitation, he made his way to the saloon bar. As he opened the door, he was taken aback by a loud cheer and an explosion of tropical colour. All the regulars were there: the boys from the club, Patsy, Albert cheerleading on top of the bar counter, and Lenny, who was attempting to limbo under a rigged-up washing line.

"Welcome to Jamaica," Lenny yelled. "Limbo, limbo, how low can you go?"

A straw hat was plonked unceremoniously on Danny's head and a glass of rum punch placed in his hand. It felt like sunshine to Danny, like coming out of the grey cloud of wedding arrangements and endless logistics.

These were his friends, his family. It was a time to forget everything you were supposed to remember.

Calypso music played to enhance the Caribbean atmosphere. Harry Belafonte on the record player was joined by Lenny in a spirited version of *Island in the Sun*, while the limbo contest got under way in earnest. Even Albert threw caution to the wind and had a go. It was a valiant effort, but he lost his balance, fell over and succeeded in tipping a glass of rum punch over his specially bought exotic Hawaiian shirt, an incident followed by a less exotic and somewhat crestfallen "Bollocks!"

Mopping himself down, Albert called for order, and rang the bar bell loudly to announce the winner of the limbo contest.

"The winner is... Jimmy Ramsbottom!"

Jimmy was another boxer from the club and part of the brotherhood. The owner of a slightly unfortunate surname, Jimmy was a flyweight and only about five foot two inches tall.

"He had an unfair advantage, he's a short arse!" shouted Lenny. "I'm the Limbo King around here!"

Half cut and the worse off for too many rum chasers, Jimmy decided to take a swipe at Lenny. Thankfully he missed, but landed a pretty useful punch into the rock-hard stomach of Patsy.

The scene changed from raucous fun to the kind of anticipation you see in those westerns, when the gunfighters have a stand-off. Patsy eyed up little Jimmy, and little Jimmy looked very nervous. The partygoers held their breath.

In one smooth motion, Patsy grabbed a bowl of trifle made especially by the landlady Maria for the party and emptied it on little Jimmy's head. Custard, cream, sponge, jam, the lot. The cherry, which had been carefully placed on top to enhance the presentation, stayed beautifully positioned on top of Jimmy's nose. The little flyweight resembled a cross between a circus clown and a piece of modern art.

There was a shocked silence, and then a lot of laughter. As if on cue, the food fight began in earnest. Sausage rolls and pork pies bounced off heads, bread rolls were hurled like missiles. Lenny had an aim that was lethal thanks to his cricket experience, and could throw a pickled egg like a return throw from the boundary. In the thick of the fight, Danny was enjoying himself hugely.

Grabbing the bar bell and ringing it as loudly as possible, Albert attempted to restore order.

"Come on lads, we don't want a full-out bar-room brawl! Calm it down. Now gentlemen, a bit of respect for a lady. May I introduce to you… Fifi Lamour!"

All eyes turned to Fifi's entrance, with only the odd pig in a blanket or profiterole occasionally still airborne. A small flying sausage from Little Jimmy narrowly missed Fifi's head.

"That's about the size of yours, ain't it Jimmy lad?" Patsy shouted, to hoots of laughter.

Fifi seemed very professional in her chosen art. Dressed in black stockings and suspenders with a mock policewoman's shirt and tie, she was still attractive, although a little bit dumpy, with dyed blonde hair and a faraway look in her eyes.

As Danny watched her gentle gyrations, he couldn't help wondering why a lady would do this. Perhaps she was a struggling single mother, or was forced to do it by a pimp. His thoughts were rudely interrupted by Fifi's ample breasts, thrust in gay abandon like two soft pillows into his face.

It was difficult to know what to do in that kind of situation, so Danny did very little, in the hope that Fifi would move on to a more appreciative audience. She did, but not before straddling Danny and wiggling a lot, which brought a huge cheer from the chaps. Submission was the best bet. Danny decided to grin and bear it.

Two raunchy songs later, Fifi's act was over. She collected her payment from Lenny and disappeared into the night. Celebrations were starting to tire, so Albert took over once more.

"We got a coach waiting to take us all up the West End to do a spot of gambling," he told the crowd, "just to round the evening off. Lenny?"

Grinning, Lenny presented Danny with his fifty-pound wedding gift.

"With this," Albert proclaimed as Danny stammered his thanks, "you can break the casino, son. Now who's with us?"

There was another cheer as the drunken revellers prepared to leave the food-sodden pub and board the waiting coach.

Maria the landlady, who had lovingly and unwittingly prepared the ammunition, was livid.

"Look at the state of this place," she bellowed. "What are you, animals?"

"It's all right, Maria, just a bit of fun," Albert tried to say, but it was no use.

"Get out of my bloody pub!" Maria screamed, and gave Albert a manly shove out into the street.

The coach driver was understandably reluctant to let the motley food-covered mob on to his nice clean coach, and was arguing with Jimmy the trifle-head flyweight. Albert stepped in to defuse the situation.

"Don't worry mate," Albert soothed. "Any mess I'll pay for."

In all honesty, the little money he owned had already been spent on Danny's party. But it was important to Albert that the celebrations went to plan.

The coach driver finally agreed to let them on. Some of the boys climbed into the coach and fell over. One or two were so legless they were unable even to manage that, so they were carried aboard. Little Jimmy was sick all over the coach driver's shiny shoes, so the coach now smelled like a cross between a pig sty and a pub. Muttering, the coach driver started up the engine and headed up to town.

Piccadilly Circus was around five miles from the East End. There was much singing, with Danny the loudest of all. Most participants joined in, usually in different keys, with a bawdy song about Salome who apparently had hairs on her belly like the branches of a tree, while the half-spoken, half-sung rendition of *Danny Boy* from Patsy almost moved Danny, sitting in pride of place at the front of the coach, to tears.

The boys did the Hokey Cokey proud and even attempted the Conga. Finally, much to the relief of the suffering coach driver, the rabble arrived at the bright lights of Piccadilly, where they more or less fell out of the coach with hearty cheers and drunken legs.

Like most big cities, London is a place that's hard to shock. But even with the average Londoner's casual take on unusual behaviour, the stag party with their Caribbean garb and piggy-back races round Piccadilly's famous fountain turned more than a few heads – particularly when little Jimmy decided to use the fountain as a washroom to remove the remnants of the trifle from his head.

"Come on, you lot!" Albert shouted, when a couple of policemen started taking notice. "Time to move on!"

He did his best to lead the party through Soho's sleazy streets. A swift head count seemed to show that all were present and correct. He found a broken umbrella in a bin and placed his straw hat on top, tour-leader style, trying to keep the rabble in check with a constant reminder to "Follow the hat! Follow the hat, lads!"

Another head count revealed the loss of three members of the clan to other establishments en route. Circumnavigating the many strip joints and ladies of the night, keeping a firm eye on Danny as he swayed along on Lenny's guiding shoulder, Albert eventually found a casino. The next task, of course, was to get this lot in. It wasn't easy.

"This is a fine place you got here," he told the anxious-looking casino receptionist. "Very classy. I got a group of hard-working lads who want to come and spend their money in your establishment in the name of harmless stag-night fun. That's OK, isn't it?"

The receptionist pursed her lips and adjusted her low-cut top. "I'll have to call upstairs to the owner, sir," she said. "If you'll bear with me?"

Albert waited while Patsy and Lenny tried to keep the boys in check out on the street. Then his heart sank like a lead balloon. None other than Tommy Costa was coming down the stairs.

This was not the grand finale to the party that Albert had envisaged.

Costa eyed the dishevelled Albert up and down.

"Hello, old man," he said in amusement. "What you doing in my gaff? Ain't it past your bedtime?"

Of all the establishments in London, Costa's place would definitely have been bottom of the list. Albert attempted to think on his feet as Costa brushed past him to see what all the noise outside was about.

In the lamplit street, Danny was happily riding around on someone's shoulders. Another of the lads was climbing up a street lamp. Little Jimmy was tap dancing and the rest of the rabble were playing football with an empty beer can while Patsy and Lenny attempted to keep order.

"Hello champ," said a smooth, familiar voice. "Having fun?"

Seeing the unlikely figure of Costa through a half-cut mist of trifle and rum punch rendered Danny almost speechless.

"It's my stag night," he managed to answer, swaying up high on his perch.

"Wonderful," purred Costa, all smiles and cordiality. "Come in and celebrate with us." He cast his eye over Danny's unruly bunch of mates, adding: "We can't let your friends in, sorry. We're too busy and the dress code demands a jacket and tie."

The refusal didn't seem to worry the other boys too much. There were plenty of other more appealing local prospects to savour than Costa's gambling den. Almost at once, they started trickling away into the night and Patsy and Lenny followed.

"Bring the kid in, Mick," Costa instructed the doorman. "Drinks on the house."

Albert was in reception as Danny was ushered through.

"What about Albert?" he asked. "Can't he come in?"

"Dress code," Costa said, without looking in Albert's direction. "You have a nice suit. He looks like he just got off a banana boat."

Danny stood his ground, swaying slightly. "I'd like Albert to come in too. He organised it."

Costa shot a grudging look at Albert. "As it's you, champ," he said.

Albert and Danny were hustled into the roulette room. Talking the whole while, Costa treated Danny like a VIP and Albert like he was invisible.

"What are you having, champ? Whisky? We'll fix you a steak sandwich and the best seat in the house. Come and enjoy yourself."

Danny's wedding gift of fifty quid evaporated in an embarrassingly short time. Albert stood by silently and watched. Even through the fog of alcohol, Danny could see that Albert was really uncomfortable in Costa's presence. But he didn't know what to do about it.

★

"It's getting late, Danny," Albert said as the clock inched towards two a.m. "Big day tomorrow."

"No need to leave just yet," Costa coaxed. "Have another drink."

Danny knew Albert was right. "I'm getting married tomorrow," he said. "Thanks for your hospitality, Mr Costa, but we should call it a night."

Costa shrugged. "Have it your way," he said.

"See you at the wedding," said Danny awkwardly.

"Looking forward to it," said Costa, pulling Danny into a hug. He clicked his fingers at the doorman. "Mick? Show our visitors out."

Outside the streets were still busy and full of nightlife. Danny felt deflated and sobered by what had been a strange ending to a happy night.

"So," Albert said as they reached the night bus stop. "Costa's coming to the wedding?"

Danny was starting to find this tiptoeing around Costa and Cohen tedious. He had his future to think of. Surely Albert could see that? He tried to play it down like it was no big deal.

"Yeah, him and Cohen," he said. "I need to keep my options open."

Albert spent the bus journey not speaking and looking out the window. Beside him, Danny couldn't enjoy the ride. He had mixed feelings about everything right now. On one hand, he thought of Wendy and her family and how excited they were to hear about the liaison with Cohen and Costa. On the other, he was wrestling with feelings of disappointment and guilt on his friend and mentor's behalf.

As the bus reached his stop, Danny gripped Albert's arm.

"I want you always to be involved, Albert," he said. "I wouldn't be a fighter if it wasn't for you."

"We'll see," answered Albert non-committally. "Good night, Danny."

It wasn't quite the answer Danny had wanted as he left the bus and watched it move off down the Whitechapel Road.

The sun was beginning to rise as Danny wearily reached home. He felt empty and alone, like he was the only person left in the world.

Going upstairs to his room, he could hear the distant sound of Ricky's snoring down the corridor. Reaching under his bed, he picked up the red and silver box, opened it and sifted gently through the contents. For no particular reason, his eyes filled with tears.

"What's happening, Dad?" he whispered.

In the past, Danny had always answered his own questions the way he imagined his father might have done. He didn't do that now. Everything seemed so futile, so pointless. Here in the early-morning hours, he felt nothing at all.

Closing the box and his eyes, Danny drifted off into an uneasy sleep.

CHAPTER EIGHT

DANNY woke up to the sound of Rosie's hairdryer. His brain felt like lead and the hairdryer sounded like a road drill as he tried to lift his hungover head from the pillow.

This was the big day. The day when he should have been feeling excited. After all, he was about to marry his childhood sweetheart and future mother of his baby. But his subconscious was still troubled by loyalty to Albert, and the reality of marriage and fatherhood without a handbook to guide him along the way was sinking in. So a black cloud hung over Danny's morning, obscuring the view.

It was already eleven-thirty, and the service was scheduled for two p.m.

Albert was supposed to arrive about twelve to begin his best man duties. Danny hoped he'd make it, not least because Albert was picking up his wedding suit and bringing it over. His only back-up – the old navy suit – was still encrusted with food from last night's shindig. He could just imagine Wendy's face if he turned up in that. A Norman Wisdom-fitting suit, smelling like a putrid larder.

As Danny eased himself into the bath and the comforting

warm water, he could hear Rosie discussing with Ricky what she should wear for the wedding. He hoped she would give the leopard-print dress a miss and wear something a bit classier, but he wasn't hopeful. As for Ricky, if he turned up in one of his Elvis outfits, Danny was ready to disown them both.

Feeling slightly more upbeat and a touch more human after his bath, Danny looked in the mirror as he shaved. He was really starting to resemble that cherished photograph in the red and silver box. This somehow made Danny feel stronger, more in control. As he looked in the mirror and smiled, it almost felt like his dad was smiling back.

The clock downstairs struck noon as the doorbell pealed out its annoying Big Ben chimes. Albert, thought Danny. Right on time.

As Ricky opened the door, Danny heard Lenny's voice. He grabbed his dressing gown and went downstairs.

Lenny looked like somebody else, dressed in his best cream suit with shoes you could see your face in and a very serious expression.

"You look sharp, Len," said Danny.

"A choc ice dressed as a pox doctor's clerk," Ricky grunted. "Now I've seen it all."

"I got something for you, Danny," said Lenny, ignoring Ricky.

As he handed over Danny's wedding suit, shirt, waistcoat and cravat, Rosie made her grand entrance down the stairs, dressed to kill in head-to-toe leopard print topped off with a giant pink hat. The impression was not unlike a movie star from a bygone era. Rosie held her head high in a cloud of cheap perfume and struck a model-like pose.

"What d'ya think?" she said, and gave her audience a bit of a twirl.

Danny and a startled-looking Lenny nodded without a word.

Ricky whistled. "Beautiful, my darling," he said. "The belle of the ball."

Danny decided the best thing was to escape upstairs as soon as possible and get dressed.

"Thanks for the suit, Len," he said. "Where's Albert, is he on his way? He was supposed to be here for twelve."

Lenny cleared his throat. "I saw Albert," he said. "He came by me garage this morning, to give me the suit and a letter he told me to give you."

Danny slowly took both the letter and the suit.

"I'll be back later with the car to pick you up," Lenny added.

"Yeah, right," said Danny, staring at the letter. "Thanks Len."

Danny headed up the stairs. Sitting on his bed, he opened the envelope.

DEAR DANNY,

Sorry, but feeling a bit rough today so I am unable to make the wedding. I send my very best wishes to the bride and groom. I hope you have a wonderful day, and I wish you both well.

ALBERT

He had half-expected this. He knew at once that the presence of Cohen and Costa at the wedding had brought on Albert's mystery illness. With no best man, and indeed no best friend, Danny felt deflated. He felt like going round to see Albert, but thought he'd better not force the issue. Besides, he wasn't sure where Albert actually lived, because he had never invited Danny round.

Danny decided he had enough on his plate today. Though he was disappointed, he tried to look on the bright side. At least a drunken confrontation at the wedding breakfast between Albert, Cohen and Costa wouldn't now spoil Wendy's big day. And Albert had been spared meeting Rosie and Ricky and their unique fashion sense.

Feeling like a trussed-up chicken, Danny was soon suited and booted and ready to go. Rosie and Ricky headed off to the church on Ricky's BSA Gold Star motorbike, with Rosie desperately holding on for dear life to her very big hat. It felt to Danny like the lull before the storm.

All was now quiet, the empty house full of memories. Danny listened to the clock's *tick-tock*, the soundtrack to his growing up. Danny's mum's pride and joy, second only to her radiogram, the grandfather clock in the hall was like the heartbeat of home. As Danny looked around at the familiar furniture and ornaments he had lived with all his life, a wave of nostalgia came over him. Soon it wouldn't be his home any more.

As the clock's second hand moved slowly and he heard the clock chime one, Danny thought about the many things the house had seen. His mum's parties, which had kept him awake. His childhood friends congregating around the gramophone and playing Rosie's records before she came home. The pet mouse he had called Micky, and how he'd cried when Micky died. His bedroom upstairs where he'd once put together the model of a Spitfire. The smell of cooking mixed with Rosie's perfume, the kitchen tap that always dripped and the stairs that creaked; all would soon be memories.

He walked into the living room, found his favourite record, *Tutti Frutti* by Little Richard, and put it on. It sounded good. Danny liked the way the music transported him back to a less complicated time.

When the record finished, there was just the tick of the clock and the dripping tap to be heard. The clock struck one-thirty, and Danny came back from yesterday to now and to the future. To the wedding.

For a small fee, Lenny had procured a nearly new Ford Cortina from one of his clients to act as a limo and to drive Albert and Danny to the church. When Danny opened the door, he saw Lenny with the polished and valeted Cortina, the usual wedding ribbons attached to the wing mirrors for the occasion. There was no Albert in the back. Danny had hoped Albert might have a change of heart, but no.

"You're looking sharp, man," said Lenny, eyeing up Danny in his wedding regalia.

"The motor looks good, Lenny," Danny replied, then stated the obvious. "No Albert?"

"Better get going," was Lenny's reply. "You go in the back, make you look more important. But I ain't wearing no chauffeur hat."

These weren't the kind of nerves Danny felt before a fight. They felt different, not unlike the butterflies he felt when he first kissed Wendy. The kind he felt when he'd first gone to Patsy's boxing gym.

As the Cortina pulled up at the church, impressing the guests outside, Danny panicked.

"The wedding rings!" he said. "Albert had the rings!"

"Don't worry," Lenny replied calmly. "Albert gave them to me."

Danny eased the collar away from his neck. He was sweating. Seeing a group of guests at the door of the church having a quick cigarette before the service focused him on his role. He'd practised this with the vicar and Wendy a few evenings ago. It was going to be fine.

Danny got out of the car, going over the choreography of the day in his mind.

"All right, Danny?"

"Good luck in there, mate."

He nodded absently at a few church stragglers, most of whom he had never met. Lenny stood awkwardly with him. They were were relieved to see the hand of the vicar at the church door outstretched in welcome.

The Reverend John Edwards had a headful of white hair, smiling eyes and a stammer. Now in his sixties, he had seen many of his congregation literally come and go, with countless baptisms and funerals. Weddings meant too much confetti strewn over the churchyard, but the vicar seemed happy to grin and bear it. His genial presence brought a sense of calm and order to proceedings.

"Where is your b-b-best man?" he asked.

Danny wiped his forehead. "He's not here. But Lenny has got the rings."

"Yeah Father," Lenny confirmed. "I can be the second-best man."

"Very good. Don't w-w-worry, I'll guide you through the service. Now, we'd b-b-better get going, I have a christening in thirty minutes. Shall w-w-we go in?"

As they walked through the large arched wooden doors, the chatting turned into whispering, like the reverence shown when visiting someone in hospital. Rosie waved furiously, poised for a good cry with handkerchief in hand. Rick gave Danny the thumbs up.

Black Lenny's appearance caused a minor stir, but respect seemed instinctively to prevail in the hallowed surroundings. Nods and smiles all round greeted Danny as he walked to the altar. He felt as if he was floating, mentally and physically. The demonic-sounding church organ provided the backdrop to this surreal dream.

He was brought back to earth when he saw Cohen and Costa standing on his sparsely populated guest side of the church. With smiles like Cheshire cats and the light from a nearby candle catching Costa's gold tooth, they gave Danny a wave. Lenny made that hissing sound he used when a job was a nuisance.

At the altar, Lenny dropped to one knee and crossed himself, which surprised Danny. He was anxious to get going. It was now past two o'clock, and there was no sign of Wendy yet.

"It's tradition for the bride to be late," Lenny whispered in Danny's ear. "Don't worry man, she'll be here soon enough."

The organist played on, a rather sombre and funereal choice. Then, silence. An air of anticipation floated through the church followed by Mendelssohn's well-used Wedding March.

Heads turned in admiration. Danny turned too.

A vision of stunning beauty in a flowing white dress with a veil across her smiling face, Wendy looked a picture as she and her father made their regal entrance. Through the ringing in his ears, Danny could hear crying. Clearly some of the lady relatives were determined to enter fully into the emotion of the occasion, Wendy's mum among them. Hopefully they were tears of joy.

"You're a lucky man," Lenny murmured as Wendy floated majestically down the aisle.

Speechless, Danny could only nod in agreement.

Reaching Danny's side, Wendy looked into his eyes and smiled. Their love was clear for all to see.

Possibly because of the time pressure of the upcoming christening, the vicar's stammer grew worse as the service got under way. It really came to prominence when he tried to pronounce "Wendy".

"Do you, Wa-wa-wa," said the vicar. "Do you, Wa-wa... Do you..."

On the third attempt, Wendy got the giggles. Danny followed. The pressure of the occasion had got to them both, and like a pair of naughty children, they were soon uncontrollable.

A stern look from Mr Bristow restored some sense of order. The probably-too-happy couple managed to confirm their vows with just the odd snort of laughter, much to the relief of both vicar and congregation. Then the vicar invited the witnesses to the back of the vestry to sign the paperwork. As Albert had not made the wedding, Danny pushed Lenny into taking his place.

And at last, with the register signed and the organ in full swing, the church bells rang out with a vengeance, heralding the emergence of Mr and Mrs Danny Watson.

Back in his bedsit, Albert could hear the church bells ringing in the distance. Rocky did her version of Irish dancing on her favourite perch, a treat she reserved for bell-ringing occasions.

Rocky was happy, but Albert felt a sadness. He had wanted to be there, but socialising with Cohen and Costa was something he couldn't stomach. Although Danny's betrayal still hurt, he felt he had let the boy down.

He looked out of his window towards the church just a few streets away.

Perhaps he had overreacted; perhaps he should have honoured his commitment to be best man. He had asked Lenny to look after Danny on his behalf, but he was full of mixed feelings. He'd had a right to be there, much more than the new duo trying to muscle in on Danny's boxing career.

He picked up the photo of his son from the sideboard, stroking his fingers over the young Tommy's face. Tears filled his eyes. Danny had helped to fill the void left by his Tommy's death and it hurt Albert to think he was not present at the boy's big day. But as usual, Albert's principles, coupled with his stubbornness, had made the decision for him.

If he had gone, any word out of place from Cohen and Costa would have led to an awkward and possibly physical outcome. Albert was no longer young, but his reflexes and punches were still sharp, and to cause a commotion at the wedding would certainly spoil the day. Danny's day. So his decision to steer clear was best for all.

The bells stopped ringing and Rocky stopped dancing. Albert wondered if Danny's mother had been at the wedding. He'd never been introduced to her, but felt he knew her from all of Danny's stories. He thought of Lenny decked out in his cream suit, looking worried when Albert had delegated his best man duties on to Lenny's reluctant shoulders.

Feeling like an outsider, Albert looked through his window at the Trinity Church steeple. Not sure if it was wanting to be a part of Danny's day or just curiosity, he grabbed his coat and hat and went out into the street.

Simon was downstairs, wrestling with a set of Victorian drawers outside his shop.

"Present and correct Albert, off to the wedding?" he asked. "Enjoy yourself."

"Will do," Albert replied, and quickly made off before Simon could interrogate him further.

Making his way towards the church, he stood a safe distance away. He could see the confetti-covered newly-weds posing for photographs, the stately horses and carriage, people getting in cars to make their way to the reception. None of them noticing the scruffy figure standing alone on the corner.

As Albert stood and watched, he thought how good Danny and Wendy looked together, how happy they were. But the smile on his face soon faded when he saw Cohen and Costa warmly shaking Danny's hand, congratulating the couple with all the smarmy good wishes they could muster. The promoters got into their expensive cars: Cohen in his white Jaguar and Costa in his black Mercedes. Not even noticing Albert, they drove away to the reception. Albert felt invisible and helpless, and he didn't like it.

He gave himself a stern talking-to. What right did he have to stand in Danny's way? Why should he feel bad about the boy he had mentored wanting to better himself? Cohen and Costa had money and power. He just had a faded glory that few remembered.

Perhaps it was time to let bygone be bygones. He would talk to Danny. And if, as he had said, he still wanted Albert to be involved, then so be it.

Mr Bristow's contacts with the local Conservative Club had led to them making a considerable effort for the wedding reception. There was still the smell of stale beer and tobacco, but there were also balloons, tables nicely set out and a banner saying "Congratulations to Danny and Wendy!" in the claret and sky-blue colours of the boxing club and local football team. All in all, a good effort.

The guests started to arrive and find their places. The bride and groom, the Bristows, Rosie and Ricky were all on the top table. In Albert's absence Lenny had been promoted to the top table as well. Luckily he had not been seated next to Ricky, as Ricky's distaste for "choc ices" could have become tricky.

Cohen and Costa, looking distinctly out of place, sat on a table with Wendy's elderly relatives, and were doing their best to be charming. Patsy had been placed next to the seat which should have been Lenny's, but now remained empty.

Looking over at the empty chair, Danny thought about Albert. The letter had said he wasn't feeling well, but it hadn't rung true. No matter how ill Albert felt, he would have been there, even if it had meant crawling there on his hands and knees. No, Danny knew better. He knew how strong-minded Albert was, and he knew exactly why he hadn't come.

Mr Bristow struck a wine glass with a spoon to make an announcement. When no one took any notice, he struck it again, this time a little harder. The glass promptly shattered, most of it straight into Mrs Bristow's lap, which did the job.

"Welcome one and all, to our wedding breakfast to celebrate Wendy and Danny's marriage," Mr Bristow announced. "I'd like to propose a toast to Her Majesty Queen Elizabeth the Second!"

Danny wasn't sure why it was called a wedding breakfast. It was four-thirty in the afternoon. Surely it should be called tea or dinner? Whatever its name, the celebratory meal consisted of rubbery chicken and overcooked veg. The revellers revelled manfully through it. Close on the heels of the beige chicken dinner came a decent trifle that reminded Danny of little Jimmy Ramsbottom.

"Ladies and gentlemen," said Mr Bristow. "I give you… the best man!"

Without Albert, the best man berth was still wide open. Lenny looked like making a speech was the last thing he wanted to do. Danny breathed an apprehensive sigh of relief as Tommy Costa stood up to to fill the void.

"My lords, ladies and gentlemen," Costa began. "I'll make this short. I have known the groom for a while now. He's a good boy with a big future in boxing who ain't punch drunk just yet. You only have to take a look at his new wife, the beautiful Wendy, to see that."

Wendy smiled and turned pink with embarrassment.

"So please join me," Costa went on with a grin, "in toasting the bride and groom."

"The bride and groom!"

Glasses clinked around the room as Mr Bristow took over, welcoming Danny into the family, thanking bridesmaids, the cake maker and as many folk as he could remember. As the applause died down, Wendy gave Danny a nudge.

"Your turn, Danny," she whispered. "Say something."

Danny reluctantly got to his feet. "Thanks for coming," he managed. "Time to cut the cake."

The three-tier cake was pretty impressive. It had been made by Wendy's Great Aunt Madge, a chain-smoking lady from somewhere north of Watford, who looked on proudly as Danny and Wendy posed for photographs next to her masterpiece.

With the cake cut and a chilling scream from Danny's mum to ward off evil spirits, a three-piece muzak-style band called Sid and the Melody Kings began to play. The line-up consisted of a chubby drummer who looked about fifteen, a clarinet player who looked about one hundred and fifteen, and the band leader, Sid, a thin grey chain-smoker who tinkled the ivories on his electric piano.

Tables and chairs were moved to the sides of the room and Danny and Wendy took to the floor for the traditional first dance. Wendy's choice – *Love Me Tender* by Elvis – was a good one, but with Ricky crooning along in his best Elvis impression, a little of the romance was lost.

Wendy and Danny cruised around the dance floor. Danny's footwork was a little suspect, but Wendy managed to guide him round in a forceful but loving way, with only a hint of a grimace when Danny stepped repeatedly on her pretty open-toed white shoes.

With a round of applause, Danny's ordeal was over.

"Ladies and gentlemen," cried Sid, the band leader. "We invite you all to join the happy couple on the dance floor!"

Mr and Mrs Bristow took up the invitation, followed by Wendy's excited young second cousin, who slid on his backside on to the dance floor just a little too close for Mr Bristow's liking, cramping the magnificence of their sedate Viennese waltz.

"Thanks for the invitation, Danny," said Cohen. "We gotta get going."

"You look beautiful, Mrs Watson," Costa added. "Like a princess."

"Please accept these small gifts as a token of our admiration," said Cohen as Costa handed over a nicely wrapped wedding gift.

Wendy unwrapped the box. Inside were two identical watches, one for a lady and one for a man.

"Goodness," said Wendy. "This is ever so generous of you."

Danny felt a little dazzled by the sight of the watches. The pots, pans and cheap tea sets from the other guests were no match for this extravagant gift.

"Here's to our future together," said Cohen with a wink.

"Together we can take on the world," said Costa.

The men shook Danny's hand, grabbed a bit of wedding cake and made their retreat.

"They're so nice," said Wendy, turning her wrist to admire her new gift.

"Yeah," said Danny. "They're all right, aren't they?"

The wedding was beginning to warm up now, helped by the beer and spirits on tap. More people took to the floor in a sparsely supported but spirited Gay Gordons.

"Ladies and gentlemen," announced Sid, "please take the floor for the twist!"

The Gay Gordons were forgotten as the floor was immediately jammed. It seemed everyone had their own particular moves, all based on Chubby Checker's hit. Ricky and Rosie led the way. Ricky's legs seemed to be having an out-of-body experience as he sang at the top of his voice in a key that was very different to the Melody Kings' rendition. Sid and his Melody Kings did their best to keep up. They weren't the perfect combination, musically, for a bit of rock 'n' roll, but they were effective enough.

Lenny danced like a demon and was the centre of attention. Ricky's furious legs were no match for Lenny's natural sense of rhythm, and he retired to the side of the dance floor to glower.

"They're good at that, the darkies," he told Rosie glumly. "Must be jigging about to those jungle drums."

The wedding day was perfect. No fights, no family feuds and a good time had by all. A special day to remember for Danny and Wendy.

CHAPTER NINE

THE morning after the wedding saw Danny once again the worse for wear. Not being a drinker, he'd had more than his fill over the weekend, and was suffering.

Wendy, on the other hand, out of respect to the unborn baby, had only sipped one glass of champagne during the whole function and nothing else. She had been up bright and early, packing for their honeymoon and raring to go.

Mr and Mrs Bristow had kindly rented the couple a caravan for a week at Clacton-on-Sea. That, plus the whip-round from the boys at the boxing club totalling a generous twenty-one pounds and ten shillings, meant the honeymooners had a week of leisure ahead of them and money in their pockets to spend.

Gingerly washing and shaving, Danny thought about the events of the previous day. It had gone well, he thought, but he still had Albert and his absence nagging at the back of his mind.

There wouldn't be time to talk to Albert before he left for his honeymoon. It would have to wait till he got back. Any liaison with Cohen and Costa would have to wait too.

Wendy banged on the bathroom door. "Danny, hurry up, we'll miss the train!"

"Won't be long!" he called back, and quickly got dressed.

The honeymoon was an exciting prospect. A train ride and a week by the sea, a welcome change from the East End streets.

"It would be nice to bring up the baby in the fresh country air, wouldn't it?" said Wendy as they watched the countryside roll by out of the train window. "Now Mr Cohen and Mr Costa are going to help you make all that money, Danny, we could buy a nice house with a garden."

"We don't want the baby talking like a country bumpkin," Danny joked, still trying to circumnavigate the Albert conundrum in his head.

Rolling down to the Essex coast, the train pulled into Clacton-on-Sea station. Baskets of flowers hung along the platform.

"Ain't it nice!" cooed Wendy.

There was the smell of the sea in the air and seagulls circled noisily in search of any fish or chip they could nick from a unsuspecting holidaymaker.

All was right in the world as Danny and Wendy found the bus to the Happy Valley holiday camp and climbed aboard.

The camp wasn't quite as impressive as the station. Dragging their suitcase into the wooden cabin marked RECEPTION, Wendy and Danny found a surly man with long sideburns waiting inside.

"Name?"

"Mr and Mrs Watson," Wendy proudly announced.

Danny grinned at her. It felt good to hear her say that.

"One week," stated their host. He handed Danny the key. "Row four, third berth down."

Wendy and Danny tracked down their love nest after about ten minutes: an ancient caravan called "Dream Days" which had obviously seen better days.

"Ready, Mrs Watson?" said Danny, determined not to show a glimmer of disappointment.

Wendy smiled up at him as he carried her over the threshold. There was an almost reassuring smell of mustiness and past fry-ups inside.

"Oh it's lovely," Wendy said. "Look, if you stand on the sofa, you can see the sea."

There was a moment of silence, followed by uncontrollable laughter.

"Mum's hop-picking cow shed was better than this," said Danny, grinning.

He and Wendy were in love, and the run-down honeymoon suite was going to be a comical experience. Now they were alone together, the surroundings didn't matter. They would be content in a cave.

After unpacking, they decided to do a recce of the Happy Valley holiday camp and its facilities. There wasn't that much to see: rows of caravans, a couple of tents, the communal washrooms and, the cherry on the sundae, a social club.

Wendy and Danny watched all the toddlers tottering about and talked about the forthcoming baby. A few names were suggested, but nothing settled on.

"Look!" Wendy pointed out a poster heralding the Knobbly Knee Contest the following afternoon. "You should enter, you'll definitely win that."

"Oi!" said Danny, laughing.

They were both anxious to get to the beach, so Wendy packed a few things in a bag and Danny sought directions from a jolly caravan neighbour.

The weather for September was decent and the sun glistened on the calm grey ocean. Danny splashed out on a bag of chips, and they found a spot they liked near the pier where they sat side by side to watch the never-ending motion of the waves, kissed by the seahorses.

"Why do they call them seahorses?" Wendy asked.

"I didn't know they did," Danny replied, putting his arm around her.

Sand castles were built and then washed away by the gentle never-ending waves. Children played, while grandparents slept in rented deck chairs. It was a typical English bucket-and-spade seaside scene, and Danny and Wendy were happy to be a part of it.

After a stroll down the pier, a cheeky look at the "What the Butler Saw" machine and a couple of goes on the pin tables, they decided to head back and get ready for a night out at the social club.

Wendy didn't think much of the communal washroom, although for Danny, it was not unlike the many changing rooms he had spent hours in at boxing tournaments.

Ready for the night and dressed to kill, with Wendy looking lovely in a dress with pink roses on it and Danny in a smart blue jacket and black shirt, they made their way to the club. The early-evening bingo session was reaching its climax, and the concentration of the participants was tangible as they waited, pencils poised, holding their breath and listening intently for that elusive winning number.

The Master of Ceremonies looked slightly bored, with his hair parted in the middle and the look of a nineteen twenties movie star about him.

"Two fat ladies, eighty-eight!" he announced. "On its own number eight, see you at the garden gate!"

"House! Over here!" rang out from a hysterically excited fat lady in the corner. Making her way to the stage through the groans of the losers, arms raised in celebration, she collected her prize bottle of sherry and returned to her table like the conquering hero.

"I don't much fancy this, Wend," said Danny, eyeing the door.

Wendy held on to his arm as the tables and chairs were cleared for the shindig ahead. "Come on Danny," she said, "it's our holiday. We should have fun. There's an empty table over there, look."

After settling Wendy down, Danny went off to the busy bar to purchase a couple of lemonades and a bag of crisps. After fighting to be served and with his purchases in hand, he made his way back to their table.

Wendy had been joined by a group of other campers there for the beer and entertainment. Danny squeezed his way to his seat. Introductions were more of a middle-class thing; working-class folk tended not to do them.

"How long you down for?" asked one of their new neighbours.

"Me and my husband are down for a week," answered Wendy with a smile.

Danny loved hearing her say that. It felt good every time, proper and as it should be.

The three-piece resident band struck up with a vengeance. This seemed to be a signal for every child in the room to head for the cleared dance floor. They ran, they slid, they chased each other, they fell over. Amidst the chaos, two very well turned-out ballroom dancers held their heads high and moved like stately galleons to the band's rendition of *Let's Face the Music and Dance*.

Most of the kids had vented their spleen by now, and the dance floor was starting to feature more grown-ups. The ballroom dancers were still at it, ranging from cha cha to foxtrot for anyone that was interested, but most of the other couples were content enough to just shuffle round. Two little girls danced on their dads' toes and loved it.

"Dance with me," said Wendy as the band launched into a suitably slow tune.

Danny was reluctant at first, but it felt good to be swaying to the music with Wendy in his arms.

"These are the good times and this is us having 'em," he whispered in Wendy's ear.

"I love you," said Wendy and kissed Danny gently on the cheek.

"I love you too," said Danny.

The Romeo on the drums gave all the girls the once-over as the band took a break and the raffle was drawn. Danny watched him eye up Wendy, but decided not to react. The drummer winked at another girl sitting close to the stage, and Danny saw him furtively disappear backstage with the girl in tow. Both of them returned after about fifteen minutes, looking flushed but happy.

There was something moving in the way that these salt-of-the-earth people sang the last song en masse.

"Good night campers, see you in the morning, good night campers, I can see you yawning... drown your sorrow, bring the bottle back tomorrow, good night campers, good night."

Happy Valley was indeed a happy place.

The holiday seemed to fly by. Danny and Wendy visited the amusement park almost every day, and had a lot of fun on the rides: Danny's favourite was the Big Dipper while Wendy loved the Big Wheel. There was only one dicey moment, when Danny was short-changed by a shady showman on the Waltzer. But sensing Danny's fighting skills, the showman grunted an apology and rectified the "mistake".

In a week of candy floss and fish and chips, Danny and Wendy were happiest going for a dip in the cold North Sea.

"You want to watch out for sewage," a beach neighbour told them gloomily towards the end of the week. "London's waste is deposited directly into the sea, you know."

This kind of took the edge off the swimming, and a quick paddle became the order of the day.

Nights at the camp were magical. Wendy and Danny would sit on the beach watching sunsets, and would cuddle together till well after the sun had gone down.

"Look," Wendy said one night. "They've got stars here. So many stars, twinkling in the sky."

"We get stars in London too."

"Not often."

"That's because at home there's too much light in the streets, so you can't see 'em," Danny explained.

Wendy looked up at the star-filled sky. "Which one of those do you reckon is our baby?" she asked.

Danny laughed. "I don't know. But I reckon he'll be our little star."

"How d'ya know it's a he?" said Wendy. "It might be a she. Imagine that! A little me. Two of us! Do you think you could cope?"

"It won't be easy, but I'll try," answered Danny, and kissed Wendy gently on the lips.

As the end of the week approached, Danny's thoughts returned to reality. He had a career choice to make. Wendy was pushing for stronger connections with Costa and Cohen and more security. But Danny was still troubled by Albert's absence at the wedding and his hostile reaction to Danny's hopes and dreams.

On the train home, Danny felt that odd combination of

looking forward to going home and feeling sad that the honeymoon was over. For Wendy, it was back to the sugar factory. For Danny, it was time for some life-changing conversations. He had to start shaping the future now.

CHAPTER TEN

BACK in East London, Albert was collecting glasses at the Live and Let Live as usual, and keeping an eye on Patsy's boxing gym upstairs.

"Ain't you got a clapped-out Ford Anglia engine to be reconditioning, Lenny?" he asked as Lenny ordered another pint of brown and mild.

"That can wait, man," said Lenny. He studied Albert. "We need to talk about Costa and Cohen, and Danny's future."

Albert turned back to the glasses. "It's up to the boy," he said.

"You keep pushing the subject away," said Lenny, tutting as he drained his pint.

"You ain't going to get nowhere with Albert, Len," said Patsy, coming to the bar.

Lenny eyed Patsy. "What's your professional opinion then?"

"He's a contender. What will be will be."

Patsy sounded almost proud. It sounded to Albert as if the big Irishman was weakening on the subject of Cohen and Costa. He'd put a lot of time and energy into Danny's progress, and Albert sensed that he had no plans to let go.

"Do you remember that conversation we had way back, Patsy?" Lenny asked. "When I asked, why do you do what you do? Why are you so committed to training these boys?"

"Some of them had got into bad company. If, by giving them a direction and a reason, I was saving them from a life of crime, that was reason enough." Patsy's eyes darted towards Albert. "And you never know. I might just unearth a future champion."

Albert silently took the glasses into the kitchen. Being a part of Danny's rise was a dream come true for Patsy. Why wouldn't he go along with Cohen and Costa's plans for the boy? Albert felt sad, for reasons he couldn't explain.

Back home at the Bristows', Wendy had been sent a rather large bunch of flowers from Costa and Cohen. There was also a message for Danny to give them a call and meet up.

"Good news, Danny," said Mr Bristow, clapping his new son-in-law on the shoulder. "You're going up in the world, eh?"

The thought of calling Cohen and Costa filled Danny with both excitement and trepidation. He felt he needed to talk to Albert first. Although he knew Albert lived in Canning Town, he'd never discovered Albert's actual address. Albert would most likely be at the park feeding the ducks in the morning. He'd find him there.

That evening, Wendy went through the holiday adventures with her parents, recounting everything from the surly man on reception to the musty old caravan, from the camp to the shady showman on the Waltzers and everything between. Danny did the best he could to enthuse alongside his wife, but his mind kept wandering to the coming meeting with Albert. So he kept quiet, nodding at the right time and shaking his head when needed.

It was good to be back in a proper bed. The caravan had been fun, but pretty uncomfortable, with its drop-down bed that had felt as if it was still occupied by a previous tenant. Danny took his mind off his worries by reaching for Wendy, and, eventually, a good night's sleep was had by all.

The Monday-morning blues hit hard.

"I wish we were back at Happy Valley," Wendy sighed as she got ready for work.

"Me too," was Danny's short reply. He probably should have been a bit more supportive, but had his own blues to turn purple.

With her sugar-factory turban on her head, Wendy gloomily left the house. Danny looked at his watch, the wedding present from Costa and Cohen. It was only eight-thirty. Albert didn't usually get to the pond till about ten, so Danny decided to pop in on his mum on the way to the park.

But by the time he got there, Rosie had already left for work. Only the sound of Ricky's snoring filled the house. Danny went upstairs to his old room. Taking the tin box from under the bed, he opened it.

"I got married, Dad," he told the open box softly. "She's nice, you'd like her."

Outside the window, homing pigeons were circling from the pigeon fancier two doors away. Danny thought how wonderful it would be to fly like a bird. Perhaps his father was that free, up in heaven, above the early wintering sky.

Downstairs, the hall clock was striking ten. Danny was shaken from his thoughts and remembered the job at hand.

At the park, he headed for the duck pond. It seemed right that this meeting should take place there. After all, it was where they'd first met seven years earlier, when Danny had been just sixteen and set to run wild.

On the path by the weeping willow tree, he saw the familiar figure of Albert surrounded by ducks, brown paper bag in hand, sharing the spoils.

"Albert! Hey Albert, how are you?"

Albert's face was expressionless. Danny tried again.

"All right, mate? I've been away on my honeymoon."

"I know," was Albert's response. "Nice."

Danny could see there was work to do here. He sat on the bench behind Albert and waited for him to finish with his feathered friends.

"I'm pleased to see you," he said hopefully. "Sorry you missed the wedding. Do you feel better?"

Still nothing from Albert. Just the sound of battling, quacking ducks.

Danny swallowed hard. "I wanted to talk to you about this Costa and Cohen thing," he said. "Get some advice."

"Don't matter what I think," said Albert. "It's down to you."

Danny realised this was it. It was time to let Albert know how he felt about him.

"Listen Albert," he pleaded. "If they can help me turn pro, and me and the family can have some money, and I get the chance of a proper boxing career, shouldn't I take it? I want you to be involved, I need you there by my side."

Albert turned to face Danny for the first time.

"Do you know what you're getting yourself into?" he said as he joined Danny on the bench.

Danny frowned. "What d'ya mean? They seem all right."

"They have a reputation, Danny. They're dangerous men."

"Maybe. But with you and Patsy with me I'd be fine, wouldn't I?"

"You think you are ready to turn pro?" said Albert. "You really think that?"

This hurt Danny. He knew he'd been swept away with the head-turning compliments from Costa and Cohen, but in the past, both Patsy and Albert had praised him and called him a contender. So why was Albert's faith now so fickle?

The ducks had deserted them and an awkward silence now hung in the air. Danny decided to change the subject.

"We went to Clacton last week," he said. "It was all right."

Albert waited.

Danny became more direct.

"I need to think of my future, Albert," he said. "My new baby. Wendy thinks it's a good idea. I'll make sure that they don't muscle in, honest. You and Patsy will still be part of the team. It could be good for all of us."

"You think so?"

"Why don't we all organise a meeting with them? See what they've got to say?" Danny suggested.

"If that's what you want," said Albert.

"I'll phone them and arrange a meeting then," said Danny.

"If that's what you want," Albert repeated.

Something in Albert's eyes told Danny that the old man knew he was serious about this. That he truly believed that his future and that of his family lay with a liaison with Costa and Cohen. Danny pressed home his advantage.

"At least if you attend the meeting, you can have some input," he said.

Albert somehow looked older. "Who am I to stand in your way?" he said.

Danny felt a flash of hope. "So it's on?"

"If that's what you want. Now, I'm off to work. Let me know when you've arranged the meeting and I'll bring a tin hat."

Danny jumped up as Albert got off the bench. "Thanks," he said. "You won't regret it."

"We'll see about that," Albert replied as he walked off.

Danny sat back down on the bench, full of relief. He watched a mother on the other side of the pond, pushing her baby in a pram through the park, and smiled. He imagined Wendy and their own bundle of joy doing the same thing in the not-too-distant future. That future felt warmer now. Knowing that Albert would be at the meeting gave him confidence. If Costa and Cohen were as dangerous as Albert said, at least Albert would be there for guidance.

Going back to Wendy's, Danny felt as if a weight had been lifted from his shoulders. He would organise the meeting.

He would keep his boxing family around him. Together they were strong.

The way now was forward, and he felt an exciting chapter was about to begin. In just over six months, he would be a father, with a career in the sport he loved and money on the horizon. A pot of gold just waiting at the end of a rainbow. He could leave the casual building work behind, perhaps buy a house for them to live in, with a garden for the little one, and a car. Not that he could drive, but that was a minor detail. A Jaguar would be fab. A house in the sticks would be nice too. Wendy wanted to move to Chigwell, where the big houses were and the air was fresher, where they had stars in the sky just like Clacton.

Wendy arrived home for her lunch break from the factory.

"I've had a chat with Albert, Wend," Danny said as he gave Wendy a hug and a quick kiss. "He's on board."

"I never understood Albert's feelings towards Mr Cohen and Mr Costa," said Wendy. "They've been nothing but charm personified."

"Well, Albert thinks different from us."

"I don't understand why you're so worried about Albert's feelings," Wendy said. "I'm just happy there's some progress on the cards. So you're fixing the meeting then?"

"Yeah," said Danny. "We're gonna sort this whole thing out."

After lunch, Danny found Costa and Cohen's business card and phoned the number.

"Danny boy," said Cohen, after Danny had been put through by a frosty secretary. "Good to hear from you. How was the honeymoon?"

"Great. Wendy says thank you very much for the flowers."

"I hope they were as beautiful as she is."

"Yeah, they were nice," Danny replied, a little awkwardly. "Can we meet up to talk about the contract and that?"

"Of course. When do you want to come in?"

"I'll talk to Albert and Patsy and see when they can make it," said Danny. "Maybe tomorrow afternoon?"

There was a pause.

"Albert and Patsy?" said Cohen.

"Yeah," said Danny. "I'd like them to be there."

"I'm not sure they have your best interests at heart, Danny. Tommy and I believe in you and your future. I'm not convinced they do."

This was not going to be as straightforward as Danny had hoped. If Cohen refused to have Albert and Patsy at the meeting, it would force Danny to make a difficult decision. If Cohen refused, it could be the end of his and Wendy's dream. But with thoughts of loyalty to Albert and Patsy, he stood his ground.

"I would like them to be there," he repeated nervously. "I think it's important."

"I see," said Cohen. "Well, if that's what you want, we can do three o'clock tomorrow. See you then."

And before Danny could say "Thanks," Cohen had hung up.

The phone call troubled Danny. In his mind Albert, Patsy and Lenny had to be a part of this. Cohen's reaction seemed to send a signal that perhaps they would not.

"Did you speak to them?" said Wendy as Danny came slowly back into the kitchen. "Is everything all right?"

"Yeah," said Danny. "We are meeting tomorrow at three."

He held back on the full story of the call. Cohen's reluctance to have Albert and Patsy at the meeting would probably have prompted Wendy to react the same way. She would think that anything that compromised their brighter future with Costa and Cohen was indeed dispensable.

To avoid any more questions before Wendy headed back to work, Danny walked into the back garden. He needed some space and some time to think. He sat on the garden bench beneath a watery grey-blue sky and watched Mr Bristow's Koi carp swimming gently in the pond for a while. He felt torn as he tried to navigate a way through the problem.

What course should he take if the involvement of Albert and Patsy meant saying goodbye to his prospects? If only his father had been there to turn to. In recent times Albert had been almost a father figure, so to turn his back on him was indeed a painful thought. But at the same time, to turn his back on what could be a brighter and more secure future for Wendy and the baby would hurt too.

As he walked along the garden path in the Bristows' well-kept garden, deep in his dilemma, the back door opened.

"Hello Dan," said Mr Bristow. "Congratulations, Wendy tells me you are signing the contract tomorrow to go pro."

Danny swallowed. "Er, yes," he said.

"Don't forget your in-laws when you're rich and famous!"

Danny smiled. Not because he felt like smiling, but in the hope that a smile would finish a conversation that he really did not want to have.

It seemed to work. Mr Bristow made his way to the pond to

feed his fish, allowing Danny to make his excuses and escape.

Grabbing his coat, he thought about Wendy: her glowing beauty, her beloved bump, how she would be the mother of his child. The image strengthened his resolve as he made his way to the Live and Let Live.

Lenny was already at the pub, sitting in his usual seat and sipping his usual drink. "So how's married life treating you then?" he asked.

"Well, I'm still married," Danny replied.

"You keep it like that."

Albert was as usual serving behind the bar and keeping an eye out for any trouble. Not that there was ever any trouble, probably due to Albert's reputation.

Danny looked around. Nothing had really changed from the first moment he'd walked in here, when Lenny had bought Wendy a drink as they were underage all those years ago. He'd been nervous and apprehensive then, but now the pub felt safe, secure, like a second home. With everything in his life changing and feeling so different, it made Danny feel good that the Live and Let Live stood unchanged and constant.

"What's it gonna be?" said Albert as Danny leaned on the bar.

"No, I'm all right," Danny said. "I just came to confirm that meeting thing with Cohen and Costa. It's tomorrow at three at their office, is that gonna be OK?"

Albert took the address that Danny had written on a piece of paper. "Still sure you want me come?" he asked.

"Of course I do," said Danny. "You and Patsy."

"And they're all right with it, are they? Cohen and Costa?"

"Yeah, looking forward to it," Danny surmised.

Albert sighed. "Right. I'll tell Patsy when he comes in."

Leaving the pub, Danny couldn't help feeling as if he had lit the blue touch paper and fireworks could erupt. He walked the damp streets for half an hour, thinking everything through. Then, instead of going back to the Bristows', he made his way to Rosie's house.

It felt good to walk the streets he'd walked as a child, looking for sense memories that would make him feel more secure. He passed the alleyway where he'd had his first kiss, a kiss from a buxom girl the kids called Titsalina: an innocent secret he had kept from Wendy, just in case. As he walked past Old Nosy Parker's house, the net curtains twitched. "Nosy" hated children, Danny remembered. He'd once kicked a football through Nosy's back window: a powerful shot, but off target. He'd never got the ball back.

The old house still felt like home. It was empty and quiet today, except for a radio Rosie always kept on to deter would-be burglars. Not that there was much to take.

Danny climbed the stairs to his room and the red and silver tin box. Opening it up as he had done so many times, feeling the cold medals in his hands, he searched for an answer to what might be a difficult choice tomorrow: a choice between prospects and loyalty.

As he looked at his father's yellowing army photograph, the doubts settled in his mind. The photograph radiated loyalty. Loyalty to comrades, King and country. He would be loyal to Albert and Patsy, come what may.

"Thanks Dad," he said, before closing the box and putting it back under his bed.

Feeling clearer, Danny left a quick note for Rosie saying he had popped in and he was sorry he'd missed her. It wasn't completely true. In a way, he was relieved to be given some time alone with his father's memory to think things through.

He thought about taking the box over with some other things he had taken to the Bristows', but decided for the time being to leave the box in the bedroom where he'd grown up. Almost as a shrine to his childhood.

As he was walking back to Wendy's, a gleaming Austin Cambridge pulled up and the window wound down.

"You want a lift?" asked Lenny.

"Nice motor, Lenny," said Danny. "Does the owner know you're taking it for a spin?"

"Doing a test drive," Lenny replied, tapping his nose. "Drop you off at the top of Wendy's road?"

The Austin Cambridge was an old car, but elegant, with a smell of leather and petrol inside. It went at a fair lick, and pretty soon, they were at Danny's drop-off.

"So, big day tomorrow, champ," said Lenny as Danny got out of the car. "The meeting and all that."

For the first time Danny felt like he didn't have to avoid the question. "Yeah," he said. "Me, Albert and Patsy are gonna hit the big time."

"Hey now, don't forget your cheerleader here!"

"Never," confirmed Danny.

And with a thumbs up, Lenny drove off.

CHAPTER ELEVEN

ON his morning run, Danny often liked to go down by the River Lee, away from the traffic and away from people or, some days, to Albert's park. Today it seemed better to do the river run. He would be seeing Albert later at the meeting, and he wasn't totally confident he could answer any tricky questions posed by Albert beforehand.

But Danny was optimistic. Things would work out.

Back at the Bristows', the family had gone to work. Danny ran a bath and sank into the water. There is something about taking a bath that allows you to mull things over, think things through. Lately, Danny had been doing his fair share of thinking through. Relaxing, he looked at the fish and sea shells on the bathroom wallpaper and felt the warmth of the water wash away his troubles.

As he climbed out of the bath, he couldn't help drawing a smiley face on the misty bathroom mirror. Most men have a little boy inside them just wanting to break through, and Danny was no different.

Wendy had ironed her favourite Danny shirt for the meeting. It wasn't Danny's favourite, but as fashion wasn't really his thing, he thought it best to go along with Wendy's opinion. The blue suit was hanging up, waiting for him. Although he felt much more relaxed in a tracksuit than a lounge suit, Danny made the effort to make an effort. Not quite looking like himself, but looking reasonably smart, he was ready to go.

He was giving his shoes a bit of a shine on the back of his trouser legs when he heard a key in the door.

"Just back for lunch and checking you're looking respectable," said Wendy, kissing him on the cheek. "Let's have a look then. Remember they said the local press might be there."

Danny, feeling like a small boy getting ready for school, stood still, arms by his side, as the inspection commenced.

"Where's the tie Dad lent you?"

"Do I have to?" said Danny, now definitely feeling about six years old.

Ignoring him, Wendy fetched Mr Bristow's favourite stripy blue tie and fixed it firmly around Danny's shirt collar. "That's it," she said, smoothing down his shirtfront. "You look lovely. I reckon, when you go for something like this, you have to look like you don't need it, in order to get it. You know what I mean?"

Left to face the world done up like a dog's dinner, Danny was hoping against hope not to bump into anyone he knew on the way. Thankfully he got to Costa and Cohen's without seeing anyone he knew well, although he did get some quizzical looks and a wolf whistle from some building-site workers he had worked with in the past.

Checking the address and with a belly full of butterflies, he rang the bell. The door opened to a swanky reception with boxing posters on almost every wall: some famous, some forgotten.

Hidden somewhere behind a mask of make-up sat a receptionist: a pretty girl in her twenties with blood-red lipstick and nails to match. Danny approached her, but was ignored in preference to an incoming phone call. Mid-conversation, the receptionist pointed to a seat.

Danny obediently sat down. Looking around the impressive reception, he took in a brown leather sofa, three chairs, a coffee table and a rather tasteless water feature gurgling in the corner, with water flowing from a giant frog's mouth. The receptionist carried on her conversation, oblivious to Danny's presence.

A feeling of anti-climax swallowed him. This was a life-changing moment, but here he was, alone on a sofa, invisible and watching a frog spout water.

He looked at his watch. Five past three. Where were Albert and Patsy? What if they weren't coming? What was he going to do?

The receptionist hung up the phone and looked at him.

"Can I help you?"

"I've a meeting with Mr Costa and Mr Cohen," replied Danny, relieved to be acknowledged.

"Name?"

"Danny. Danny Watson."

The receptionist opened a diary. "You're not down here," she said. "What time was your appointment?"

To Danny, the word appointment seemed dead on. After all his upbeat anticipation, it now felt like he was waiting for the dentist.

"They said three o'clock, me and two others," he said.

"So where are the other two?"

Danny adjusted his collar. "On their way," he said hopefully.

The receptionist looked disbelieving. "I'm sorry," she said, "but I can't see any meeting listed for three o'clock, and Mr Costa and Mr Cohen are out at lunch."

Feeling completely crestfallen, Danny was not sure how to respond.

"Shall I wait then?" he said.

She sniffed. "That's up to you. But I don't know if they will see you."

Danny had built this meeting up in his mind. He'd made all those arrangements with Albert and Patsy and been forced by Wendy into dressing up. He was even wearing a tie. And now here he was, all by himself and being given the cold shoulder.

"I'll wait for a bit," he said, with as much dignity as he could muster.

He was about to pick up a boxing magazine from the coffee table to disguise his discomfort when the doorbell went. The receptionist sighed and pressed the buzzer by her desk, grudgingly opening the door.

To Danny's great relief, it was reinforcements.

"Sorry we're late, son," said Patsy. "Bloody buses."

"We're with him," Albert told the receptionist. "We can go in now."

"Like I told the other gentleman," stated the receptionist, "Mr Cohen and Mr Costa are not back from lunch and I have no record of a three o'clock meeting."

Albert snorted. "Bollocks to that. Call the bloody restaurant and tell 'em to get their arses in gear."

The receptionist started spluttering when the door swung open for a second time. In walked Costa and Cohen, followed by a large, Greek-looking minder. The minder gave Danny, Albert and Patsy a suspicious once-over. Danny recognised him from his drunken stag night in Costa's casino.

"Danny boy," said Costa. "Sorry we're late. Our meeting overran."

"Come through, Danny, you're looking good," said Cohen as he shook Danny's hand.

They both ignored Albert and Patsy. The Greek minder's eyes stayed hostile.

"No calls, Mavis," said Cohen. "Offer our guest a drink, will you?"

Mavis smiled thinly. "Tea or coffee, Mr Watson?"

Danny didn't like the way Albert and Patsy weren't included in the offer. "No thanks," he said. "You know Albert and Patsy, don't you, Mr Costa, Mr Cohen?"

But there was not a flicker of recognition from either man.

★

Albert gritted his teeth, holding back his anger. No point winding these clowns up just yet. It would only reflect badly on Danny.

"Do you still want us to come with you, Danny?" he asked, trying to be polite. He knew he needed to be there, to protect Danny in this shark pool.

"Yeah, of course," said Danny eagerly. "The meeting is with all of us, ain't it?"

"Whatever you want," Costa replied with a false smile, putting an arm round Danny's shoulder.

Inside Cohen's palatial office, Albert stood beside Danny with mixed feelings. He could see that the boy was overawed as he looked at the richly furnished room with its comfortable furniture and private pool table. Patsy hadn't cracked his face yet. Albert just felt utter disdain.

Cohen sat behind an enormous leather-topped desk. "Take a seat," he advised. "We have a lot to get through."

Albert and Patsy chose the sofa. Danny picked a chair closer to the desk. Costa stood with his arms folded.

There was some initial small talk about the wedding, the honeymoon and Wendy's health, all of which irritated Albert. Listening to Costa and Cohen assuming the stance of concerned family members didn't ring true. Albert could see through them both like they were two dirty panes of glass.

"Danny," Costa said at last. "Jack and I believe in you. We think you could have a successful and lucrative boxing career."

Cohen took hold of the reins. "Like Tommy says, you could do well as a boxing professional. Forget these piddling amateur fights, where you're lucky if you get expenses. How long have you been on the amateur circuit?"

"Nearly seven years," answered Danny.

Costa nodded. "Time to move up," he said.

"Danny," said Cohen. "With the right team behind you, you could not only make a name for yourself, but secure your whole family's financial future."

Albert watched Danny listening to Cohen's persuasive banter. His heart felt heavy.

Costa took over. "As you most probably know, Danny, we promote and manage some top fights and fighters."

"And that's what you need, son," said Cohen. "We think that we're the team to make you a big fighter, to make it happen."

"A winning team," Costa confirmed.

Albert sat quietly and said nothing. Like a poker player with a good hand, he was letting nothing show.

Patsy joined the discussion. "You know," he said, "I'm not too sure that the boy is quite ready to turn professional yet. But he's a good fighter, yes."

Danny's eyes darkened. Albert wanted to warn Patsy not to pour cold water on Danny's dreams and push him closer to the Costa/Cohen camp. But the damage was done.

"How little faith, Patsy," said Cohen. "That kind of thinking is not what you need, is it Danny?"

"I don't want the boy to get hurt," said Patsy. "That's all."

"Oh, I think he can take care of himself," said Costa.

"That sounds good to me," Danny chipped in. "I want to do well, I want to earn decent money."

"Of course you do," said Cohen in a sympathetic way. "You sign with us and we make it happen."

There was a moment or two of silence. Cohen lit a large Cuban cigar and leant back in his chair.

Albert had seen and heard enough.

"So what's in the contract?" he said bluntly. "Why don't you take Danny through it?"

"Of course Albert old chap," Cohen replied. "Tommy? Do the honours."

Costa handed Danny a copy of their standard management contract and proceeded to go over the terms.

"One, you sign with us for ten years, during which we have the right to terminate the agreement at any time. Two, we arrange and promote all your future fights. Three, you agree to be fit and ready for the scheduled fights. Four, we have the right to appoint trainers and training camps and regimes either here, or abroad. Five, you will make yourself available for all press and promotion for upcoming fights. Six, our commission will be fifty per cent of your purse and one hundred per cent of the night's takings – after expenses of course."

"Of course," mimicked Albert.

"Simple, straightforward and honest," said Cohen, ignoring Albert.

The money didn't worry Danny too much. As Costa had said, fifty per cent of something was better than the hundred per cent of nothing he had been fighting for so far.

He reflected on clause four: Costa and Cohen's right to appoint trainers and training camps. This was the crunch. The mountain he hoped he would not need to climb. He had made loyalty the top of his list as he looked through his father's box of memories yesterday, but faced with the reality of jeopardising the chance of a better future, this was going to be a tough decision.

He wondered why Albert and Patsy had kept quiet as Costa had read out the clauses. Was it because they didn't want to influence his decision, or were they just not that concerned?

Danny looked at Albert, then Patsy. With his mind made up, he turned back to Cohen and said, "I can't sign this."

Cohen's eyes widened. "Sorry?"

"I can't sign this," Danny repeated.

Cohen silently exhaled a cloud of blue cigar smoke.

"Why, Danny?" asked Costa. "What's the problem?"

"Clause four," Danny said. "I want Patsy and Albert to be my trainers."

There was a huge intake of breath as Costa and Cohen looked at each other. Albert's eyes almost filled with tears.

"That's right," Patsy said defiantly.

"Gentlemen," Cohen said as he looked at Costa. "Can you give us five minutes?"

Albert, Patsy and Danny left Cohen's office. Danny wordlessly shook their hands in a gesture of loyalty and brotherhood before they sat together on the brown leather sofa in the reception area.

Minutes passed, with just the tick-tock of an overdecorated

clock filling the room, the gurgle of the frog fountain and the sound of an ambulance bell hurrying through the streets.

The office door opened and Costa beckoned them back inside.

"Danny," Costa said. "Because we believe in you, I've managed to convince Jack to let things stay as they are with Albert and Patsy. You have our word on that."

"But no other changes," said Cohen. "All right?"

Danny felt a rush of relief. He grinned at Albert and Patsy. Patsy grinned back.

"So are we ready to sign?" Costa said in a showbiz voice. "We've got the local press outside wanting to get a picture."

"Yeah," said Danny happily. "I'll sign."

A photographer was brought in, and hands were shaken. Danny signed the contract, awash with optimism and relief. He'd got what he wanted, and Albert and Patsy were going to be part of it.

"That's my boy," said Patsy as Danny walked beside his friends down the Whitechapel Road with a spring in his step. "You come through, Danny. It may be a bit early, but we'll take it slow. You're turning professional, son, and I'm looking forward to working with you."

"Thanks Patsy," said Danny.

Albert just grunted.

"You boys join me in a celebration drink in the Blind Beggar?" Patsy asked, rubbing his hands.

Danny had never been in the Blind Beggar, but he knew its reputation for shady underworld activity.

"Probably bump into Costa and Cohen there," said Albert

sarcastically. "It's just the kind of place where they hang out, I reckon."

The Blind Beggar had just opened for the evening. As they entered the pub, a few heads turned.

"Albert! Over here!"

In the corner, a stocky, well-dressed man with a face that looked as if he had had a two-week fight with Rocky Marciano got to his feet. "Albert Kemp my old son!" he said. "Slumming?"

Albert's face broke into a smile. "Harry Baldock," he said. "As I live and breathe! Still standing, then?"

Harry Baldock grinned. "Standing with the best of them, old son," he said. "Who are your friends?"

Albert made the introductions.

"Harry was a boxer in his day," he told Patsy and Danny. "One of the best fighters I ever went up against. Harry, young Danny here is a true contender who's about to embark on a professional career. You should keep an eye out for him."

"I'll do that, Albert old son, I'll do that. Who's for a drink?"

They had a couple of pints at Harry's table. Although Danny was enjoying the company and the stories of the good old days, after a couple of hours of Albert and Harry's reminiscences, he wanted to get back to Wendy. So, with fond farewells, he left them to it.

I'm on my way, he thought from the top deck of the trolley bus, looking down at the twists and turns of the streets he knew so well. *It's finally happening.*

Towards the end of the journey, the conductor came by and punched his ticket.

"Don't I know you?" he asked, looking at Danny's face.

"I doubt it," Danny answered cheerfully as he readied himself to jump off the bus. "But you will."

The Bristows were in the living room watching television. Danny tumbled out his news.

"Wonderful!" said Mr Bristow approvingly. He flicked the tie round Danny's neck. "That tie always worked for me."

"Do you want a cup of tea, Danny?" asked Mrs Bristow.

"No thanks. Where's Wendy?"

"She's in bed, she felt tired. Probably still awake though."

Danny took the stairs two at a time.

"It all worked out, Wend," he said, bounding into their room. "I signed the contract, like I told you I would. Everything's gonna be all right."

"That's great," Wendy mumbled, half asleep.

Danny kissed her forehead and gently put his hand on the ever-growing bump. "We're on our way," he said. "You, me and the baby."

Wendy smiled and closed her eyes.

Creeping round the darkened room, Danny was relieved to get his dog's-dinner outfit off. Sliding quietly into bed with one more kiss on Wendy's cheek, he fell into a contented sleep.

The next morning, amidst the usual semi-chaos of most working families – the hurried breakfasts, getting ready, fights for the bathroom – Danny thought happily about what lay ahead. No more hod carrying. He had left the building sites now, and hoped they would soon be a distant memory. He had been given this opportunity, and he had to grab it with both hands, focus and train even harder than before.

He decided not to take his usual running route to the park, but go straight to the Live and Let Live gym. When he got there, only Daisy the cleaner was in, polishing the brass and making the place presentable for the lunch-time opening. Daisy had a curious habit of whistling like an insanely happy milkman whilst she cleaned, which suited Danny's mood this morning.

He persuaded her to unlock the door to the upstairs gym. There was almost a church-like feeling about the darkened theatre of dreams at this time of the morning, and as Danny turned on the lights, he saw the familiar surroundings as if for the first time, the faded posters of past fighters gazing down on him as if to inspire and guide. He looked at the poster of Albert, proud and in his pomp, and almost bowed his head the way a churchgoer bows to the altar.

His eagerness to get going and train hard turned into a reverent awareness of gladiators past. Danny thought about their trials and hardships, their victories and defeats, their dreams and nightmares. He was following in their noble footsteps, and he felt he could not let them down. His commitment would pay homage to those that had gone before him. Heroes, like his father, warriors of the past, faded but still glorious.

With a deep breath, Danny began to work through

the exercises he had been through so many times. There was a strength in him today that he'd rarely felt before. He was now a professional boxer, and this was where he truly belonged. This was where his future would be shaped.

CHAPTER TWELVE

AFTER weeks of hard training under the watchful eyes of Albert and Patsy, there wasn't a single fight on the horizon. Danny was beginning to wonder if Costa and Cohen had changed their minds. Perhaps the inclusion of Albert and Patsy had dampened their enthusiasm.

"You should telephone them and see what's going on," Wendy suggested.

But Danny was apprehensive. If it was bad news, he didn't want to hear it.

"They're like bad pennies," was Albert's take on it. "They'll turn up."

And turn up they did.

After a phone call to the Live and Let Live from Cohen and Costa's receptionist, the officious Mavis, Danny was asked to meet his new managers at the gym the following Friday, at eleven o'clock in the morning. The news came as a relief, but also with a tinge of worry. Danny was hopeful that the meeting would be positive, and not a "Thank you and goodbye".

"At least something is happening," Patsy said as they waited in Patsy's office for Costa and Cohen to arrive.

At eleven-fifteen, the familiar smell of overpowering after-shave wafted into the gym.

"Danny," said Costa warmly, wrapping Danny in a hug while Cohen gave a half nod to Albert and Patsy. "Look at ya, getting better-looking every day! We've got some good news."

Cohen was more business-like. "We have arranged your first fight, Danny," he said.

"Great! When?" said Danny eagerly.

"Six months' time."

"Who's he fighting?" asked Patsy.

"Reece Davies," said Costa.

"Reece Davies?" echoed Patsy. "The ex-British champion, the boy from Tiger Bay? Reece 'the Dragon' Davies?"

"That's him."

Danny turned at the sudden gasp of air from Albert.

"You look worried, Albert," remarked Cohen.

"Davies is a formidable opponent," Albert said evenly. "He may be in his thirties with his title-fight days behind him, but are you sure Danny's ready for him?"

"You need to believe, fella," said Costa.

"Yes indeed," said Cohen. "The Dragon is on the way down, and our boy is on the way up."

"A fight like this will generate a lot of interest, new boy against an ex-champ," said Costa, with a knowing wink to Danny. "I reckon we will sell tickets by the shed-load."

"There will be local and hopefully national press to do, and of course a press conference after the weigh-in," Cohen said.

After weeks of nothing, now things were moving just a little too fast. This was serious and it was happening. Danny glanced at Albert, but Albert was staring at the floor.

"Right," Danny said.

His first instinct was to get to the nearest punch bag and get punching. He was in prime condition, but would that be enough to put up a show against this experienced adversary? The conversation flowed around him, but Danny felt detached, his mind on the forthcoming make-or-break contest. This was being thrown in at the deep end all right. Danny wanted to make sure he wouldn't drown.

"We'll be in touch," declared Cohen, shaking Danny's hand.

"Speak soon," said Costa as he pulled Danny into one of his prolonged hugs.

A stunned silence hung in the unusually fragrant air as the two promoters left the gym. Patsy broke the silence.

"Right, Danny," he said. "The Dragon is a tough fighter and we got work to do, so let's do it."

"You can do this, Danny," said Albert after a moment. "You have to do it."

The big debut fight with the Dragon was fixed for the Saturday of the second week of April, not long after the baby was due. Posters were up in the streets of London, and Danny had been interviewed by the *Stratford Express* and *East London Advertiser*. Momentum was growing. There had even been an article or two in the national papers' sports pages.

Danny and the team had watched recent footage of a

Davies fight filmed on a dodgy cine camera and shot by one of Patsy's friends. Watching the shaky black and white images, over and over again, looking for strengths and weaknesses. But as Albert said, there weren't many chinks in his armour.

Albert was worried, but didn't let on to Danny. He did not want to damage the boy's confidence, but this looked to him like a mismatch, a very difficult fight for a young boxer making his professional debut.

Danny and Patsy on the other hand were upbeat, dedicated and focused on the job in hand. The odd visit from Lenny to watch Danny spar and lift the spirits meant the camp was feeling boosted, confident and happy.

Albert tried to be positive, but in his heart, he was troubled.

After a sleepless night, he finally made a decision to telephone Cohen and voice his worries. Using the phone in the hall of the pub in a quieter moment, he dialled the number.

Mavis answered, using her almost-posh telephone voice.

"Please hold, and I will see if Mr Cohen is free."

Albert waited, not really sure what he was going to say.

Mavis was back. "Mr Cohen wants to know if it's urgent?"

Assured that it was, she put Albert through.

"Albert," said Cohen. "To what do I owe this pleasure?"

"This first fight for Danny, I'm worried about it," Albert said. "I think the boy could get hurt. And with all the build-up, if he gets battered, his career could be over before it's started."

"Too late to change it now, old timer. But don't you worry. We have invested *heavily* in Danny, know what I mean? The underdog bites back and all that? See you there."

The call left Albert bemused. What did Cohen mean?

Was it simply that they had spent money on the promotion, or that they intended to invest in Danny's future? It had to be the latter. Perhaps he should take a longer-term view, and look past this upcoming tussle. Perhaps Costa and Cohen did care about Danny's future after all, and were in it for the long haul. Maybe they were not the shady couple he thought they were.

"Oi, Albert!" shouted Maurice from the bar. "It's getting busy out 'ere, you working or what?"

Still puzzling about motives, Albert reported for duty. Sure enough, the lunch-time drinkers were starting to form a crowd. The Live and Let Live was as popular at lunch time as it was at night, with the dockers there on their lunch break as usual and Lenny's regular lunch-time visit already in progress.

Lenny always brought in his own lunch. At first Maurice had barred it, but after pressure from Albert he'd given in. Lenny's packed lunch had now become part of the fabric of lunch time in the pub.

The pub menu included the usual pub fare like meat pie and mash, chicken and chips, and ham or cheese and pickle sandwiches, all prepared under duress by Maria, Maurice's Italian wife. Maria had left Italy at nine years old when her father came to England, and had worked in her father's cafe in Billingsgate. Now more Cockney than most of the dockers, she had taken on her father's mantle in the firm belief that cuisine was in her blood.

She had asked her husband if she could introduce some more varied and upmarket dishes, but when her suggestion of prawn cocktail was shot down in flames, she let it slide. Anyway, the workers were happy and her sausages had quite a reputation.

"Hello Len," said Albert as Lenny approached the bar. "The usual?"

"Yeah, thanks Albert. How is it going with Danny? Not too long now before the big fight."

"He's doing good. Training hard and looking pretty sharp."

"Nice," said Lenny. "Gonna put some money on him, invest in success."

Albert's mind shot back to the phone call with Cohen. *Invested heavily.*

"What are the odds?" he asked.

"Three to one," said Lenny as he rubbed his hands together. "Not great odds, eh?"

Albert would have expected the odds to be more like ten to one. After all, Danny was an unknown, while the Dragon with his big, mainly Welsh following was a star. Perhaps when Cohen said "invested", they had put money on Danny winning.

The pub rush started to ease. Lenny said goodbye with his usual "Oh well, some of us have to work", and Albert collected and washed glasses.

Everything was as it always was, but Albert had this black cloud hanging over him and he wasn't really sure why. He put it down to anxiety over the upcoming fight. The weigh-in, maybe. It was nerves, pure and simple.

To take his mind off the conundrum, Albert went to help Maria clear up in the kitchen.

Maria was grumbling as usual about her never-ending workload and her lazy husband. Albert dried up pots and pans with the odd nod of understanding, which he hoped would soothe her sometimes savage breast.

He had seen Maria blow her Latin temper a number of times, and had learned that the best option was to sympathise and keep quiet.

Job done, he made his way to the dry cleaners to pick up his one suit. He wanted to look smart for the big weigh-in next week. Next stop, Harry the barber.

The fashion for the time was for longer hair, but that was strictly for the young, or "the beatniks" as Albert called them. For Albert, the customary short back and sides was the way to go.

With suit in hand and a tidy haircut, Albert made for home.

"Who's a pretty boy?" Rocky squawked in greeting.

This was more or less the extent of Rocky's vocabulary. Seeing how Rocky was a girl, she was obviously addressing her owner. So Albert took it as a compliment, thanked his bird, and filled her tray with some fresh bird seed before sitting down in his favourite armchair. Rocky settled on her favourite lampshade and Albert took a nap.

With the baby's birth due any day, Wendy and Mrs Bristow were packing her hospital bag in readiness for the big event. Danny was as involved as he could be, but his mind was on the fight and the face-to-face meeting with Davies at the weigh-in the following week. His hands went cold and his stomach turned as he carried the thought of what was to come, and as much as he wanted to concentrate on Wendy's apprehension, it wasn't easy.

As Danny prowled the back yard, deep in thought, he heard a cry from Wendy that brought him rushing inside.

Mrs Bristow was semi-hysterical. "Danny! Her waters have broken! We've got to get her to the hospital. Call a taxi, quick!"

Danny found a number as quickly as he could and called with shaking fingers.

"Ten to fifteen minutes," he told Mrs Bristow a little breathlessly, trying not to look at the way Wendy was writhing and moaning in pain. "Get her ready to go, all right?"

His mind now was in overload. The fight, the baby, Wendy's welfare. There was still the prospect of a new and exciting life ahead, but all of a sudden it seemed a long way off.

As he prowled up and down the street waiting for the promised cab, Danny forced himself to prioritise Wendy and the baby. The weigh-in and fight would have to wait.

At that moment a fairly clean, but rather battered taxi turned into the street. He waved to the driver and went inside to fetch the girls.

On the way to Howards Road Hospital, Wendy gripped Danny's hand tightly, her face grey with pain.

"It'll be all right, won't it?" she said in a scared voice.

Danny reassured her the best he could. Looking at her, he wished he could take the pain away. She looked so vulnerable and child-like.

At the maternity ward, Wendy was led away by a friendly

Irish nurse, who told Danny and Mrs Bristow to wait in reception.

"I'll come and fetch you when Wendy is settled," she said kindly, her gentle accent going some way to calming Danny down.

After a short while, Danny and Mrs Bristow were ushered into the maternity ward. Wendy, now in a robe and in a hospital bed, smiled a weak hello.

"You all right?" said Danny anxiously.

Wendy burst into tears. "They said there's a complication with the baby," she sobbed.

Danny's heart thumped hard in his chest. "What? What complication?"

"Mr Watson?" said a voice.

Danny whirled round to see a doctor and nurse standing behind him.

"Mr Watson," the doctor repeated. "I explained to your wife that the baby seems fine, but is not engaging in the position it should for a successful natural birth. I'm afraid we need to carry out a Caesarean."

Wendy looked like the scared little girl Danny had first met in school. He wanted so much to take away the fear and the worry in her face.

"Is there no other way?" Wendy's mother pleaded.

The doctor shook his head. "We should operate as soon as possible."

Danny couldn't believe this was happening. Holding Wendy close, he could feel her sobbing, although she was making no sound.

"This operation, Doctor," he said, feeling terrified. "It's safe, ain't it?"

"As safe as it can be. I'm sorry, Mr Watson, but we have no choice."

Looking around the ward of ten or twelve expectant mothers, Danny could see that some of the inmates already had their newborns by their side, their ordeal of childbirth over. One of the babies began to cry. It sounded like a mewing kitten, helpless and in need of its mother's attention. This world felt alien to Danny. His world was a man's world. He was touched by the sacrifices women make for their children. It was something he had never quite realised.

He lifted Wendy's face up with his finger and looked into her frightened eyes. "You need to be a brave little soldier, Wend," he said quietly. "It'll be all right. Your mum's here, I'm here, your dad's on his way, you hear me?"

Wendy slowly nodded her head, like a child reluctantly agreeing to go to bed. The nurse gently took her hand, helped her off the bed and led her away.

Mrs Bristow sat on a chair in the waiting room as Danny paced up and down the corridor, desperate for news and a happy outcome.

A flustered Mr Bristow rushed in.

"What's happened?" he said. "Where's Wendy?"

"She's had to have a Caesarean, Brian," said Mrs Bristow. "She's in the operating theatre now."

Wendy's parents sat together, motionless. Danny went on

pacing the corridor, his heart aching. There was nothing they could do but wait, and wait they did.

As Danny heard cries of pain coming from a nearby delivery room, he began to think of his own mother, Rosie. She may not have been the best mother, but she was his mother. He should remember that.

He decided to telephone her at work to tell her that Wendy was having the baby. He was touched by her reaction.

"You're not to worry now, Danny," Rosie said. "Everything will be fine. I'll come by after work and see how you're all getting on, all right? Give my love to Wendy and stay strong."

When Danny returned to the ward, the doctor was in conversation with Wendy's parents.

"Congratulations, Mr Watson," he said. "You have a beautiful baby girl. Both mother and baby are fine."

The emotion was just too much. Danny's legs went from under him as if he had been hit by a knock-out punch, and he slumped to the floor. The next thing he knew, the lovely Irish nurse from earlier was helping him back on to his feet. The name on her badge said "Nurse O'Malley".

"It's all right, Mr Watson," she soothed in her Cork accent. "It happens more times than you'd think."

Danny felt embarrassed but elated as he got to his feet. His parents-in-law were both smiling fit to burst.

"So now," said Nurse O'Malley. "Would you all like to see the mother and baby?"

Mr Bristow looked at Danny with watery eyes. "You go on your own, son. We'll see them in a minute."

Nurse O'Malley led the way along the same corridor that

Danny had been pacing like a caged tiger barely twenty minutes earlier as he waited. The good news still had not totally sunk in. He needed to see Wendy and the baby with his own eyes.

As he walked into the ward, Danny saw clearly for the first time his beautiful baby, secure and content, lying in her mother's arms.

"Isn't she lovely?" Wendy said, her face radiant and happy. Danny thought how beautiful she looked.

"Indeed she is," said Nurse O'Malley. "A beautiful six pound and five ounce baby girl."

Danny reached out and took the bundle of joy for the first time. Tears filled his eyes as he looked down at this small, helpless miracle.

"She's got your nose, Wend," he said.

Wendy smiled. "And look at her little red ruby lips."

"A little Wendy," Danny said, almost bursting with pride and love. He felt completely different now. He felt like a man. He was a father to a baby girl, and this wonderful thing filled him full of pride and selfless love and a modicum of apprehension.

"Not a little Wendy," said Wendy. "A little Ruby. That's what we should call her, Danny. Ruby."

Wendy and baby Ruby were going to stay in hospital for a few days to get over the operation. Visitors en masse duly came to see the newborn. Albert bought some grapes, Lenny a box of chocolates, Rosie a little pink dress.

"You have to be a father to a daughter," said Albert as he took Ruby in his arms for the first time. "And a good one."

Danny was determined to be just that.

CHAPTER THIRTEEN

IT was time to concentrate and focus on the task ahead.

Mother and baby were doing well back at home. As proud as Punch and keen to help, Mr Bristow had furnished the happy parents' bedroom with a cot, and Mrs Bristow was proving a godsend with all the night feeds.

In the days before the birth, Danny had felt nervous about the head-to-head. Now a fearless determination prevailed. He had the extra incentive of his new baby girl. Her future was in his hands.

On the day of the weigh-in, Patsy arranged for Albert, Danny and Lenny to meet him at the Live and Let Live at two o'clock. Lenny had agreed to drive them to the venue, but again refused to wear a chauffeur's hat.

At two-thirty, Danny materialised.

"Sorry," he said, gasping a little. "The baby."

Albert, Patsy and Lenny all nodded sympathetically.

"Test driving this one and all, Len?" said Albert as they all got into the swanky Humber Hawk parked outside the pub.

"You can't say I don't offer a thorough service," said Lenny cheerfully.

"So, Danny," said Albert as they drove to the York Hall, Bethnal Green where the weigh-in was taking place. "Why did you decide on Ruby and not Alberta for the baby, eh?"

Danny laughed. "I reckon Ruby is a good name. It seems to suit her."

"I had an aunt called Ruby," reminisced Lenny from the front seat. "Best cook in Jamaica. Her jerk chicken was magic."

At York Hall, there were people already going in. As Danny got out of the car, there was a spontaneous cheer from well wishers, and people surged forward to shake his hand and ask for his autograph. It was obvious that the fight had attracted interest and caught the imagination of fight fans. Local boy, in his first professional fight, against a seasoned ex-champ. That natural British instinct to support the underdog was gaining momentum.

Danny and his entourage were shown into the hall like visiting royalty. Lenny looked like he was loving it, while Patsy took it in his stride. Albert stayed by Danny's side as the team was shown to a room at the back of the hall and asked to wait.

Tommy Costa appeared, sweating and behaving like a mother hen.

"The press is going crazy for this, Danny," he said. "Tickets are sold out. It's gonna be a night to remember."

Sold out. The news turned Danny's stomach. He could hear the assembled fight fans in the hall, a chant from Davies's followers of "Dragon! Dragon!" This was really happening.

Cohen appeared, as business-like as ever.

"Danny, you're to sit on the stage on the right. Davies will sit on the left. Davies will do the weigh-in first and then it will be your turn. After the weigh-in, we'll have a press conference and some photos. Got it?"

Danny took it all in, his mind racing. There was a surreal feeling of slow motion to the proceedings.

"Danny! Danny!" greeted him from a partisan cluster of supporters in the hall as Danny climbed on to the stage. The flashbulbs were going crazy as he blinked in the spotlights.

Another chant struck up, louder than the first.

"Dragon! Dragon! Dragon!"

Danny did his best not to feel intimidated, but watching Davies walk through the hall like the king of the ring was terrifying. Proud as a peacock, the Dragon hit the stage with his arms raised in triumph, like the fight had already been won. Shooting an ice-cold look to Danny, he took his seat.

The official prepared the weigh-in procedure as the fighters stripped and stood face to face. The hostility in the Dragon's eyes was palpable. Danny stared him out the best he could, doing his best to keep any trace of fear from flickering in his eyes.

Davies was ten stone, twelve pounds: just two pounds inside the welterweight limit. He was shorter than Danny, but solid like Welsh granite, with muscles that looked ready to burst and a neck like a raging bull. Danny weighed in at his usual ten stone ten pounds, giving the Dragon a slight weight advantage.

As the fans cheered themselves hoarse, the Dragon's shaved head glistened in the spotlight. This was a man from the Valleys, a hard man born from a line of miners. His record was impressive too. He had never been knocked out and had twenty-three contests to his name, with nineteen wins, a draw and two losses. Importantly, in his last two fights – one of which had been for the British title – he had lost on points, and was now looking to find that purple patch back to the title to avoid entering the twilight of his career.

At thirty-four, he was ten years older than Danny.

Danny and his camp hoped that the age difference would go Danny's way. Danny had a reach advantage too, being the taller man, plus a hunger that maybe Davies had lost in the sweat and tears of his past battles. It all felt like wishful thinking, seeing the prime shape the Dragon was in, but Danny was intent on giving it his all. This was Danny's chance and he was not going to let it slide.

With the weigh-in done, the press conference started. Cohen was on stage to fend off any awkward questions and to organise the photo session. A few staged pictures were organised, with the two fighters staring at each other, each doing their very best to look as mean as possible.

Then the questions began.

"Dragon, why did you agree to fighting a relatively unknown fighter like Danny Watson?"

"For the money and as a stepping stone back to my title," came the Dragon's reply.

"Danny, you have been given the chance to fight a British ex-champion in your very first professional fight. Do you think you might be out of your depth?"

Albert couldn't hold back. "Have you seen Danny fight?" he shouted at the journalist, raising a cheer from the fans.

"I would like to thank Mr Cohen and Mr Costa for this chance and I intend to do my best," Danny said.

Cohen took up the baton. "Danny is a worthy contender and we believe he has a great future."

"Yeah, but not against me," drawled the Welshman.

Cohen, at that point, decided to call an end to the press conference. With the applause, jeers and cheers from fight fans ringing in their ears, the boxers and their entourages left the stage.

Back in the dressing room, the verdict was that the event had gone well.

"I liked your humility out there, Danny," said Costa, slapping Danny on the back.

"Davies is over the hill and no match for you, Danny," Cohen assured him. "You've got youth and hunger on your side. That Dragon ain't gonna breath no fire."

Albert stood back and listened to the words of comfort, but was not comforted or convinced that Davies was past it. He felt deep down that this was going to be a very difficult fighter to overcome.

Lenny left to fetch the car. As Danny was held up for a few autographs, Albert was stopped by Harry Baldock, the old boxer and friend he had recently met in the Blind Beggar.

"Your boy's looking good, Albert," Harry said as they shook hands.

"Yeah, he's a good boy, Harry," said Albert. He lowered his voice. "But between you and me, I'm not sure a fight like this is right for him. This early, he could well come unstuck."

Harry smiled knowingly. "I think the odds are stacked in your boy's favour," he said with a nod and a wink. "Know what I mean?"

Lenny pulled up beside Albert with a toot of his horn. Patsy and Danny were already on the back seat.

"I'd better get going, Harry. See you at the fight."

Driving back to Canning Town, Harry's words tumbled around Albert's head. There had been something about the nod and the wink that made Albert uncomfortable.

He didn't want to think too hard about what Harry had meant.

With the fight scheduled for the next day, Patsy wanted Danny to spar for the rest of the afternoon and complete a training session. Arrangements were made for the trip to York Hall the following evening. Lenny was going to pick them up at six, with the fight scheduled to start at nine.

"Good to get there early," said Patsy. "Give you time to prepare and focus."

They worked through the afternoon, going through Danny's exercises. As Danny picked up his bag to leave, Patsy gave him some final advice.

"Try and get a good night's sleep. And no argy bargy with Wendy, OK? It'll weaken your legs."

Danny had no problem agreeing with Patsy's suggestion. After all, Wendy had only just returned from childbirth. Argy bargy was not an option.

The thought of getting back to Wendy and baby Ruby was

much more exciting than the trauma of the weigh-in and the grinding training session.

Danny almost flew upstairs to see them.

Ruby had just woken up and was in Wendy's arms, gurgling softly to herself. Danny looked at his wife and daughter with an overflowing sense of love. Taking Ruby in his arms, he looked at her beautiful little face, her tiny nose (a replica of her mother's), her blue eyes blinking in the daylight. Looking down at this miracle strengthened his resolve for the fight to come.

"She's got my ears, you know," he told Wendy as he kissed Ruby's tiny forehead. "Good job she ain't got my nose."

It was a moment to treasure. The three of them, there in their borrowed bedroom, away from the world of boxing and violence. Safe from the outside difficulties that surrounded a working-class life.

The night's sleep was a decent one. Perhaps Ruby knew that Daddy had a big day coming, and apart from one restless night feed at two a.m., she left Danny reasonably undisturbed.

CHAPTER FOURTEEN

IT was almost like Danny had wings as he ran back to the house after his morning jog in the grey, drizzly light. Wendy and Ruby were taking a late-morning nap, so as quietly as possible, he took a shower. As the warm water cascaded over him, he thought of the night ahead, and his rendezvous with the Dragon.

Patsy and Albert's words went round and round in his head. *Keep your distance. Don't get involved in a brawl. Use your reach advantage. Keep moving.*

Showered and changed, he sat down to re-watch the old footage of the Dragon's past fights, on a fairly ancient projector that Albert had borrowed from his downstairs neighbour Simon. Once again, Danny analysed any possible weaknesses in the fighter's armour. He could see very few. The power of the Dragon's punches was formidable. His nerves were tingling as he watched his opponent floor a worthy contender. "Keep moving" was the answer. "Keep your distance" was definitely the tactic.

Ruby woke up. Turning the projector off at the sound of her gentle cry, Danny went upstairs. A tired but happy

Wendy was changing the baby's nappy. Danny had mastered a few nappy changes, but lacked the expertise of fixing the safety pin without a struggle. His nappy prowess was no match for the baby's adoring mother.

Standing there watching his wife and daughter put everything into perspective for Danny. It reminded him of the importance of succeeding in this quest for a secure future for the two people he loved the most.

Nappy changed, Danny took Ruby in his arms.

"She smiled at me," he said.

"It's probably wind," Wendy replied.

"No, she definitely smiled at me," insisted Danny.

Wendy gave him a concerned look. "Are you feeling OK?"

Danny handed Ruby back and rolled his shoulders, trying to ease the tension. "I just want to get on with it," he said. "Get it over with."

"Be careful, won't you?" said Wendy as she cradled Ruby against her shoulder. "We love you, don't let him hurt you."

Danny's eyes filled with loving tears. It felt so safe to be here in their little room, safe from the battle to come, safe from the cuts, bruises and hostility. Part of him just wanted to stay here, cocooned with the people he loved. But, like his father before him, he knew he had to go into battle with his head held high and a brave heart beating in his chest.

"Don't you worry," he said. "It's gonna be all right. I'll tell you all about it when I come home."

There would be life after this ordeal. It was a good thought. For months his focus had been on the fight and his powerful opponent. Now, knowing that his family would be waiting for him after the fight, Danny felt not only a sense of purpose, but a sense of security.

The Humber Hawk pulled up outside at six o'clock on the dot. Danny looked through the window at the car, and his boxing family waiting inside on the plush leather seats, and with a belly full of butterflies, kissed Ruby and Wendy a meaningful goodbye.

"Don't look so worried," he said, holding Wendy close. "It's time to be positive now. I'm going into battle for the people I love, and I'm gonna win. All right?"

As Danny got into the Humber Hawk's back seat, he could see Wendy and Ruby at the bay window of the house. Wendy was waving Ruby's tiny hand as if she was waving goodbye. He blew them both a final kiss and the car moved off.

"How you feeling?" asked Albert.

"He's feeling good ain't he, 'cos he's gonna slay the Dragon," said the optimistic Lenny. "Just like St George, ain't it?"

Danny was relieved that Lenny had answered for him. At that moment, he wasn't really sure what he was feeling. He knew he had a job to do, and he had trained and worked hard for this moment, but there was still a part of him that wished he could just stay with Wendy and the baby, safe and secure and away from the battle to come.

The drive to Bethnal Green was dream-like. Danny watched the streets pass by without really seeing them, his mind well and truly on the coming fight.

The traffic was beginning to build as they turned into the street to York Hall. The fight fans were starting to arrive. The reality of all these people paying to watch and the lines of fight fans waiting outside the hall scared Danny more than he'd expected.

Patsy patted his shoulder. "Look at that, Danny," he said. "They have all come to see you win."

Danny nodded, his mouth dry, his hands ice cold, resisting the urge to come back with "Maybe they have come to see me lose." Right now, that was what he was feeling.

They got through the milling crowd and the car made its way to the back entrance and the changing rooms. A small gathering of fight fans waited for an autograph or a photo, and Danny obliged, before Tony Costa scooped him up and led the way to his room.

In the hall, fight night was well under way, with the first scheduled contest already in progress. Danny had not wanted to arrive too early, as sitting and waiting was a recipe to stir up nerves and too much time to think was dangerous. But Patsy knew best. They all needed a little time in this place to properly prepare, and focus was important.

Costa was almost too upbeat. "It's gonna be a night to remember, Danny boy," he said jubilantly. "Every ticket sold out weeks ago, how about that?"

If this was meant to cheer Danny up, it didn't. It only seemed to bring on the nervous gravity of the occasion.

"The boy needs some time, Tommy," said Patsy, ushering Costa out of the room. "We'll see you out there, all right?"

Costa reluctantly left and Danny's warm-up began. Hitting

pads and skipping ropes, Albert reminded Danny of tactics while Patsy worked on his confidence.

"You're looking sharp, son. You're moving well. Keep going, that's it, that's good."

The Watson–Davies fight was top of the bill. Patsy was bandaging Danny's hands in readiness when the fight official came in.

"Ten minutes please, gentlemen."

A flow of adrenalin shot through Danny's veins. He sought reassurance from his father's medal, which he had placed inside his sports bag, taking it out and turning it over in his fingers.

"You're gonna win this," said Lenny. "Make your father proud. Go well, I'll see you after."

The official returned as Lenny headed out to find his ringside seat. "Time to go," he said in a matter-of-fact way.

Danny kissed the medal for bravery and followed Albert and Patsy into the crowded auditorium.

Cohen had laid on a bit of showbiz for the gladiators' entrances, with spotlights blazing and fanfares sounding. The crowd rose to its feet to greet them. As the lesser-known and the undoubted underdog, Danny entered first. "Danny! Danny!" echoed around the hall as he walked with Albert and Patsy through the crowd, flanked by security men.

Danny and Patsy entered the ring. Albert stood by Danny's corner. Danny went through some shadow-boxing moves and waited for the Dragon's entrance. He didn't have to wait for long.

"Dragon! Dragon! Dragon!"

In the Dragon came, led on by a Welsh flag held high by one of his entourage. The noise of the crowd rose in a deafening crescendo as Davies, his trainer and cut-man bounced into the ring.

The referee called both fighters together.

"A nice clean fight, no holding, eight four-minute rounds, clear?"

Danny heard the instructions, but was intent on looking the Dragon straight in the eye. He was not going to be intimidated like at the weigh-in.

But this time Danny saw a different look in the ageing warrior's eyes. The cockiness had gone. In its place there was a flicker of guilt, a look of resigned sadness.

The boxers returned to their corners. With a few last words of encouragement, the announcement of "Seconds out!" rattled the speakers in the smoke-filled room and, with a roar from the crowd, the battle commenced.

Danny did as he was instructed, keeping a good distance from the Dragon and using his longer reach. But the explosion of violence from the Dragon that Danny and his camp had expected was more like a damp squib.

Round one went by without much drama. Danny landed a few jabs and the Dragon hit Danny with a decent body shot. Honours were even as the fighters felt each other out.

Round two was more of the same. Danny felt surprised at the Dragon's lack of aggression. The crowd, who had paid good money to watch some decent action, were beginning to get restless.

"Time to change tactics," Patsy said in the break between

rounds two and three. "Stop back-pedalling now and go on the offensive, all right? We need this fight to catch fire."

Danny settled in his gum shield as the bell for round three rang out. He went straight on the offensive, pushing the Dragon round the ring with a barrage of quick jabs. The Dragon answered back with a few wayward haymakers that were easy for Danny to avoid. The crowd were becoming more and more frustrated by the lack of action, and a few boos began to resonate around the room.

At the end of round three, Patsy and Albert were right in Danny's face.

"You're ahead Danny, keep it going!" said Albert.

"Yeah, same again!" said Patsy.

Round four started. Now on the front foot, Danny was definitely the aggressor, and the Dragon was backing off, dropping his guard and bouncing off the ropes. Danny pushed forward, relentlessly forcing his opponent into his own corner. It looked like the Dragon was indeed struggling, when a straight right from Danny hit him fair and square, smack on the chin.

The Dragon went down like a pack of cards.

"One, two, three, four..." the referee counted as the Dragon lay still on the canvas.

The crowd, who had initially greeted the knock-down with stunned surprise, started getting vocal. Amid the cheers from Danny's followers were boos of derision from most of the rest.

"... eight, nine, ten!" counted the ref.

That was it. Danny had beaten the ex-champ, knocking him out for the very first time in his illustrious career.

There was joy in the ring. Albert and Patsy lifted Danny on to their shoulders. Lenny clambered into the ring to celebrate.

But in the hall, pandemonium had broken loose. Boos were ringing out, chairs were being thrown. The Dragon's followers were frustrated and angry because of the lack of fight in their man.

The referee lifted Danny's arm. "And the winner is... Danny Watson!"

A mass of derision and boos greeted the decision. The crowd's reaction confused Danny. He'd won fair and square. He had knocked out the legendary Dragon.

"What's all this about?" he shouted at Patsy as the noise level continued to rise. "I won, didn't I?"

"They're just bad losers," Patsy shouted back, leading Danny out of the ring, away from the fracas and back to the safety of the changing room.

Grinning broadly, Cohen and Costa were waiting for Danny with a bottle of champagne.

"Brilliant, Danny boy," said Costa, kissing Danny on the cheek.

"You gave him a boxing lesson," agreed Cohen.

"But what about the crowd?" said Danny, still stunned by the reaction.

"Don't you worry about that," Costa soothed. "Bad losers, those Welsh gits."

The wonderful reality of winning started flowing through Danny. So much had rested on the result, and he had come through. He had actually won.

Costa cracked open the champagne with a flourish. So much of a flourish that it looked for a moment as if he would spray the crowded dressing room with it the way racing drivers did. But in the nick of time, he poured the fizzing liquid into some plastic glasses instead.

"To the future," he toasted, handing the glasses out.

"To the future!"

Albert stood quietly to one side, watching the others drinking champagne and laughing. He felt troubled. He was a wise old fighter, and he'd seen that the Dragon had had no fire in his belly. Davies had not come to fight.

He watched Danny's face as he tasted champagne for the very first time. The boy's happiness radiated around the room. Albert decided that, if this was indeed a hollow victory, he was in no way going to let on. To put a damper on Danny's great night would be wrong. Best to enjoy the surprise win and keep his reservations to himself.

Lenny, merry and a little drunk after several glasses of champagne, went to bring the car round. As the team left York Hall, congratulations and handshakes followed Danny to the waiting car.

"How about that then?" said Danny jubilantly as Lenny drove them home. "How about bloody that?"

Lenny broke into a tuneless calypso about cricket from

Whitechapel to the Blackwall Tunnel. Patsy, not to be outdone, attempted a chorus of something Irish about Galway Bay. Albert just sat, quietly piecing parts of the jigsaw together.

We have invested heavily *in Danny…*

I think the odds are stacked in your boy's favour. Know what I mean?

By the time they reached the Bristows' house, Albert had come to the conclusion that the fight had indeed been fixed.

"Good night, son," he said as Danny got out of the car, happy and barely bruised, heading to the front door and his waiting family. "Well done."

The juxtaposition of the boy's delight and Albert's own sadness was hard to take. Albert was an honest man, full of high principles. If the Dragon had been paid to lose and given a pay-off for his imminent retirement, it left a very sour taste in his mouth.

"Drop you back at your flat, Albert?" Lenny offered.

Albert roused himself. "Cheers Len, that would be good."

Neither Patsy nor Lenny pressed him to invite them in. It was clear that Albert wasn't in a party mood. As Lenny pulled away, Albert stood on the street outside his flat, thinking over the night's events. The cobbled street seemed to sparkle under the street lamps, and the gentle rain on his face didn't help wash away his worries.

The taste of victory, right or wrong, was a big step up for Danny. What had the boy got himself into? What other tricks did Costa and Cohen have hidden up their sleeves?

In Simon's shop window, Albert saw a pair of well-used

boxing gloves hanging from a shelf laden with bric-a-brac. So much for the Noble Art.

Albert climbed the stairs to his flat and he turned on the light. Rocky came to life with a chirp and a hop as he walked over to her cage and stroked her blue feathered head.

"I'm whacked, mate," he said. Rocky leant her head to one side as if she was listening. "It's been a funny old night, Rocky. A funny old night."

The next morning, he was anxious to see what the newspaper sports writers had made of last night's contest.

He was first to the newsagent, where he bought most of the morning papers, much to the surprise of Norman, the corner-shop keeper. Norman had rosy cheeks and always seemed to be sucking one of his own boiled sweets.

"See you later, Norman," said Albert as he paid for the papers and tucked them under his arm.

Norman tucked his boiled sweet into his cheek and watched as Albert left the shop.

Sitting down at the bus stop, Albert took a deep breath and opened the first paper. There, on the back page, was a photo of Danny, his arms raised in victory. The headline read NEW BOY WATSON'S SURPRISE WIN!

Nervously scanning the review of the fight, Albert was pleasantly surprised. There was no mention of a fix, just surprise that a young unknown could knock out an experienced old warrior. The write-up went on to lambast the Dragon's fans, calling them bad losers.

Albert pressed on through the pile of newspapers. None of them raised any suspicions. Danny had been covered in praise.

He headed round to the gym to see Patsy.

"What a night!" Patsy said by way of greeting.

"Yes indeed," agreed Albert. "Have you seen the papers? Young Danny is the talk of the back pages."

Patsy took the newspapers and scanned the sports pages, occasionally reading out loud particular sentences that were positive, like "Watson's tactics were spot on" and "This boy could go far". Albert listened. It pleased him that Patsy was enjoying the post-mortem, but in his heart it still felt like a hollow victory. Anxious to air his misgivings, he decided to come clean.

"Danny came out of it well," he said. "Considering."

"Considering what?"

"It just seemed too easy. Like the Dragon wasn't up for it."

Patsy put down the paper he was reading. "What d'ya mean?"

"Well like I said, it seemed like Davies didn't want to fight," said Albert.

Patsy tutted. "That's because he couldn't. Danny fought the perfect tactical fight, like we told him. That's all."

It seemed to Albert that Patsy's euphoria may have clouded his judgement. However, he began to question his own take on the fight. Perhaps the contest hadn't been a fix after all. Patsy, with his vast experience of the fight world, would have seen what Albert felt he had witnessed, but no. The big Irishman was walking the purple patch of a winning trainer, and was not to be shaken off.

"I wonder what Cohen and Costa's next plan is," said Albert.

Patsy shrugged. "Well they ain't put a foot wrong yet, Albert," he said. "You should stop being so suspicious and be a bit more trusting. Danny must be on cloud nine this morning. The last thing he wants is to be shot down in flames."

For Danny's sake, Albert decided to keep his misgivings to himself. Patsy went on devouring the back pages while Albert doodled on a piece of paper on the desk.

"Do you know something, Pat?" Albert said after a moment. "They reckon they can tell people's personalities from what they doodle. *Doodle*. Funny word ain't it?"

"Amazing," said Patsy with his head in the papers.

Albert shifted in his seat. "What time's Danny coming?"

"He's late already," said Patsy.

They both heard Danny's footsteps as he climbed the stairs to the gym.

With a smile as wide as the Norfolk Broads and with Ruby in his arms, Danny walked into Patsy's office.

"How are the best trainers in the world?" Danny said, passing the little bundle to Albert.

It was a long time since Albert had properly held a baby in his arms. He remembered to support Ruby's head, a throwback to when he had held his own baby son so long ago. He looked at her innocent sleeping face, helpless and trusting. A feeling of warmth and protectiveness welled through him. Lifting Ruby up, Albert looked again at her little face. Untouched by bad things, she looked like an angel.

After a suitable amount of fuss was made of the baby,

especially by Patsy, who couldn't make his mind up if Ruby looked more like her mother or her father, Danny got down to business.

"I got the fight purse," he said. "And the good news is, I've got some dosh for you both. Fifty quid each. Not bad for a night's work."

He proudly presented them both with a wad of one-pound notes. Albert's first instinct was to refuse the money, but mindful of Danny's euphoria, thought it best to just say "Thank you" and accept it.

"Why is the money from you and not from Costa and Cohen?" he asked.

"They pay me and I pay you. That's the arrangement. That's the way they want it."

"Right," said Albert. "I hope they paid you well."

Danny grinned. "After their commission, I got two hundred smackers. More money than I've ever seen in my life. Good, ain't it? Here's to the next one."

Albert felt his suspicions surface again. "I wonder how much they made?" he said.

"It don't matter, does it?" said Patsy briskly. "The boy done well and has made a mark."

"Thanks, Patsy," said Danny, looking pleased. "Me and Wendy are going to look at a town house in Chigwell this afternoon. If it's as nice as the estate agent reckons, I'm gonna put a deposit down. Wendy's dad and mum are gonna help a bit."

"That's great," said Patsy.

"Yeah. It's a bit far to bike it to here from Chigwell so I might buy a car too," said Danny. "A Jag."

"Big plans," Patsy teased.

Albert listened, but kept his focus on the baby in his arms. The promise of a better life for Ruby was doing its best to overrule his doubts and questions. "That's a good thing, Danny," he said, trying to be upbeat. "Make sure it's got a garden for the little one."

"It has, Albert. You'll have to come and see it. I've got a meeting with Tommy and Jack in the morning to talk about the next fight."

The Tommy and Jack reference was not lost on Albert. Gone was Mr Costa and Mr Cohen. Clearly, Tommy and Jack were getting closer to Danny and extending their influence.

"That's good, Danny," said Patsy. "We need to keep looking to the future. What time do you want us there?"

"No, you're all right," said Danny. "It's just me this time. I'm having lunch with them, they said for me to come by myself. But I'll tell you all about it later."

Ruby woke up with a gurgle and a cry.

"Better get going," said Danny, scooping Ruby out of Albert's arms. "She's hungry, I'll get her back to Wendy. See you soon."

Albert listened to Danny making his way back down the stairs, his footsteps echoing around the gym.

"How about that, Patsy?" he said. "Looks like we've been given the elbow."

"No, it's fine," said Patsy. "He don't want us hanging on his shirt tails, that's all."

Albert scratched his head. "Yep, of course," he said. "I'd better get downstairs, do some work. See you later."

"Yeah. See you later, champ."

Lenny was already sitting at the bar. He leapt from his seat and engulfed Albert in a hug.

"What the bleeding hell are you doin', Lenny?" Albert spluttered, fighting him off.

"That's for the winning trainer, Albert!" Lenny cried. "What a win, man, me bet came up! Danny is the king of East London! Come on now, let me buy you a drink."

"Not now," said Albert. "Maybe later."

"You can be a miserable old bastard, Albert," Lenny remarked. "Cheer up, Danny is on his way to the top!"

When Danny got back with his precious cargo, Wendy was getting ready to view the Chigwell house. She was flustered but excited, making double sure that Ruby's baby bag was full of all the baby-changing and feeding necessities for the trip.

Danny read the property particulars over and over. "It's got a dishwasher," he said in amazement.

"Don't need one," said Wendy as she put Ruby's baby bag over her shoulder and they wheeled the pram out of the door. "I've got you!"

Travelling by bus from the East End into the Essex countryside was a truly pleasant change. The air felt fresher, cleaner. There were trees and fields.

"This is great," said Wendy in delight. "It's so much better for Ruby to grow up here."

"I bet the schools are good," said Danny.

Getting off the bus, they found the address and walked

down the cul-de-sac of newly-built houses to find number seven. Waiting outside was the pinstripe-suited estate agent, property particulars in his hand and a welcoming smile on his face.

"Mr and Mrs Watson? Roger Hancock, nice to meet you." He reached into the pram and tickled Ruby's cheek. "And who's this precious bundle?"

"This is Ruby," Wendy proudly answered.

"How lovely. Now shall we take a look at this very desirable property? Lucky number seven!"

After unsuccessfully trying two or three keys, Roger Hancock let them all inside. He seemed to have a fixation with cupboards, opening every one, with a colourful explanation for the purpose of each. Danny and Wendy both found it irritating. All they wanted was to see the house.

"I like the look of it from the outside," Danny said. "With its car port under the first floor, it looks American."

Roger Hancock looked slightly bemused. "It does indeed!" he said. "And all at a bargain price!"

The house had that unmistakable smell that new-builds have: the smell of fresh paint and plaster. Above the car port was a kitchen, a large open-plan lounge with a small balcony and large sliding glass doors.

"A beautiful room and wonderful modern kitchen," purred Roger. "And plenty of cupboards!"

"It's lovely," said Wendy, looking around.

"Where's the dishwasher?" asked Danny.

On his second attempt, the first cupboard door proving to be a washing machine, Roger revealed the dishwasher.

"Nice," said Danny approvingly. "What are the neighbours like?"

Roger Hancock winked. "Oh, in an area like this, I'm sure they are fine."

After a good look at the lounge and kitchen and every cupboard on the first floor, Roger led the way through the magnolia-coloured decor to the second floor. With much gusto, he opened the door to the brand-new bathroom.

"The finish and choice of materials in these particular new-builds is flawless," he said.

Danny stared at the little ceramic piece of equipment beside the toilet. "What's that?" he asked.

"A bidet. A brand-new and fashionable piece of kit."

"What's it do?"

Roger Hancock cleared his throat. "Well," he said. "Let's just say it is used instead of toilet paper. Very popular in Arab countries I believe."

"Ugh," said Danny.

"Oh Danny, it sounds hygienic," said Wendy with a slightly posher voice than usual.

They went on through to the master bedroom, which was big and light. It was nice to see the trees outside.

"And you should hear the sound of the birds singing in the morning!" said Roger Hancock enthusiastically.

Danny looked out of the window. "Is that the garden?" he said.

"Yes," the estate agent confirmed. "It's small but manageable. I'll show you on the way out. And remember, in addition to the garden, there are many nice country walks in the area."

He became conspiratorial, and whispered quietly as though the walls of number seven had ears. "And of course, Bobby Moore the West Ham footballer lives just down the road."

This did impress Danny.

For the sake of privacy and to have a chat, the couple went out to the little garden. It felt good to get away from Roger Hancock's sales pitch. Buds were opening on bushes and trees were ready to play their part in the spring miracle.

"What do you think?" Danny asked Wendy.

"I love it. It's perfect!"

Danny looked at Wendy's face, her eyes sparkling with excitement, standing there with their daughter in her arms. This was his chance to buy a home for his family, away from the smog and dirt of London.

"I like it too," he said. "It just feels right. The money might be a bit tricky though."

"We'll be all right," said Wendy as she took his hand. "You got Tommy and Jack behind you now."

"Albert and Patsy too," said Danny. "Right. I'll make him an offer."

Danny put on his best business head, and went back in the house to confront the waiting Roger Hancock, leaving Wendy waiting outside in the garden.

Five minutes later, he returned. Wendy put down the dandelion clock that she'd been blowing for Ruby and looked eagerly at him. "Well?"

Danny worked hard on his poker face, not allowing it to show a thing.

"Come on, Danny," Wendy begged.

Danny walked towards Wendy and Ruby, picked them both up, swung them round, and whispered in Wendy's ear: "It's ours."

"Oh, Dan," Wendy whispered with tears of joy in her eyes. She kissed him smack on the lips. Danny responded by kissing Ruby gently on the nose.

They stood together on the garden path, Danny's arm protectively around Wendy, and looked up at their new home in wonder. This was it. Their new beginning.

Walking back to the bus stop, Wendy was full of plans for their new home. There was talk of colour schemes, curtains. Danny felt it was important to get a swing and slide in the garden for Ruby.

"Wendy, d'ya know what?" Danny said as the bus cruised back down the familiar streets of East London. "I bet they have stars there too, like Clacton."

Wendy was full of excitement as she told her mum and dad all about their new house. Plans were made for the Bristows to see it the next day, when Danny had his lunchtime meeting with Costa and Cohen.

"Delighted that you're moving up in the world, Danny," said Mr Bristow, shaking Danny's hand. "But we're a little sad that you'll be moving out."

Mrs Bristow wiped her eyes. "We've got used to having you and little Ruby around," she said. "And we've so enjoyed being close to your new-found success, Danny."

"Watching Ruby's progress day by day is something we'll

miss," said Mr Bristow wistfully. "But not the night feeds. I tell you what, I'm looking forward to some order being restored in this place. Being woken by your little princess at two in the morning and a house full of baby paraphernalia hasn't been ideal, I suppose."

"But it's been an acceptable cross to bear," said Mrs Bristow.

The next morning, after the Bristows left for Chigwell, Danny went out into the small but well-kept garden. He looked up to the sky and whispered: "Things are going really well, Dad. Thank you for your help."

He felt sure, as he had felt so many times before, that his father was looking down on him, helping and guiding him.

Still buzzing with the excitement and thoughts of having a place of their own, he decided to take a morning run to the park and tell Albert the good news. It was strange to think, as he ran through the familiar smog-laden streets, that in just a few weeks, it would be time to say goodbye to it all. He reflected on the years of growing up in the neighbourhood, the scrapes and adventures of his childhood. He thought about those wayward friends that he grew up with. Vince for one had landed up in prison: something to do with a botched robbery attempt on a bank in Romford. Ironically, one of the gang had become a policeman somewhere in Norfolk. Another had emigrated to Australia for a better life. Danny's life was changing for the better too, and he was looking forward to meeting up with the man that had set him on this path.

The familiar sight of Albert in the park, bag of bread in hand, surrounded by his family of hungry ducks, made Danny smile. With so many things changing, the constant routine of Albert felt reassuring.

"Morning, Albert!"

Albert turned. "Hello Danny, all right?"

"I've got some good news, Albert. I'm buying a house in Chigwell!"

Albert sat on the bench. "That's a bit posh Danny, I'm pleased for you. When do you move in?"

Danny joined him. "In a couple of months. I've gotta get one of them mortgages, I think."

"Right. Lots to do then."

"Yeah. You'll have to come and see it."

This was a good feeling, Danny thought. Just the two of them, generations apart, sat side by side. No pressure, no distractions.

"None of this would have happened if I hadn't met you all those years back," he said.

"So it's my fault, is it?" said Albert with a smile.

"Yep, all your fault," Danny agreed. "I could have been in jail now, like a couple of my mates from school."

"Well it's free board and lodgings," Albert observed. "None of that mortgage lark."

Danny laughed. "I'll need to buy a motor though, if I'm living in the sticks. I need to get to Patsy's and that."

"See Lenny, he'll sort you out with something decent," advised Albert.

"It's going well though," said Danny. "I've got that lunch

meeting with Tommy and Jack later, in an upmarket Chinese restaurant in Limehouse called Wing Wong or something. You ever had Chinese food, Albert? I ain't. Is it right they cook up cats?"

Albert scratched his ear. "I wouldn't know, son. But if you're meeting Costa and Cohen, maybe they should cook up a couple of rats."

This took Danny aback. He knew Albert was suspicious of Costa and Cohen, but had hoped the recent triumph and success would have eased his fears.

"It will be interesting to see what plans they have in the future for us, won't it?" he said, trying to put a positive spin on things. "I'm not sure why they didn't want you and Patsy at the meeting."

"It's your future," said Albert. "We're the past, me and Patsy."

"No," said Danny uneasily. "You're a part of it."

The two men went quiet, and watched a small boy with his grandfather playing with a remote-controlled boat on the pond, scattering ducks in its wake.

"Listen son," said Albert. "Costa and Cohen want control. They don't want me interfering. I've given this a lot of thought and I think it's best if I bow out."

Danny felt winded. "You what?"

"I'm sorry boy," Albert said gently, "but I've made my mind up. Best if you go your way and I go mine. I'll still keep an eye on what you're up to, and I'm sure Patsy will still be with you, but you don't need me. I can't rub shoulders with Costa and Cohen."

Danny felt like his world had turned upside-down. From being on top of it all, he was now drowning in a sea of confusion. He had trained so hard and Albert had been his inspiration, but now with success within their reach, Albert wanted out. He couldn't believe it.

Albert put his arm around Danny's shoulder. "You're moving up, Danny. Those two have contacts and power. You don't need an old stick-in-the-mud like me."

Danny felt choked. Albert was not a man to change his mind when it was made up. His first reaction was to ditch Costa and Cohen, but there was the new house, the baby, Wendy to think of. He needed to think this through. He needed time to defuse the bomb that Albert had tossed in his lap.

"All right Albert," he managed to say. "I've gotta go, speak to you later."

Albert looked into Danny's eyes. "Goodbye son," he said.

At the park gates, Danny looked back to see Albert still sitting on his bench. A cloud of sadness engulfed him as he walked the streets back to the Bristows'.

Albert stayed where he was, staring at the trees gently swaying in the wind.

He had tried wrestling with his principles, but couldn't shake off his misgivings. Costa and Cohen had fixed Danny's fight to fast-track him into a money-making machine. Albert had too much respect for himself and the noble art of boxing to do anything so shady.

Costa and Cohen had recognised his honest old-fashioned

outlook and saw him as a drag on their scheme of things. As much as he cared for Danny, he could not be a part of something crooked. He could not be party to the dangerous liaison that could eventually lead to Danny's downfall.

With a heavy and empty heart, Albert made his way home.

CHAPTER FIFTEEN

DANNY was still in a state of shock when he reached the Bristows'. He was relieved that the house was empty. He needed some time to think, to be alone. He made his way through the back door and into the garden, looking up at the clouds in search of answers. None came.

Deep in troubled thought, he heard the front door open.

"We're back, Danny!" Wendy called. "Mum and Dad love the house, it's going to be so good for Ruby!"

Danny made his way inside, past a couple of smiling garden gnomes along the path.

"You know, Danny," said Mrs Bristow in excitement. "I wouldn't put curtains up. The modern thing is those Venetian blinds."

"Albert's leaving the team," Danny blurted out.

The chatter stopped for a moment.

"Oh well," said Wendy. "If that's what he wants. He's probably too old for this game now anyway."

"Albert's important," Danny said angrily.

"Not so much now you've got Tommy and Jack looking after you, eh?" said Mr Bristow.

Danny felt his anger and frustration begin to boil over.

"You don't understand," he bit out. "None of you understand."

Grabbing his coat, he walked out of the house and slammed the door. None of this was the Bristows' fault, he knew, but it felt like it.

He walked aimlessly around the streets until it was time for lunch. Arriving at the Chinese restaurant at Limehouse, he felt a mixture of emotions towards Costa and Cohen. It was their fault that Albert was leaving the team, and yet they were his best option if he, Wendy and Ruby were to move forward.

He looked through the window at a line of nasty-looking orange ducks hanging on a spit. Seeing the ducks so bald and lifeless sent his mind back to Albert and the lively birds that he nurtured and fed. Albert would be disgusted to see this.

He was just about to go in when a car pulled in at the kerbside.

"Danny boy!" said Tommy Costa.

"Hello Danny," said Jack Cohen.

The two men greeted Danny with hugs and handshakes and led him into the restaurant, to what was obviously the best table in the house.

"You're looking great, Danny," said Cohen warmly.

"Like a true champ," said Costa.

A Chinese waiter brought over some menus. Costa with his usual grasp of the good life ordered champagne, while Danny, who decided his brain was already pickled enough, ordered a lemonade.

Most of the dishes on the menu read like gobbledegook.

"We look after this place," Cohen said as Danny struggled his way through the choices. "It's all good stuff, Danny. Have what you want."

Danny's eyes went to the "English Dishes" section. "I'll have an omelette," he said, thankful for something he recognised.

Lunch was ordered and quickly served. After some small talk and enquiries about Danny's family, Cohen kicked off a more meaningful conversation.

"Things are going even better than we hoped, Danny."

"Like a dream," said Costa.

"And this is just the beginning," said Cohen through a mouthful of chicken chow mein. "The world's at your feet, son."

"I suppose you wanna know what the plan is," said Costa, building a pancake of duck and plum sauce.

"We have lined up a fight with another real contender," said Cohen. "If you win, you could be on your way for a shot at the British title."

"What d'ya mean, *if* he wins?" chimed Costa, winking at Danny and raising a glass of bubbly at him.

"Albert's leaving the team," Danny said, unable to hold it in any longer.

Costa and Cohen looked at each other.

"That's a shame," said Cohen unconvincingly.

"Probably his health or his age. Don't worry about it, you got us," Costa said and put his hand on Danny's knee. "That's all you need, Danny."

Danny felt a little uncomfortable. The hand on the knee was not good.

He decided to remove himself.

"Where are the gents?"

He got back at the table to see Costa and Cohen clinking glasses. The banana fritters had arrived.

"I bet you wanna know about the fight we've lined up," said Cohen.

"It's a cracker," enthused Costa.

"We have got you a fight with Billy Livermore, a big contender for the British title," said Cohen.

Costa jumped in. "A match made in heaven. You have just got to outbox him and we reckon you'll be on your way to a shot at the title."

Danny had heard of Livermore: a bruiser from Manchester with a knock-out punch to match. He started to feel a little easier about Albert jumping ship. The charm and positive plans from Costa and Cohen reassured him that he was on course, with or without his old mentor.

"When is it gonna be?" he asked eagerly. "Sounds good."

"There are a few things we still need to finalise," said Cohen. "It could take six months to a year, but we know it will be in Manchester."

"Sounds a way off," said Costa, "but you need to be ready, Danny."

"Don't worry about that," said Danny confidently. "I'll be ready."

"Do you still think Irish Patsy is the right man for the job?" asked Costa. "You know, with Albert gone and everything?"

This question took Danny aback. Now that Albert had jumped ship, he was not going to lose Patsy too.

"Yeah I do," he said firmly.

Costa shrugged. "Fair enough. See how it goes."

Lunch seemed to be on the house. Danny asked if he could pay his way, but Cohen shrugged away the suggestion.

"Don't you worry about that," he said as the waiter fetched their coats. "We have an arrangement with the owner. We look after him and he looks after us."

The thought of protection money came into Danny's head. He pushed it away.

"I'm buying a house," he said as the three men walked to the door.

"Nice," said Costa. "Whereabouts?"

"In Chigwell," Danny answered proudly.

"Stick with us, Danny boy, and you'll soon be able to buy the whole of Chigwell!" said Cohen.

Handshakes and hugs followed. Danny stood on the pavement and watched their white Jaguar drive off. Six months to a year? He'd be ready, with or without Albert.

Now that the dust had settled and Costa and Cohen had delivered their charm offensive, Danny started feeling resentful towards Albert. Clearly Albert didn't have the same belief in him that Costa and Cohen had. Danny wanted to tell Albert what the plan was, to talk about Livermore and the fight ahead, but he couldn't. Albert had let him down.

He headed for the gym to tell Patsy about the forthcoming fight. The Live and Let Live bar was quiet, and there was no sign of Albert. Danny felt relieved. Bumping into Albert might be a little awkward. Danny was not sure how he would react.

The light was on in Patsy's office and the sound of light snoring could be heard. Danny knocked.

"Patsy?"

Patsy jerked awake. "Sorry, just having one of those power naps. What's happening?"

"We've got a fight with Billy Livermore in about six months' time," said Danny.

Patsy went pale. "Christ!" he exclaimed. "That's a bit of a jump. Have you told Albert?"

Danny sat down opposite Patsy. "Albert's decided he don't want to be involved any more."

"Is that so?" Patsy sounded concerned. "Why's that then?"

"Costa and Cohen," Danny said bleakly.

Patsy shook his head. "That's sad," he said. "What do we do now then?"

"We train hard, Patsy," said Danny in determination. "You and me."

Patsy played with a well-chewed pencil on his desk. "So they want me involved, do they?"

"Of course they do," Danny said. "And I do too."

Patsy nodded. "This Livermore is a tough nut to crack," he warned. "You'll need to be at your best."

"I will be with you beside me."

"So you will," said Patsy in agreement. "So you will. Eleven o'clock after your morning run tomorrow? See you then."

Leaving the gym, Danny was relieved that at least Patsy was still in his boxing family. He'd thought for a moment, because of Albert's withdrawal, that Patsy might pull out too. But now confident that Patsy was still up for it, he made his way home to tell Wendy the news and give Ruby a cuddle.

Everything was going to be fine.

Patsy needed time to think.

He knew that Albert had misgivings about the dangerous liaison with Cohen and Costa. Patsy knew they were shady, but being the trainer to a top professional fighter had always been his dream. Maybe the fight with the Dragon had been a fix, but it had put Danny on the map. And it had put Patsy on the map too.

Patsy had known Albert since he'd first come over from Ireland. He'd seen Albert fight towards the end of a talented and illustrious career. Albert had strong principles. The word "cheat" was not in Albert's vocabulary. But sometimes in life, Patsy thought, you had to compromise. And if to compromise meant that he would be respected as a top trainer, then compromise he would.

After feeding Rocky the budgie and washing up later that afternoon, Albert sat down on his well-worn and friendly armchair. It felt cold. He would have fed the gas meter and lit it for warmth, but until he got paid he couldn't afford to.

The money from Danny still lay on the sideboard. It was as much as Albert could do to touch it, let alone spend it. It represented everything he hated about the dark and criminal underbelly of boxing.

He felt more alone today than he had in a while. Rocky was doing her best to cheer him up, but her perch dancing wasn't really helping. Albert knew he had done the right thing by cutting ties with Danny; he couldn't be a party to the shady world of Cohen and Costa. But still, he worried about the boy and where they would lead him.

He thought back to the day they'd first met, when something in the boy's eyes had reminded him of his own lost son.

"How far you've come, Danny," he said to himself. "How far you've come."

Not one to wallow in self-pity for long, he decided to get out of the flat and pay Lenny a visit.

True to form, Lenny was washing a car.

"Albert man," he said, squinting up at his visitor. "You look like you're running out of petrol. Cup of tea? I'm just finishing."

"Yeah," said Albert gratefully. "Cup of tea."

He followed Lenny to his sitting room at the back of the workshop and took his usual seat.

"How's the boy?" said Lenny, boiling the kettle.

"Fine, I think," said Albert. "He's got another fight coming soon."

"Who's he fighting?" asked Lenny as he handed Albert a mug.

"I don't know, Len," Albert admitted.

"What, his managers ain't told you?"

"I'm not involved any more," said Albert, taking a welcome sip of his tea.

Lenny frowned. "Those bastards got rid of you?"

"Not directly. It was my choice, Len. I think it's best."

Lenny set his own tea down on the worktop. "What are you saying, Albert?" he demanded. "You threw away a chance for glory, a chance to have money? Why, man? Why?"

"My glory may have faded, but money and glory ain't everything," said Albert with dignity. "Honesty, fair play and truth in the sport I love makes money worthless."

Lenny sipped his tea, then made his familiar hissing sound. He shook his head. "Principles, principles," he said. "You know, boy, people go to war on principles. What good does that do, eh?"

"It's just the way I am," said Albert. "I can't change."

"You're a fool to yourself," said Lenny, angry now. "How can you watch Danny's back if you're not around?"

Albert bent his head over his tea. "I know, Len," he answered. "I'm sorry. Now, subject closed."

CHAPTER SIXTEEN

LIFE without Albert watching and advising was difficult for Danny at first. But Albert had made his decision, and Danny had to move on.

Danny had been promising his mum that he would bring Ruby round and visit for weeks. It was always a point of friction between Wendy and Danny, with Rosie complaining that she wasn't seeing Ruby or her son nearly enough. The truth was, Wendy thought Rosie was a bad influence. So, the Bristows' house was definitely out of bounds for Rosie Watson, and Danny's visits to his mum's were limited.

Danny pushed Ruby through the streets to Rosie's house for a rare visit. Keeping the peace between his mother and Wendy was tricky, and he had often been stuck in the middle since moving out. It was true that Rosie's lifestyle of partying, drink and fags probably wasn't ideal, but she was still his mother, and through all her failings, there was indeed love.

Danny rang his mother's doorbell. The door opened so quickly that it was clear Rosie had been waiting in the hall.

"Danny darling!" she gasped, grabbing Ruby. "Oh look at her, look at her! Come to Nanny!"

Rosie seemed sober and unlikely to drop her grandchild today, Danny decided.

"Ain't she got big?" cooed Rosie. "She'll be walking soon. Oh Danny, she's lovely!"

To Danny's surprise, the house was spick and span. There were no empty bottles, no over-full ashtrays. The kitchen was cleaner than Danny had ever seen it. A cake sat on the kitchen table, next to the best china tea set that usually only came out at Christmas.

Danny was touched by Rosie's efforts. "The place looks nice," he said.

"Well it's not often I get to see you and Ruby," said Rosie, with just a touch of venom. "So I wanted to make it nice."

"I know," said Danny. "It's just been so busy. Where's Ricky?"

"He's gone to Stratford," Rosie replied. "He's doing his Elvis thing in a pub or something called the Two Puddings. How about a nice cuppa? Look, I bought a cake too, your favourite. Angel cake."

"Thanks Mum," said Danny, whose last taste of angel cake had been when he was about nine.

"Oh, and I bought some rusks for Ruby."

With Ruby happily on Rosie's lap, they sat down for cake and tea.

"Lots of good things happening, Mum," said Danny, angel cake in hand. "I told you about the new house?"

"Yes you did Danny, I'm pleased for you. Only I probably won't get to see you at all when you move away," said Rosie, suddenly crestfallen.

"Of course you will," said Danny, knowing in his heart

that his mum was probably right. With Wendy's attitude towards Rosie's lifestyle, the visits would be rare, if at all.

He drank his tea and watched his mother playing with Ruby. Ruby seemed so happy bouncing on her nan's lap. Danny wished he could change Wendy's attitude, although he knew that Rosie's performance as the perfect nan and mother was very unusual. After all, she was never a great mum to Danny, putting him a firm second to her well-known gallivanting. But still, it was good to see Ruby happy in her nan's presence.

Rosie did all the things that grandparents tend to do. There was "Walkie round the garden!" and "Tickle under there!" – a firm favourite with the sweetly chuckling Ruby. "Peek a boo!" went down a treat too. It was clear that Rosie was loving having Ruby all to herself for once, and Danny was happy for Rosie to have this special time with the grand-daughter she hardly knew.

"Ooh look at the time," Rosie said at last, briskly handing Ruby back to Danny. "I better get going. I've got to get to that pub to see Ricky do his thing. Silly sod forgot his Elvis wig."

The saying "Leopards never change their spots" floated through Danny's mind. "Yeah, Mum," he said, trying to paper over the cracks. "We better get going too. It was good to see you."

Rosie more or less bundled them out the door.

Danny made his way back home, taking the scenic route through the park. He wheeled the pram with the sleeping Ruby to the duck pond and sat down on Albert's bench.

There was something about this familiar spot that helped him think. Danny looked around at the budding trees and early flowers heralding the beginning of spring, and watched ducklings following their mother with relentless energy. The loss of Albert was the only grey cloud on this beautiful day.

All was as it always was, but Danny couldn't help feeling uneasy. He had a loving wife, a beautiful daughter, a new home to look forward to. But sometimes, too many changes could be overwhelming.

Where would these uncharted waters take him? Perhaps it was the thought of moving away from the area he had known since he was a baby that was confusing him. And then of course, there was the battle to come. "A life-changing contest," Costa had said. Danny's life was already changing.

For the better on paper, but what about in reality?

His thoughts were broken by Ruby's crying. Danny looked at her cherry-red face and open mouth. She looked like a baby bird, waiting hopefully for its mother to return with food. Reaching into the bag hanging on the pram, Danny picked up the baby bottle of milk his mother had filled before they left. Taking Ruby in his arms, he tucked the bottle teat between her little red lips.

As he watched her feeding, all the grey clouds in his mind disappeared.

Seeing her so helpless and dependent on him cleared his thoughts. The desire to get things right and build a happy future for his baby girl welled up in him, a feeling as strong as the oak tree that they sat under which shaded them from the sparkling sun.

With Ruby fed and happy and trying to munch on one of Rosie's rusks, Danny wheeled the pram out of the park again. "We should get back, Ruby," he told his daughter. "Mummy will be wondering where we are."

At the last minute, he decided to make a detour to Lenny's garage.

Lenny was in his usual position underneath a car.

"I've brought someone to see you, Lenny," Danny told Lenny's legs.

"Is that you, Danny?" came Lenny's voice from underneath an exhaust pipe.

"You remember Ruby, Len," Danny said as Lenny slid out from underneath the car. "Ruby? This is your uncle Lenny."

Lenny's face lit up. "Ain't she got big?" he said, as Ruby wriggled and fretted in Danny's arms. "Beautiful too. Good job she takes after her mother. Let me wash me hands so I can hold her."

"She's all yours," said Danny.

As soon as Lenny took her, Ruby stopped fretting and became still and serene.

"I think she likes me," Lenny said proudly. "She's got taste."

Lifting the little girl high in the air, Lenny then started to sing a soft lullaby, making up the words as he went along. Ruby was hooked, a wondering smile spreading across her little face.

Danny loved seeing them together. "You look like the perfect grandad, Lenny," he said in admiration.

Lenny finished his song. A mesmerised Ruby had already fallen into a happy sleep in his arms. Taking Ruby from Lenny, Danny put her gently in the pram.

"She is lovely," Lenny said, looking down at the pram. "You're a lucky boy."

"I know," said Danny. "So did you hear about Albert? Leaving and that?"

Lenny made a face. "He told me," he said. "He thinks a lot of you, Danny, but not a lot of Costa and Cohen."

"That ain't a reason to leave," said Danny, fishing for answers.

"He's got his reasons," was Lenny's enigmatic reply. "He didn't want to talk too much about it."

It seemed to Danny that Lenny either wouldn't or couldn't throw more light on Albert's decision.

"I know where he lives," he said aloud. "Above that junk shop. I could go and have a chat with him, maybe. You know, away from the Live and Let Live."

"Not a good idea," said Lenny. "Albert don't have visitors. He has let me in his flat only twice all the years I've known him. So Danny, I hear Costa and Cohen are working for you, got your next fight planned?"

Danny reluctantly dropped the subject of Albert. "Yeah, they're doing good. I'm fighting Billy Livermore in a few months' time."

Lenny whistled. "Now that'll be a tall order," he said with a smile. "But don't you worry. Your number-one fan will be there to support you."

This statement of loyalty meant a lot to Danny. With Albert gone, he'd felt sort of abandoned. Having Lenny around at least would be something.

They wished each other warm goodbyes and Danny

headed back to Wendy's house. As he pushed the pram along the cobbles, Danny allowed himself to focus on the task ahead. Albert or no Albert, he was going to give the Livermore fight all he had. His family deserved it. His future depended on it.

The next few months were busy. Danny tried to avoid the distraction of moving, leaving most of it to Wendy and her willing parents. His priority was to be fit and ready for the fight.

Lenny had kindly lent him a Ford Zodiac, and after a handful of lessons and a near-botched driving test, Danny was soon driving back and forwards to the gym. Patsy had Danny working well, and the occasional sighting of Albert at the Live and Let Live was not as awkward as it could have been.

It was true, though, that things with Albert were different. Albert never watched Danny train any more, and their conversation was little more than small talk. Albert would occasionally take Patsy aside and ask how Danny was doing, but that was the extent of his involvement. There was a chill between Danny and Albert now, although their relationship had not entirely frozen over.

On the other hand Costa and Cohen were getting closer to Danny every day. There were almost daily visits to check on progress. They brought sports writers to interview Danny, photographers to capture the boy, and food supplements to aid his concentration.

"Vitamins, are they?" said Patsy, examining the supplements one day.

"Only the best for our boy," said Cohen.

"Whatever they are, they're working," said Patsy as they watched Danny pummel the pads with renewed aggression. "His stamina, strength and energy have all improved."

"How's his temper?" asked Costa, casually examining his fingernails. "Along with the benefits, these vitamins can sometimes get a fighter a little worked up."

"Short," said Patsy.

Cohen and Costa nodded as if they'd expected that.

"There's always side effects," said Cohen. "Worth it though, right?"

Patsy watched Danny work through his routine. "Worth it," he agreed.

After each tough training session, Danny would climb in his borrowed Zodiac and drive home to his new house and family.

Wendy and her mum had performed miracles in Chigwell. Most of the moving boxes were now empty, and furniture was being delivered daily. Ruby loved being in the garden. The new house was starting to feel like home.

Danny loved the house. He felt a sense of achievement having put a roof over his family's head. As for the sky-blue Zodiac, he especially loved the bench seat and the column gear change. It wasn't a Porsche, but he did feel like one of his heroes, James Dean, as he motored from East London to leafy Essex. He had paid Lenny a deposit, and promised to pay the balance from the takings of the upcoming contest.

Things were good in Danny's life. Patsy was pleased with his progress, and although Danny still missed Albert and his words of wisdom, there was a job to do and he had to be ready.

Days were peppered with the odd press interview and a lot of serious preparation for the big fight. Patsy and Danny had watched film footage of Livermore nearly every day, looking for a weakness, a soft underbelly, an opening that Danny could attack.

"He's over-confident," Patsy told Danny as they watched the footage. "Look, he drops his guard too much. He's strong coming forward but not so secure in defence. Pushing him back will be a good option, I reckon."

Cohen found a couple of new sparring partners for Danny, fighters that mirrored Livermore's aggressive style. Danny found it useful, but was of course aware that the real thing would be a tougher nut to crack.

As the months passed, Danny and Patsy started to frequent Costa's club in Soho. The good life was seductive, and without a firm date for the fight, it was easy to drift into late nights and too much alcohol.

One night, Danny observed Costa roll up a five-pound note into a tight tube and sniff some white powder through it.

"What you doing?" he asked.

Costa pinched his nose. "Just a little pick-me-up," he answered, smiling. "Here, try it."

Danny took the note and copied Costa, sniffing the white powder. The buzz was almost immediate. He liked it.

"You got any more of that?" he asked.

Costa was more than happy to supply Danny with the cocaine whenever Danny asked. Danny started asking too often. Before long, Wendy and even Ruby had become second to Danny's new lifestyle.

Arguments were becoming frequent events. Danny's mood swings and short temper made him difficult to live with.

"You've changed so much," a tearful Wendy said one night. "You hardly acknowledge Ruby when she calls you Daddy. You ignore me too. It's like we're not even here. What's happening to you?"

Danny felt twitchy and ill. "What's happening to you, you mean?" he bit back. "You ain't the girl I married. All you care about is bloody Ruby."

"So?" Wendy spat. "Don't you think you should care about her too?"

Danny got up. "I don't need this."

But Wendy was in full flow. "It seems to me all you care about is going out all night," she said, following him out of the room. "This is not working, Danny. I've had enough, you hear me? When you are here, it's like you're somewhere else!"

"Maybe I should be somewhere else then!" Danny shouted.

Sensing the hostility, Ruby began crying, reaching out for her mother to pick her up.

"Now look what you done," Wendy said as she picked up Ruby and tried to comfort her.

As Danny looked at the tears rolling down Wendy and Ruby's faces, he felt nothing.

Wendy seemed to flinch as she looked into Danny's eyes. Lowering her voice so as not to upset the already distraught Ruby, she delivered an ultimatum.

"You've got to change, Danny," she said.

"Bollocks," said Danny irritably. "What do I need to change for?"

Wendy wiped the tears from her and Ruby's eyes. "You're not the man I married either," she said. "You're someone else, someone I don't know." She took a deep breath. "I think you need to leave."

Danny saw red.

"Good idea," he yelled. "What a fuckin' good idea."

Ruby started crying again like her little heart was broken. Danny ignored her. He went up to the bedroom, stuffed some clothes and belongings into his bag, snatched up his coat and car keys and walked out the door. He felt nothing but blind rage. Not an inkling of remorse or sadness. Nothing at all.

Danny was suffering cold sweats the whole way to London. Pulling his vitamins out of the glove box, he knocked back a couple of pills and wondered where to go. He thought about Rosie's place, but decided to drive to Costa's instead. Costa had a flat above the club. Perhaps he could stay there. Good life downstairs, cocaine on tap.

At the club, Costa was holding auditions. Twitching by the bar, Danny watched the scantily dressed girls parade up and down. Costa's preference would have been a parade of scantily dressed young men, but he had his mainly male clientele to consider.

"All right, Tommy," Danny said during a break in proceedings. "Do you reckon I could stay in your flat for a while?"

"Why?"

Danny wiped his nose. "Me and Wendy have broken up. I need somewhere to stay till I get myself together."

Costa put his arm round Danny. "Of course you can, son," he said. "You're one of the family."

Months passed. There was still no fixed date for the fight, and training sessions were becoming less frequent. Danny made many excuses, and Patsy grew tired of hounding him. Danny was living in a different world now, physically and mentally. The drugs and the nightlife engulfed him. The focus on his boxing career became almost non-existent.

Patsy had told Albert about Danny and Wendy's break-up months earlier. Albert's first thoughts had been with the little girl.

"What about Ruby? Idiot, what's the matter with him?"

"I don't know, Albert," Patsy admitted.

Albert felt heavy-hearted. "Do you think this fight with Livermore is ever going to happen?"

Patsy grunted. "They're certainly taking their time about it."

Albert felt more worried than ever. "How's he training? I haven't seen him for a while."

"Not so good. He's finding it hard with no date fixed for the fight."

Albert sighed. "Say hello to him, will ya?" he said. "It must be tough, not knowing. Like you're in limbo."

Wendy and Ruby were making the best of things. Wendy's parents were a godsend, doing their very best to soften the heartache. Mr Bristow helped Wendy with money and Mrs Bristow gave her time.

Months went by without any contact from Danny. He even missed Ruby's second birthday. Wendy did all she could to put Danny out of her mind, but it wasn't easy, especially when Ruby said "Daddy" and pointed to their wedding photograph.

Wendy had thought about putting the photo away, but decided that would be putting away the good times they'd had. So she left it there, sitting on the shelf, reminding her every day of what they'd lost.

She felt like her life was sitting on the shelf beside the photograph. Ruby filled much of her time and much of the space left in her heart, but at night the heartache would come and almost overwhelm her.

Danny seemed lost in his twilight world of drugs, drink and late nights. Cohen was the first to notice.

"The boy won't be worth nothing if he carries on the way he is," he warned Costa one night.

Costa shrugged. "He's a young fella, he's just having a good time."

★

Danny was not having a good time. His moods swung like a pendulum, and he suffered acute fatigue that only the cocaine and his vitamins seem to cure. Costa had made a few advances, suggesting drugs for sex, but Danny managed to keep his distance.

Through the dark times, Danny's past life would come to him in flashes. Wendy, Ruby, Albert. Whenever this happened, he would steer his thoughts to drugs, numbing any remorse or pain. To wallow in a stupor was better than facing the truth.

One afternoon, as Danny lay in bed with his usual pounding headache, there was a loud knock.

"Danny?" said Cohen through the door. "It's Jack. You in there?"

Danny tried to get his mind in gear. He stumbled from the bed and opened the flat door.

Cohen looked at him. "Look at the state of you," he said. "Tommy was supposed to keep an eye, but here you are like a deadbeat. What's the matter with you?"

Danny muttered something about being tired. Cohen cut through his stammering.

"I've got some news about the fight," he said.

"Yeah?" was all that Danny could muster.

Cohen prodded him in the chest. "The fight is in two months. You better sort yourself out, you're in a fuckin' state."

Marching over to the bedside table, Cohen grabbed Danny's cocaine stash and threw it out the window. Danny ran to the window, but it was too late.

"Sort yourself out!" shouted Cohen, and slammed the door behind him.

Danny went into panic mode, his heart beating like a drum. This jolt from the real world was a shock. He could only think about one thing.

He needed to get to Patsy.

He dressed and washed and went to his car, full of cold shivers, hot sweats and blurred vision. He took a couple of vitamins to ease the symptoms as he drove East. Making it to the Live and Let Live, he parked erratically by the side of the road and went in.

Albert was getting things ready for opening time.

"Danny! Where you been? Blimey, it's been ages! How are you? How's Ruby? She must be a handful, growing up fast I bet."

Danny leant against the bar. He felt completely exhausted. "Dunno," he said. "I ain't seen her."

"Since when?" said Albert.

"Dunno. A year maybe? Get us a drink, will you Albert? I got a pain in my head today like a fuckin' hammer."

For a moment, Albert was too shocked to respond. Patsy had told him Danny and Wendy had split up, but he'd never expected that Danny would abandon his daughter.

"I was sorry about you and Wendy splitting up," he said.

"These things happen," Danny said. "Where's Patsy?"

"Not here yet, should turn up soon."

"Where's that drink?" Danny asked.

Albert pulled himself together. "Do you want an orange juice or something?"

Danny shook his head. "Jack Daniel's."

"I don't think so," said Albert. "You're training, ain't you?"

Danny slammed his hands on the bar. "Who are you to tell me what to do?"

Albert noticed Danny's hands were shaking and he was sweating.

"You all right, Danny?" he asked.

Danny shook his head like he had water in his ears. "If you ain't serving, I'll wait upstairs."

Albert watched Danny go. The boy was a different person. Patsy had not said that Danny had changed so much. Then again, Albert remembered that Patsy hadn't seen him for a few months.

He was deeply concerned. He wanted to help put back the sparkle in Danny's dead eyes. But how?

Entering the empty boxing gym was like opening a door to memories. Danny sat at the ringside, shaking and thinking. He regretted talking to Albert the way he had, but it was too late now. How was Patsy going react to the order of "all systems go" from Cohen? Patsy knew full well that Danny was out of shape and struggling.

"Albert said you were here," said Patsy, regarding him from the door of the gym.

Danny rubbed his eyes. "Cohen's fixed the Livermore fight for a couple of months' time."

233

"I thought it was never going to happen."

"I think I did too."

"So are you gonna shape up?" Patsy said, his eyes hard. "Pull yourself together, train hard?"

"I'm gonna try," said Danny, nodding. "I'm gonna try."

"Tomorrow at ten?"

"Tomorrow at ten."

Patsy shut himself in his office as Danny went down the stairs again. Lenny was at the bar.

"Now where have you been?" Lenny shouted, coming over to Danny to shake his hand. "Such a long time! Good to see you, Danny, you lost a little weight. Hey man, you got cold hands. Cold hands, warm heart."

"Warm heart?" Danny said wearily. "Not at the moment. See you around, Lenny." And he nodded a goodbye to Albert and left.

The Livermore weigh-in was a week before the fight. Danny caught the train to Manchester along with his entourage: Patsy, Costa and Cohen. Instead of his customary tracksuit, Patsy had a grey tweed suit on and, with a nod to Ireland, a green tie. Danny had got ready with Wendy's words in his head: to be a champ, you have to look like a champ. So he was wearing a Prince of Wales check suit and an open-neck sky-blue shirt. Costa and Cohen were immaculate as usual, in mohair.

As the train rumbled north, the excitement and nerves began making themselves felt. Danny took a few vitamins to steady himself. Costa, full of the white powder, never stopped talking.

"You take a break, a holiday, when you win this fight, Danny. Go to my house in Cyprus. You don't have to worry about the Turkish trouble, you and the family will be happy and safe."

Danny just nodded.

He looked out the window as the train passed towns he had never heard of. He looked at the back gardens and houses alongside the track and wondered what the people inside did, what their lives were like, what secrets lay behind their back doors.

Costa kept on talking. "We're getting a lot of famous people at the club these days. One night we thought Frank Sinatra was coming but he didn't."

Danny tried to look like he was listening to Costa's endless chat. His mood swings had been getting worse lately, along with the hot and cold sweats that accompanied them. He could be happy and then, in a second, depressed and short-tempered. Wendy had suffered the changes like a saint to begin with, making excuses for Danny that he was anxious and nervous about the big fight on the horizon. Not any more.

Danny didn't want to think about Wendy.

The train finally pulled into Piccadilly station.

"Why is it called Piccadilly?" asked Danny, rousing himself. "Piccadilly is in London."

"They're copy cats," was Patsy's view.

"So where we off to, Jack?" asked Danny as Cohen hailed a taxi.

"Same place as the fight," said Cohen. "Free Trade Hall."

Patsy launched into a local history of boxing as they drove through the strange, wet streets of Manchester.

"Boxing in the late fifties was in the doldrums here in Manchester. But thanks to fighters like Billy Livermore, nowadays it's become quite a force. Loads of boxing cubs up here are actively engaging the kids."

"As far as I'm concerned, anything north of Manchester is whippets, strange accents and flat caps," said Costa.

Since leaving the amateur circuit and joining the professionals, Danny had noticed the changes in the venues, with personal dressing rooms and facilities laid on. Free Trade Hall was no different. Security men were at hand, and everyone seemed so full of respect that it bordered on servility.

Danny sat on a bench in the changing room, staring at the coat hooks on the cream-painted wall. Patsy was checking up on the gym equipment for Danny's pre-warm-up for the fight, now just a few days away.

"It's strange without Albert, ain't it Pat?" Danny said to the medicine ball in Patsy's hands.

"Yeah, a bit," said Patsy. "But we'll cope."

"A lot of things have changed ain't they?"

Patsy didn't answer.

Outside the door, Danny heard the rumble and mumble of the folk filling the auditorium.

"There are hundreds of people out there to watch the weigh-in and we're stuck in this room, hidden like we're prisoners," he said. "Do you reckon that's a part of fame and fortune? You lose your freedom?"

Costa put his head round the door before Patsy could answer.

"Ready champ?"

Danny's reflexes felt as sharp as a razor, his mind was racing, and he felt anger pulsing through him. The vitamins he'd taken on the train were clearly taking effect.

"As ready as I'll ever be, Tommy," he said.

Costa patted him on the shoulder. "The place is packed, Danny. Wait till you see it."

The update was meant as a positive, but was not what Danny wanted to hear. The reality of the situation – hundreds of people, press, photographers and the like – released a case of serious nerves and paranoia. Danny's hands were suddenly ice cold with terror.

The Master of Ceremonies' voice rattled through the tannoy.

"Ladies and gentlemen! From London, a rising star in the boxing world, Danny Watson!"

With a shove from Patsy, Danny stumbled into the spotlights. Unlike at the Dragon weigh-in, he heard cheers. This time, Danny had support and a following. As he passed through the crowd accompanied by security men, there were handshakes, pats on the back and goodwill wishes. Danny had been out of the ring for a long time, and folks were pleased to see him back.

Danny reached the podium as a fanfare heralded the entrance of Livermore. The reaction of the crowd was close to boiling point now. The welcome Danny had received was dwarfed by the cheers and applause that greeted Livermore.

Manchester born and bred, he could do no wrong in his home town.

Danny watched as Livermore and his entourage made their way to the podium. Livermore was a powerful-looking man, the son of a West Indian father and a Lancashire girl. Climbing on to the podium, he raised his arms in the air as if he had already won the fight.

Livermore was a different proposition to the Dragon. Walking over, he shook Danny's hand and raised Danny's arm with his. There was even some warmth in his eyes.

Danny was a little taken aback. It was usual that there was respect between fighters, even before a fight, but it was rarely shown. Livermore's friendly reaction felt a little weird.

The men weighed in. Both were inside the weight limit. They took their seats to answer questions from the press. Danny hated this bit, but knew it was all part of the game.

"Danny, your rise has been almost meteoric. There has been some talk that your last fight against Reece 'the Dragon' Davies was too easy. What do you think your prospects against Billy Livermore will be?"

This felt a little tricky, given that Danny was sitting next to Livermore. He decided to be modest.

"Billy's a good fighter, I know that," he answered. "But I intend to give it my best shot."

"Billy, you have a good record and are probably just one fight away from a title fight. Will winning the fight open the door to a title shot?"

"It's gonna be a tough fight," answered Livermore. "But I've got experience on my side. I respect Danny Watson, but there will be only one winner on the night and that's gonna be me. And yes, the title in time will be mine too."

Livermore's followers rose to Billy's battle cry with cheers. They started chanting, "Billy! Billy!" in true football fashion.

The press conference went on.

"Danny, I hear that one of your team, Albert Kemp, has left the camp. Do you think that will have any bearing on tactics and the outcome?"

Cohen jumped in. "Mr Kemp's departure was a mutual decision," he said smoothly. "Danny is well prepared, believe me. It's going to be a great contest. I'd like to thank you all for coming. That concludes the press conference."

Danny was pleased the trial was over, and even more pleased that the Albert question had been fended off by Cohen. He shook hands with Livermore and the two boxers posed for photographs.

Danny couldn't stop looking at Livermore. This was a boxer that had been well and truly round the block, battle-scarred from many fights in many smoke-filled venues. And yet somehow, instead of hostility, there was a look of "We're in this together" in his eyes. Billy Livermore was a sportsman, courteous and gracious.

"That Livermore seems a decent bloke," said Danny back in the changing room.

"Yeah," agreed Patsy. "He's a proper professional, but don't let that Mr Nice Guy act fool you. He needs to win this fight and he means to do you damage."

Danny nodded. "I suppose I'm standing in the way of his title shot."

"You are. If he loses to you, his chances will be limited."

"No pressure then," said Danny. He was only half joking.

With the weigh-in and press stuff over and done with, Danny and Patsy made their way back to Piccadilly station, leaving Costa and Cohen in Manchester to sort out the box office and logistics for the fight the following week.

The journey home felt longer. Danny and Patsy passed the time watching the sights and countryside as they headed south. Patsy talked about a new heavyweight called Cassius Clay and his recent win over the seasoned and scary fighter Sonny Liston.

"He has a lot to say for himself. They call him the 'Louisville Lip', but he looks good. He talks the talk and it looks like he can walk the walk. Very fast for a heavyweight, but a bit too cocky for my liking."

Danny listened, but found it hard to concentrate. After a day like today, some time by himself was what he needed. In recent weeks he'd had a very low boredom threshold, and Patsy and his talking could have easily lit the fuse to his short temper.

When they reached London, Danny offered Patsy a lift.

"No thanks, Danny, I'll take the underground. See you in the gym in the morning."

Danny felt relieved. He couldn't have taken much more of Patsy's company. Getting in his car, he took a couple of vitamins from the glove box and put on the radio. After a bit of fiddling, he managed to get a crackly signal from one of the new pirate radio stations, Radio Caroline. Radio Luxembourg was decent enough, but that only seemed to come alive in the evenings, and that was if you were able to actually tune in and get it. Meanwhile, the Beatles were heading an onslaught of what was termed "The Liverpool Sound" and Radio Caroline was full of it.

As he drove, a record from a band called Freddie and the Dreamers came on. "Not the Liverpool Sound this time," said the disc jockey, "but the pride of Manchester."

It seemed appropriate given Danny's lightning trip up North. People had seemed really friendly in Manchester. It was colder, but the people had been warmer. Danny thought about Billy Livermore and his dignified confidence.

He reminded himself that, although Livermore seemed a decent bloke, he was standing in his way. Danny resolved to replace respect with the will to beat him.

In an attempt to prepare for the fight without too many distractions, Danny had moved out of Costa's and in with Rosie. He still paid the odd visit to Costa's for a gram or two, but at least he was trying.

"How was your day then?" Rosie asked when Danny got in. "What's it like up North?"

"The people seem friendly, but it's a bit cold and wet. The bloke I'm fighting seems like a gentleman, you know?"

"That makes a change," said Rosie. "There's not many of them around." She frowned. "Wait a minute, ain't you supposed to hate him?"

Danny rubbed his forehead. "Don't worry Mum, I don't have to hate him. I just have to hate losing."

"You don't seem to mind losing your wife and daughter."

Danny put his head in his hands. Rosie had brought this up several times lately.

"You know what you need to do?" Rosie pointed to a photograph of Ruby sitting on her mantelpiece. "See that little girl. Why don't you phone Wendy and try to make peace? Make arrangements to see her?"

"I don't need this today, Mum," Danny said.

Rosie dumped Danny's beans on toast in front of him.

"Well, I'm off down the pub to meet Ricky. Phone her, Danny. That little girl needs a dad. I'll probably be late, don't wait up."

Danny felt tired and very alone. After being the centre of attention at the weigh-in, he was back with his mum in the house he'd grown up in. What did that make him?

After a few minutes, he went into the hall and looked at the telephone.

He knew the number off by heart. Picking up the receiver, he listened to the dialling tone for a while. When the dialling tone stopped and was replaced by crackling, Danny put down the receiver and went upstairs to take some more vitamins.

Feeling brighter, he returned to the phone and dialled the number.

"Hello?"

Danny clutched the receiver and closed his eyes. Just hearing Wendy's voice was wonderful.

"Hello?" Wendy repeated. "Anyone there?"

"It's me," said Danny.

Wendy went silent. Danny could hear Ruby singing in the background.

"It's Danny," he said.

"I know."

Danny clutched the receiver more tightly. "How's Ruby?"

"What do you want?" Wendy asked coldly.

Danny felt lost. "I don't really know, Wend," he said.

Wendy sounded a little softer. "You're still alive then?"

"Just about," said Danny.

"You all right?"

Danny sobbed, "I miss you both," and put down the receiver.

He went back into his mum's sitting room, wiping his eyes. He decided to look over Patsy's notes for the fight to take his mind off his broken heart.

He knew them inside out.

Attack. Be offensive. He is weaker going back.

Look for his guard to drop. Jab and move. Keep pushing forward.

Watch for his right upper cut in close, it's a big one.

For the first time in months, Danny went to his bedroom to get out the red and silver tin box. Opening it, he picked up his father's medal, feeling the cold metal in his hands. His mind went back to the beginning of his career, when Albert would bring the medal for bravery to the ringside. A sudden feeling of panic washed over Danny as he looked at the photograph of his dad in his army uniform.

"What's happening, Dad?" he whispered. "What's happening?"

★

The night before the big fight, Rosie packed Danny's overnight bag and turned into a caring mother.

"Have you got your tickets?" she said, fussing around him. "What time is the train? Do you know where you're going when you get up there?"

Danny appreciated his mother's attention, but his mind was elsewhere. He checked his watch. Lenny was going to pick him and Patsy up, and all three would take the train from Euston.

Dead on two o'clock the doorbell rang. Lenny was looking smart and, on this rare occasion, out of his customary blue overalls.

"Hey Danny, how you doing?" he said. "Come on now, we better get going. There's no knowing what the traffic will be like in Central London."

Danny couldn't find much conversation in the car on the way to the station. Struggling with nerves and in a monosyllabic mood, he wasn't much better on the train. Lenny attempted to distract him with various topics, but Danny wasn't biting.

Patsy headed to the buffet car to buy them cups of tea.

"Albert wishes you the best, by the way, Danny," Lenny said.

Danny focused. "Does he? How is he?"

"He seems OK, a bit quiet," said Lenny. "You know Albert."

"I thought I did," Danny answered.

Back in London, Albert was walking to work as usual. It was a lovely evening, with kids still playing in the street and neighbours chatting about this and that on the front step. He couldn't help smiling at the familiarity of it all.

Around the corner, he saw some small boys playing cricket against a wall. The batsman took his guard armed with a plank of wood, doing his best to protect the stumps chalked on the wall. Albert watched one of them bowl and waited to see the result.

The bowler delivered a full toss. The batsman, with a mighty swing of his bit of wood, hit the well-worn tennis ball sky high. The bowler ran to catch it – straight into the path of an oncoming car.

Without thinking, Albert rushed into the road and pushed the boy clear of danger. Someone was screaming. Dimly Albert heard the screech of brakes, before he found himself tossed like a rag doll into the air. For a moment, everything went black.

The next thing Albert knew, he was lying in the road and staring at the sky. There was blood all around him. One of the cricket players was crying. "I never saw him!" someone – the driver, Albert guessed – was protesting. "He just come out of nowhere!"

"Here you are, love, a cup of strong, sweet tea'll set you right. Don't you worry about the old fella, the ambulance will be here in a minute."

Through the wails and shouts, Albert heard the distant sound of an ambulance bell. He lay quietly, unable to move, as people clustered around, peering down at him, some with concern and others with blatant curiosity.

"You all right, fella?"

"What happened, then?"

Albert stared up at them. He wanted to apologise for wasting their time, but he couldn't find his voice. His head was throbbing like he'd taken a knock-out punch.

The crowd parted as the ambulance arrived.

"Out the way, there you go. All right, sir? We'll have you in the hospital in a jiffy."

Strong hands lifted him off the road and on to a stretcher. A vicious stab of pain shot up Albert's leg.

As the ambulance sped through the streets, a medic did some tests on Albert, shining light into his eyes, testing his temperature and blood pressure.

"Stay with me, sir."

His head wound was cleaned and dressed, his legs gently strapped together. Normally as strong as an oak, Albert was not too happy with the fuss, but not really capable of arguing the point.

He shortly found himself being wheeled into the Accident and Emergency Department of the Royal London Hospital in Whitechapel, formerly known as the Whitechapel Infirmary for the Poor. That distinctive hospital smell was unmistakable. Albert gazed up at the passing fluorescent lights on the ceiling as nurses wheeled him along to the X-ray department.

"Head blow, is it?" said the waiting doctor.

"A few broken bones too, Doctor, by the looks of it."

Albert was hurting, but didn't show it. This was all a nuisance, but a nuisance he had to endure.

Two hospital porters lifted him into the space-age X-ray machine.

"Lie still for us, sir, would you? Nice and still now."

The machine purred into action. The pain in Albert's head was now competing with the pain in his body, and winning.

X-rays done, Albert was taken to the hospital ward and a waiting bed.

The ward was full of mainly older men groaning and coughing, with a little meaningless babble from a lost soul in one corner.

The matron bustled over as soon as Albert was settled. An attractive, portly woman with a soft West Country accent, she smoothed Albert's pillow and folded her arms.

"Comfortable are we, Mr Kemp? What have you been up to?"

Albert gazed up at her no-nonsense face, her pristine uniform.

"I had a fight with a car bonnet," he replied.

The matron tutted. Her manner was business-like, and she had the perfect balance of authority and caring about her.

"Well, it looks like the car won," she said. "Now, the doctor will study your X-rays and should be with you in a little while. I just have to fill in some details. Are you all right to answer some questions?"

"I'll do my best," said Albert weakly.

"Good boy."

With Albert feeling like a helpless kid, "good boy" seemed about right.

"So," said the matron, consulting her notes. "Your name is Albert Charles Kemp, we know that. Date of birth?"

Albert's head was pounding. It was difficult to think. "Ninth of November, eighteen ninety-eight."

"So you are aged sixty-eight?"

Albert felt faintly astonished. Was he really that old?

"Apparently," he said.

"Blood group?"

"I don't bloody know," Albert quipped, feeling irritated now.

"We'll soon find out," said Matron. "Next of kin?"

Albert felt hollow, thinking of Vera and Tommy. The only other person he could think of was Lenny, but Lenny was not a relation.

"No next of kin," he said.

He'd never thought about himself like that before, all alone in the world. It made him feel sad and empty. He wondered if anyone knew what had happened, or where he was.

Matron gently took his hand. "Thank you, Mr Kemp. The doctor will be with you in a minute."

Albert felt anxious. He had arranged with Lenny that Lenny would telephone the Live and Let Live with an update after Danny's fight tomorrow night, but here he was, marooned in a hospital bed. It was a poxy nuisance, that's what it was.

The white-coated doctor sported a polka-dot bow tie. "How are you feeling, Mr Kemp?" he asked. "You've had quite an accident. Having studied your X-rays, I'm pleased to say that your head injuries are superficial and the cuts and bruises will heal in time. Not such good news on the rest of you, though. I'm sorry to tell you that you have broken your left leg in two places, fractured your right wrist and broken two of your ribs."

"But apart from that I'm fine," said Albert, trying to lighten the diagnosis.

The doctor looked back at his notes. "The nurses will arrange to put a plaster cast on your leg and wrist. I'm afraid we can't do much about the broken ribs, but they too will heal in time. I'll prescribe some painkillers for you."

The seriousness of his predicament was beginning to dawn on Albert.

"So when can I go home?"

"As soon as you're well enough," said the doctor. "Now just rest."

The groans and delirium of some of his fellow patients rattled in Albert's aching head. He hated the situation he was in. He felt imprisoned, and he didn't like it.

A pretty nurse materialised at the end of his bed.

"Hello Mr Kemp," she said cheerfully. "I've got some tablets for you. Here, take two now and I'll come back in a couple of hours so you can take some more."

Albert obediently swallowed the painkillers.

"Well done," said the nurse, patting his hand.

Albert could understand why people sometimes fell in love with nurses. This one's angel-like presence was really quite special.

"Next, we will have to put a plaster cast on that leg of yours and..." She stopped to look at Albert's notes. "And your right wrist. You have been in the wars, Mr Kemp, haven't you?"

Albert lay back, resigned to fate's cruel blow.

CHAPTER SEVENTEEN

UP in Manchester, Danny and Patsy had found their way to the hotel and checked in. Lenny had gone for a cheaper bed-and-breakfast option in nearby Salford.

Marvelling at the luxury of the hotel and his comfortable double room, Danny took a couple of vitamins, lay back on the bed and looked over the room service menu. He couldn't believe how expensive everything was. Throwing caution to the wind, he rang down and ordered steak and chips, before settling down for a quiet night watching the big TV in his swanky room. Wendy and Ruby floated into his thoughts but he did his best to erase them. They hurt too much.

His phone rang early the next morning.

"Meet me for breakfast," Patsy barked. "Most important meal of the day."

Heading downstairs, Danny was pleased to see Lenny in reception.

"Got tired of slumming it," Lenny said, tearing his eyes from the chandelier hanging overhead. "Thought I'd see how the other half live."

Danny slapped him on the back. "Good to see you Lenny," he said. "Come and have some breakfast."

In the dining room, Patsy was already tucking into a full English breakfast. Danny and Lenny ordered tea and headed for the buffet.

"They got some stuff here," said Lenny, going for the scrambled egg and bacon. "Look at that, smoked salmon! Who eats that for breakfast?"

Danny opted for corn flakes and a couple of bananas.

At the table, the talk soon turned to the big fight.

"Good night's sleep, Danny?" Patsy asked.

Danny thought of his comfortable bed with its crisp white sheets. He was already starting to feel edgy. "Slept like a log Patsy, thanks for asking," he said. "What time are we going to the hall?"

"There are a couple of fights before you, and the fight is scheduled for around nine. I reckon if we leave about seven, it will give you time to ready yourself."

Danny's palms were already sweating. "Don't worry, I'll be ready," he said.

"I got a call from Cohen this morning," Patsy went on, oblivious to Danny's nerves. "Every ticket has gone. He reckons they could've sold hundreds more."

"You're a popular boy, Danny," Lenny said through a mouthful of bacon. "You know, I think I'll try that smoked salmon after all."

★

The ward noises of pain and discomfort hadn't let up all night, and on just an hour or two's sleep, Albert wasn't happy.

"I reckon the food in prison is better than this muck," he grumbled to the genial West Indian lady that delivered his porridge. Forcing himself to eat a couple of spoonfuls, he zoned in on the tea and a piece of toast.

The ward grew even louder after breakfast. Albert reached for the ear plugs for the radio, desperate to get away from the sounds of suffering. As the nondescript hospital muzak numbed him to his surroundings, he let his thoughts drift to Danny and his trial to come.

Lenny had said he would phone the Live and Let Live after the fight to let Albert know how it went. Albert realised the Live and Let Live didn't yet know he was in this nuthouse.

He waved to a nearby nurse.

"What is it, love? Do you need a bed pan?"

Albert winced. "No," he said firmly. "Can I make a phone call?"

The nurse looked relieved that the bed pan was not on top of Albert's list. "I'll get a porter up," she said. "He'll take you to the phone at reception."

Albert hadn't really thought about his lack of mobility until a miserable-looking porter arrived with a wheelchair, bundling him into it like a heavily bandaged sack of potatoes. Had it really come to this?

Down in reception, he dialled the pub. After a few rings, Maria answered the phone.

"Maria? It's Albert."

"Where the bloody 'ell are you?"

"In hospital, with me leg in a poxy plaster."

Maria's tone of voice didn't change much. "Why the bloody 'ell you do that?"

"An accident, I was trying to save a kid," said Albert. "I just wanted to let you know why I'm not at work and where I am."

"Well that's a bloody nuisance," she said. "It means I'll 'ave to do everything myself."

Maria's word for the day was obviously "bloody", Albert thought.

"Lenny is going to call me at the pub tonight. Can you let him know I'm in hospital in Whitechapel?"

Maria sniffed. "If I get time. When are you coming back?"

"Could be a while."

"Bloody 'ell." There was that word again. "I'll let Lenny know."

While painkillers pumped through Albert's veins, adrenalin pumped through Danny's as the hired limo and driver drove him, Lenny and Patsy to the Free Trade Hall. They were greeted at the side door by security, Costa carrying an umbrella to shield Danny from the persistent Manchester rain.

"All right Danny?" said Costa with all the care and concern of a mother hen. "Looking good, champ."

Lenny knew this time was for Danny to prepare and made himself scarce. Patsy knew Danny and his moods, and set about going through some warm-ups to help relax him and prepare.

As Danny hit some pads, he could hear the crowd in the hall echoing along the corridor as they cheered and booed the earlier fighters. He tried to concentrate on his pre-fight routine, but it wasn't easy. After a spell with a skipping rope, he went to his travel bag to fetch his dad's bravery medal.

"Patsy," he said, feeling awkward. "Can you bring this to the corner for me?"

"You bet," said Patsy. "You know your dad is looking down on ya, don't you Danny?"

Danny swallowed as he handed over the medal. His mouth felt dry. "Yeah, Patsy," he said. "I know he is."

They heard the end of the previous fight, a mix of cheers and boos for the winner floating down the corridor like a distant fog. Danny's head felt like it was about to explode. He wanted more pills, but he'd taken three today already.

Patsy helped Danny on with his dressing gown. Danny still wore the colours of the West Ham Boxing Club where he started: a claret-coloured gown, and shorts with edging of sky blue.

Danny's blood felt sluggish in his veins.

"I'm not sure I'm ready, Patsy," he blurted in panic, almost pleading. "I don't feel right."

Patsy became brisk. "You're going to be fine. Courage now, Danny. Do it for your da."

There was a knock on the door. Cohen and Costa stood in the corridor flanked by five or six beefy security guards.

"Time to get it done," said Cohen. "You ready for it?"

Danny's head was banging like a drum. He looked vacantly at Cohen.

254

"He's ready, Jack," said Patsy, gripping Danny by the shoulder. "Let's get out there."

They walked to the auditorium, flanked by security. Danny felt like he was being smothered. He didn't want to be fussed over and treated like royalty. He just wanted that bell to go and to get this over with.

The crowd were on their feet to greet them, pushing and shouting as Danny was led to his corner. To take the edge off his nerves, Danny shadow-boxed around the ring like a pre-programmed robot.

More fanfares and searchlights heralded the local hero's entrance.

The noise was incredible. Livermore was a local boy made good, and the partisan crowd appreciated it.

"Billy! Billy! Billy!"

Danny stood in his corner, feeling nothing. Waiting.

Albert was suffering from more than just the pain and bruises. One of the ward residents, two beds along, was delirious. His moans and cries reminded Albert of the poor souls he had tried to rescue in the Blitz, a truly terrible time in London's history that was etched into Albert's memory.

He tried to focus on Danny and his big fight. How was the boy doing? Was he nervous? Did he have his father's medal? He tossed and turned in his bed, trying and failing to get comfortable. When would Lenny ring? Had Maria let him know where Albert was?

He looked around at the hospital ward, bare and surgical with its smell of disinfectant and cleanliness. He hated being laid up like an invalid. He wanted to be at work. He wanted to be in his own flat. If and when Lenny got in contact, he'd ask him to go to his flat and feed Rocky.

Making the best of it, Albert drifted in and out of a twilight sleep.

"I want a good clean fight," the referee told Danny and Livermore as they stood face to face. "No holding, and when I say break, you break."

Danny and Livermore touched gloves and returned to their corners. The roar of anticipation from the crowd was so loud, Danny could hardly hear.

"Seconds out!"

Ding ding!

"Round one!"

It was to be a ten-round contest. Both boxers showed respect in the first round, feeling one another out, keeping their distance and throwing the odd jab.

Patsy was in Danny's ear at the end of round one.

"You're doing good, Danny. Keep your distance. Keep your powder dry, wait for the right moment. Out you go, son."

To the delight of the crowd, round two saw Livermore on the offensive.

He caught Danny with some powerful hits, one straight left uppercut almost lifting Danny off his feet. When the bell rang out, Danny was shell-shocked and relieved to get back to his corner.

Sitting Danny down on his stool, Patsy slapped Danny's face.

"Listen to me. You need to get fighting. Jab and move forward. Stop backing away, take the fight to him. Are you listening?"

Danny nodded through the haze in his head.

"Go forward," he mumbled. "Yeah. Where's the medal?"

"Right here, son," answered Patsy, holding the medal up for Danny to see.

Livermore was first out of his corner as the bell rang. The noise of the crowd was deafening. Danny got slowly to his feet with Patsy's words resonating in his head.

The punches came fast and furious in this round. The lace of Danny's glove caught Livermore just above his right eye, followed by a ferocious and lucky right hook which drew blood. A vicious body blow to the ribs from Livermore had Danny gasping for breath.

Cheers and applause greeted both boxers as they made their way back to their corners at the end of the round. The contest had changed dramatically from the cagey first couple of rounds. The crowd was now witnessing a battle royal, and they loved it.

Danny was feeling the effects of his recent lifestyle. This was the toughest contest he had ever been in. On the far side of the ring, Livermore was being attended to by a frantic cut man, who did his best to stem the blood dripping into Livermore's right eye.

"Seconds out!" shouted the referee. "Round four!"

It was obvious that Livermore, with his vision impaired, was now going for a knock-out. Danny struggled to avoid the massive hooks and crashing uppercuts that his opponent was now throwing, and ended up on the ropes with a head full of stars. His head was just beginning to clear when Livermore came in for the kill.

Livermore's sight may have been clouded by his own blood, but his aim was true. Danny swayed like a punch bag as Livermore rained blow after blow on him. He was defenceless, lost and broken.

"He's blown it, Tommy!" Danny dimly heard Cohen shout. "Between you and them drugs, this is down to you, you've fucked him up!"

Danny's vision was blurred, every ounce of strength drained from his body. He felt like he was in a dream. The noise of the crowd seemed distant, almost as if it was in the next building. Everything was happening in slow motion.

Through his exhaustion, Danny was aware of Patsy throwing in the towel, bringing the contest to an end. He let Patsy lead him back to his corner.

The referee took Livermore's hand as the Master of Ceremonies announced: "Ladies and gentlemen, the fight was stopped by Watson's corner! Your appreciation for the winner and title contender, Billy Livermore!"

With very few exceptions, the crowd rose to its feet, cheering as Billy was carried shoulder-high around the ring. Danny felt almost invisible.

"Please show your appreciation for the brave loser, Danny Watson!" cried the Master of Ceremonies.

A few cheers rang out, but they were drowned by boos. Overcome, Danny sank to his knees and rested his head on the canvas. He was done.

Lenny could accept Danny losing, but to lose in the fourth without putting up a fight? That was difficult to take.

He made a quick exit from the post-mortem now taking place in Danny's room. He needed to find a telephone and call Albert with the bad news.

As he waited for the phone box, Lenny tried to think of ways he could soften the blow. Both Danny's loss and the way that he lost would upset Albert.

The minute the phone was free, Lenny checked his watch. Ten-thirty. Perfect. Albert would just be finishing his shift. He put his money in and dialled the Live and Let Live.

"Hello?" said a voice on the other end.

"It's Lenny. Can I speak with Albert?"

"I ain't seen him. Hang on, I'll ask behind the bar."

Lenny faintly heard "Anyone seen Albert?" against the tinkling of a piano and a rendition of *The Lambeth Walk* at full swing in the background.

"Who's that?" Maria barked.

"It's Lenny, Maria. Can I speak to Albert? I got some news."

Maria sighed. "I hope it's good news. He's only in bloody hospital."

"No," gasped Lenny. "What happened?"

"He was trying to save a kid from being run over and got hit himself, silly sod."

Lenny was almost lost for words. "Where is he?"

"Whitechapel. What's the news?"

Lenny pulled himself together. "It's all right, don't worry," he said.

Putting the receiver down, he stared at the wall in disbelief.

"You finished mate?" said a grumpy voice behind him in the foyer. "There's people waiting here."

Lenny came out of the box. He felt numb, helpless. His best friend was in hospital and he was miles away. In a matter of seconds, the bad news had got a whole lot worse.

Lenny slowly made his way back to Danny's changing room. He could hear the euphoria echoing along the corridor from Livermore's entourage. He stopped, listened and thought. Should he tell Danny and Patsy about Albert? The news would put an even bigger dampener on the night.

In the changing room, Lenny sensed the hostility from Cohen. Costa's customary champagne sat unopened on a table. Danny's loss had taken its toll physically; mentally the boy looked shot as well. Patsy sat beside Danny, his face like stone.

"You were a bloody disgrace out there, Danny," Cohen was hissing. "A fucking joke."

Danny looked blearily up at Lenny. "I'm sorry Len," he whispered. "I messed up."

Lenny decided the time to tell Danny about Albert should wait. Pouring more rain on the kid's parade right now would be wrong.

"Tell Albert I'm sorry I let him down," Danny groaned.

"Just wasn't your night, man." Lenny backed towards the changing-room door. "See you back in London, all right?"

Walking away through the rain, Lenny thought of the irony of the situation. While Livermore was on top of the world, the world was on top of Albert.

The last train back to London had left. Lenny's only option was to get to Piccadilly station bright and early and catch the early-morning train home.

CHAPTER EIGHTEEN

SEEING the Sunday papers at the reception desk the next morning, Lenny grabbed several and turned to the back pages.

The coverage of the fight was full on. There were glowing reports for Livermore, but Danny was heavily criticised. The press felt he hadn't been ready, and had let himself down. It didn't make happy reading at all.

Lenny ate the egg and bacon served by the bed and breakfast owner: a strange man with a beard and a rather effeminate apron, who talked of wanting to be in Blackpool rather than in a backwater in Salford.

"They appreciate good service in Blackpool," he sniffed.

Lenny checked out and bought a couple more papers to read on the journey. He was surprised how busy the train was. Down the corridor, he heard a couple of fight fans discussing the big fight.

"I lost money on that Watson, he was rubbish. 'Definite title hope'? What a joke!"

"Future champion," said another, laughing sarcastically. "He couldn't box my old nan."

Lenny kept quiet. He could hardly defend Danny after

such a poor showing. Besides, by the time the train got to Crewe, Lenny had fallen asleep.

Back in London, Albert was making his usual complaints about the prison standards of the food. Minutes felt like hours in this place. He hated being cut off from the outside world. He wondered restlessly if Lenny had called the Live and Let Live with the result of Danny's fight. He wondered if Lenny had got the message that he was in hospital.

After one final attempt at a spoonful of tasteless beige fodder, Albert fell asleep. It was easier to sleep in the day. The moans and groans from his co-residents seemed less ominous than in the night.

Albert felt a warm hand shake him awake.

"Wakey wakey, Albert," said his motherly Jamaican nurse. "You need to take your pills. And I've got a nice surprise for you. Your friend is here to see you."

As Albert blinked in the unforgiving fluorescent lights, he saw Lenny at the end of his bed, newspapers under his arm and a bunch of grapes in his hand.

"What you doing in here then?" Lenny asked.

"Bloody good question," replied Albert, wincing. "Some tosser in a car knocked me arse over tit!"

Lenny laughed. "You look like someone from one of them Carry On films," he said. "Look at you! One leg in plaster hoisted in the air, one arm in plaster in a sling round your neck, all topped off with that damn bandage round your head. You've been done up like a kipper, mate."

"Like a beached whale," agreed Albert. "You got the message from the Live and Let Live then? Tell me, how did Danny do?"

"You can see for yourself," said Lenny, tossing the newspapers to Albert with a sigh. "Not so good."

With some difficulty, Albert turned to the back pages. It made for painful reading, and not because of his cracked ribs. He read the damning reports one after the other, as Lenny and the nurse talked wistfully of the sun, nightlife and beaches in their faraway homeland of Jamaica.

Albert set the papers down. His heart felt as broken as his bones.

"That's bad, Lenny," he said. "He must be upset."

"Yeah man," said Lenny. "In the fourth round, it was like he never turned up. Now what about you?"

"I've got a broken leg, a broken arm, some broken ribs and this stupid bandage round me bonce. But apart from that, I'm fine."

Lenny could no longer hold back his laughter. Albert was reminded of the phrase "It only hurts when I laugh" as his broken ribs warned him off joining in.

"How long you gonna be in here?" asked Lenny, regaining his composure.

"They say if I'm a good boy, I can hobble out in a few weeks."

"That's not so bad," said Lenny. "Is there anything I can bring you? Anything you want me to do?"

"You could take my flat keys and feed Rocky. She must be starving," said Albert.

"Anything else?"

"Some pyjamas," said Albert, thinking. "Oh and I don't like the food in here. Next time you come, bring us some fish and chips and a bit of bread pudding. I'll give you the money."

"No problem," said Lenny. "You can have it on me."

Shaking Albert's good hand, Lenny winked at his new Jamaican lady friend and left.

Albert returned to the back pages.

"Danny Watson lost last night," he told the man in the next bed a little glumly. "A technical knock-out."

His neighbour grunted. He obviously had more on his mind than a boxing match. Taking the hint, Albert went back to the write-ups, reading them over and over again and shaking his head.

Danny and Patsy sat silently on the train back to Euston, studying the fight write-ups, punctuated by bacon sandwiches and watching the English countryside and towns roll by. A couple of kids had asked for Danny's autograph, but Danny hadn't felt up to signing anything and they had left. Patsy, suffering a serious hangover, seemed only capable of the odd grunt. Conversation was not an option.

Danny felt as if he had lost everything. Resting his head in his hands, he thought about Wendy and Ruby. What a tale he had to tell his little family. *Daddy just lost your future because he was stupid.* How disappointed Albert must be. Not because he lost, but by the way he lost.

The taxi dropped Patsy home and then drove on to Rosie's

house. Through his burning sense of guilt, Danny was surprised see bunting and a large white sheet draped over the front door saying: WELCOME HOME DADDY.

"Somebody's popular," the taxi driver remarked.

Danny paid the fare, unable to look away from the banner. "Yeah," he said slowly. "I think that's me."

The front door opened. Danny stared at Wendy, standing on Rosie's door step with Ruby at her side.

"I took the bull by the horns," said Rosie, looking pleased with herself. "Me and Wendy's mum persuaded Wendy to come down here to welcome you back. I want to see you two kids back together, where you belong. You have Ruby to think of, Danny."

"Don't rush this, Rosie," Wendy warned, her eyes on Danny. "I know what you've been through, Danny. I know that when you fight, you're all alone. It don't matter who's in your corner and who supports you, the pressure is all on your shoulders. I've seen you battle to secure our future, but I've been battling too. I…" She stopped, looking upset.

Danny reached for her, but Wendy pulled back.

"Look at your face," she said. "Did he hurt you?"

"I messed up, Wend," he said, feeling broken. "I'm so sorry. I missed you both so much."

He reached out to Ruby next. Ruby backed away behind Wendy's legs.

"She doesn't know you Danny, I'm sorry," said Wendy. "I'm not sure that I do either."

This hit Danny hard. He felt so ashamed, so inadequate.

"We'd better go," Wendy said. She looked at Rosie, lurking

in the hallway. "Your mum asked us to come over and welcome you back. Sorry you lost. Come on, Ruby darling."

"Now Wendy," Rosie began, "it don't have to be like this—"

"I'm sorry," said Wendy.

She put Ruby's coat and hat on and they left. A piece of Danny went with them.

Lenny climbed the stairs to Albert's flat and let himself in. He stood for a moment and looked around at Albert's world. It seemed strangely empty without him. The well-worn armchair, the boxing belt and the photos on the sideboard seemed lonely.

Rocky swayed from side to side on her perch, copying her missing master's voice. "Hello mate! Hello mate!" she screeched, delighted at the company.

Lenny found Rocky's bird seed and, after blowing off the used husks, filled the budgie's food tray to the brim. Rocky was hungry, and tucked in for all she was worth.

Changing the budgie's water and cleaning out the cage, Lenny looked around the flat, looking to grab a couple of things from home to lighten Albert's stay in hospital.

"Maybe if I take Albert something from home, he might feel a bit better. Like he's not so much in hospital," Lenny told Rocky.

The budgie responded with a manic fly-past, aiming for Lenny's head. Lenny reacted like a big girl's blouse, screaming and waving his arms about, and only calming down when Rocky settled on the lampshade.

Lenny looked around at Albert's possessions. The glittering boxing belt would be too much to take, too ostentatious. He settled for a couple of photographs on the sideboard instead. Behind the photo frames, Lenny saw a book of birds and water fowl and, reckoning that Albert might be missing his ducks, he decided to take that too. It would be something for him to read.

With a last check, he settled the happy Rocky safely back in her nice clean cage and tapped on the bars.

"See you tomorrow, Marion," he said.

Next up: fish and chips, and off back to Albert. Loading the booty into his newly acquired second-hand Austin Cambridge, Lenny headed to Whitechapel in search of fish and chips.

Lenny suspected that bringing fish and chips into a hospital might be frowned upon. Sticking the newspaper-wrapped cod, chips and a pickled onion (Albert's favourite) up his jumper, and with the book and photos under his arm, he marched into the hospital.

Albert was sitting up when Lenny reached the ward.

"It's good to see you, Lenny," said Albert.

There was a melancholy quality to Albert's voice. Lenny sensed that Albert, who had always felt invincible, now felt vulnerable, and didn't like it.

As if by magic, Lenny produced the fish and chips from under his jumper. The two men looked at each other like naughty schoolboys and began to laugh. Albert's chuckles were punctuated by a few ouches from the broken rib department, but Lenny was full on, tears running down his face as he sneaked the rations into Albert's waiting lap and under the covers.

Matron came by, inspecting the ward. She hovered, her nose twitching.

"What's that smell?" she asked. "Smells like fish."

"Sorry Matron," Albert said. "It's my friend here, Lenny. He works in Billingsgate Fish Market." He looked at Lenny. "I told you to take a bath before you came here, didn't I Len?"

An outraged Lenny could only nod his head in reluctant agreement.

Matron looked Lenny up and down with disapproval, then continued with her inspection. No sooner had she gone than Albert was tucking in. He didn't even offer Lenny a chip.

"I brought you some stuff from home too, make it feel a bit less like a hospital," Lenny said, and showed Albert the book and photos.

"What d'ya wanna do that for?"

"Thought it might help, that's all."

Albert sighed. "Stick 'em on the side. How was Rocky, all right?"

"You mean Marion?" Lenny teased. "She was fine."

Albert broke into a smile. "Thanks mate," he said. "I appreciate it. Seen Danny and Patsy since you got back?"

"Not yet. I'll probably see them at the gym tonight."

Lenny felt uncomfortable. He had not let either Danny or Patsy know that Albert was laid up in hospital yet.

"What did Danny say when you told him about me?" asked Albert. "Probably couldn't care less."

"He was really upset," Lenny lied.

Albert looked pleased and surprised. "Was he?"

Lenny cleared his throat. "I'd better be off," he said. "Give me the evidence."

Checking for Matron, Albert passed him the empty fish and chip paper stashed under his pillow.

"Thanks, Lenny mate," he said.

"Yeah," said Lenny. "See you tomorrow."

Lenny was suddenly eager to get to the Live and Let Live to let Danny and Patsy know Albert's unhappy fate. He felt guilty that he had told Albert a lie, and wanted to put it right as soon as possible. He drove to his workshop and parked his car, then walked on to the pub, thinking how much things had changed – and not for the better.

Inside, Maria was manning the bar for the sprinkling of early-drinking locals.

"Did you see Albert, Len?" she asked.

"Yes, I paid him a visit," said Lenny.

"And how was the silly sod?"

"Grumpy but all right."

"So when is he coming back?" Maria demanded. "I get no help from that lazy sod," she added with venom, pointing at Maurice.

"I think it's gonna take time," admitted Lenny. "He's bust up pretty good, leg and wrist and ribs."

Maria uttered a few Italian swear words under her breath as Maurice silently poured Lenny his usual.

"All right, Maurice?" said Lenny.

"All right," Maurice grunted.

Maurice was a man of few words who seemed to have

the world on his shoulders. Maria's nagging over the years had taken its toll, worn him down, and he seemed almost detached from the world around him. He drank too much and was hardly ever without a slim, cheap cigar stuck tentatively in the corner of his downturned lips. Lenny could only remember seeing him smile once, when a horse he had backed came in at thirty-three to one and Maurice secured, unusually for him, a win at the bookies.

Lenny accepted Maurice's usual lack of bonhomie and headed off to make more meaningful conversation with a couple of locals. They had just started discussing Danny's loss, when the man himself came bouncing through the door. –

"You got back then, Lenny?" Danny said. "You missed a good drink."

To Lenny, Danny seemed high on something, his eyes unfocused and his hands trembling.

"Yeah, I bet," Lenny remarked. "Drowning your sorrows ain't no bad thing. But I needed to get back as soon as I could."

"Why's that, Len?"

Lenny patted the seat beside him. "Sit down, Danny," he said. "I've got something to tell you. I should have probably told you last night, but I couldn't add to your problems. It's about Albert."

Danny's eyes stopped darting around the pub and fixed on Lenny at once.

"Sit down," Lenny repeated.

Danny sat down. "You're making me nervous, Len," he said. "What's happened to Albert?"

"Albert got knocked down by a car a couple of days ago," said Lenny. "He's in hospital."

Danny's face went pale with shock and disbelief. "When?"

"The same night as the fight."

All the air seemed to go out of Danny. He looked down at the faded red carpet that covered the bar floor. "How bad is it?"

"It's pretty bad. Broken bones, the lot."

Danny slammed the table with his fist. "If he had been with us, this wouldn't have happened, stubborn old git! Where is he?"

"In the hospital in Whitechapel."

"So what, you've seen him then?"

"Yeah," Lenny said, smiling slightly. "I took him some fish and chips."

"Typical," said Danny. "I'm gonna go and see him."

"We can go together if you like," Lenny suggested.

"I'll come and get you at two," Danny said.

Danny went upstairs to the gym to calm down. The lights were out, and as he stood trembling at the top of the stairs, he could see the shadows of the punch bags and the ropes around the ring from the street lights. The smell of leather and sweat pervaded the emotive surroundings.

He remembered the very first night he'd walked into the place. It had felt strange, like another world then. But now, it felt like *his* world. A world of late he had forgotten. Warm thoughts of Albert filled him. The old man had been the spark that lit the fire.

Albert was here in spirit. Danny could feel him. Taking one last look at the darkened gym, he nodded respectfully.

"Thank you, Albert," he said.

The next afternoon at two o'clock sharp, Danny pulled up at Lenny's garage, armed with a bunch of flowers and a bunch of bananas.

"Ready when you are, Lenny," Danny said, flowers in hand.

"Oh you shouldn't have," replied Lenny, taking the flowers from Danny and doing his best blushing-bride impersonation.

"They're for Albert, you git," said Danny, snatching the flowers back. "I just wanted to know if you reckon he'd like 'em."

Lenny clapped him on the back. "I don't think he'll think much of them, but he'll think a lot of the thought behind them."

"So I should take 'em then?" asked Danny, now in two minds.

"Yeah man, he'll be pleased to see you, and the bananas."

"What about the flowers?"

"Beautiful."

They got into Danny's car and headed for the hospital.

"So he's in a bad way?" Danny asked as they drove.

"He's a war horse," Lenny said reassuringly. "He'll be all right."

Danny squinted through the windscreen. His eyes had been doing something funny lately, blurring and giving him bother.

"Do you want me to drive?" Lenny asked.

Danny shook his head. "No you're all right. My eyes get a bit blurry sometimes."

"You should get 'em tested," said Lenny.

Danny said nothing.

As they approached the hospital, Danny had mixed feelings. Things of late with Albert had been a little frosty. He wanted to see Albert, but wasn't totally convinced Albert wanted to see him. There was that other feeling you get too, a feeling of apprehension when visiting someone in hospital, when you want to see them, but don't want to see what they have become.

Danny parked up and walked to the hospital entrance with Lenny.

"Come on, it's this way," said Lenny.

They walked down the corridors. Danny tried to tune out the cries of pain and reflected on mortality. He was a young and fit man who hadn't been around sick and hurting people much. Maybe losing a boxing match was not the end of the world. There were worse things in life.

"Tough times for some folk," Lenny said, noticing Danny's change of mood as they took the stairs.

"When I go," Danny told Lenny, "I don't wanna go in a place like this. I wanna go under a big oak tree in a field in the country, with Wendy and Ruby by my side."

Lenny put his hand on Danny's shoulder. "I understand, man," he said.

Danny brought his thoughts back to the purpose of their visit. "So where's Albert then?"

"He's up here on the left. Come on."

Albert was napping when they reached his bed. Danny was shocked to see the state he was in. He and Lenny stood at Albert's bedside, unable to decide whether to wake him or let him sleep on.

Albert made the decision for them by opening one eye.

"Afternoon Albert," Lenny said. "Look who's here to see you."

Albert raised his head with difficulty. "Hello Danny."

Danny tried to cover his shock. "Blimey Albert," he said. "You have been in the wars."

"You could say that," Albert agreed.

"It's good to see you," Danny said truthfully. "Did you hear about the fight? Technical knock-out, they called it."

"Lenny told me all about it," Albert replied. "I'm sorry, Danny."

Danny fiddled with his collar. "So how you feeling?" he asked. "Are they looking after you?"

"They're good people," said Albert. "Lenny's been to see me a few times, brought me a few bits from home. But I just wanna get out of here, really."

Lenny had brought Albert a couple of photos, a boxing magazine, some tea bags and a bird book. One of the photos caught Danny's eye. It looked like the one of his father. They probably all had them done like that in the army. Reaching up, he wiped his forehead. He was sweating profusely. Thoughts of the pills in the glove compartment of his car were beginning to overwhelm him.

"You need to put that fight with Livermore out of your

mind," Albert observed, watching him. "It's done. On to the next, right?"

"Not that easy though, is it?" said Danny. "I feel I let a lot of people down."

Albert just smiled back in an understanding way.

Danny couldn't stop thinking about his pills. "Well," he said. "It's been good to see you. I better get going, you know. Things to do."

Albert nodded. " Come by again if you can, it was good to see you."

Danny wiped his nose. "Will do," he said. "You staying, Len?"

Lenny nodded. "Don't worry. I can make my own way back."

"Right," said Danny, backing towards the door. "See you both soon."

Albert watched Danny leave. He didn't like the look of the boy.

"He seems a bit shook up, Len," he observed.

"Yeah," said Lenny. "Losing the fight and his break-up with Wendy must be hurting."

"Keep an eye on him, will you?"

"I'll do my best."

Calmer now that he'd had his pills, Danny thought about how sad it had been to see Albert bedridden as he drove home. He'd always been full of energy with a sparkle in his eyes, so this different Albert had been a shock. He'd looked old. Danny had never thought of Albert as old, but it was obvious the accident had hit him hard.

He thought about the army photo on Albert's bedside table and the resemblance to the photograph of his dead father.

Kemp.

Kemp had been Danny's surname before Rosie changed it to his step-father's name, Watson. Danny wondered why he had not noticed the coincidence before.

Albert was Albert Kemp.

The moment he reached Rosie's house, Danny went straight to the tin box, took out the photo and studied it.

"Kemp," he said aloud.

Seizing the photo and popping a couple more pills for good measure, Danny jumped back in his car and headed back to the hospital.

When he got to the ward, Lenny was still there.

"Albert," said Danny, rushing to Albert's bedside.

"You're back soon," said Albert, looking startled. "Did you forget something?"

Danny grabbed one of the photographs on Albert's bedside table and studied it. His hands couldn't stop shaking.

"That's my son," said Albert.

"But that's my dad," Danny blurted, holding his cherished photo next to Albert's.

Danny and Albert stared at each other in shell-shocked silence.

"Your dad was Tommy Kemp?" said Albert at last.

"I never thought about the surname," Danny said. His head was spinning. "Mum changed it to Watson when she married my step-dad, Watson's all I've ever known. But yeah, his name was Tommy. Tommy Kemp."

Albert leaned forward. "What's your mum's name?"

"Rosie Watson." Danny couldn't believe he was having this conversation.

"Do you know her middle name?"

"Yeah, she hates it," Danny whispered. "It's Olive."

Albert sank back in his pillow. He looked older than Danny had ever seen him. "Rosie Olive Watson is your mum," he said, almost to himself. "Did she tell you about your dad and what happened?"

Danny shook his head. "No, not much. I always thought it was too painful for her to talk about."

"It was painful," said Albert quietly. "Yes. Within days of being told that Tommy had died in battle, she was off like a bullet, living with another man. Pregnant with Tommy's baby. Pregnant with you."

Danny's legs felt like they were about to give way beneath him. "You knew about me?"

"Her behaviour angered us," Albert said simply. "Me and Vera. It caused a massive family rift. I ain't seen Rosie since, and I never saw my unborn grandchild. She – you – moved away. I had no idea where."

Lenny, who had been sitting as still as a stone, came to life.

"Wait now," he said, looking bewildered. "You saying what I think you're saying here, Albert?"

"Reckon I am." Albert hadn't taken his eyes off Danny. "Looks like I'm your grandad, Danny."

A wide-eyed Lenny broke into uncontrollable laughter.

"Grandad!" he spluttered.

"Keep it down please," said a passing nurse.

"Grandad!" gasped Lenny, a little more quietly.

Danny was struggling to take it in. There had always been a bond between him and Albert, but this was incredible. They were family. Albert was his dad's father. Albert was his grandfather.

He could not help himself. He bent down and hugged Albert.

Something stirred in Albert's eyes. "Nice, son," he whispered in Danny's ear. "But this is really hurting my ribs."

Danny pulled back, half-laughing. "Sorry! I couldn't help it. This is… This…"

"We've got a lot to catch up on, Danny," said Albert steadily.

"We have, Grandad," agreed Danny, catching hold of Albert's hand with tears in his eyes. "We have."

CHAPTER NINETEEN

OVER the next few weeks Danny visited his new grandfather every day. Lenny came too, although Danny was not really convinced if the visits from Lenny were for Albert, or for the nurse from Lenny's home town of Kingston, Jamaica, who always seemed to be on the ward.

When he'd got used to the idea of having Albert as his grandfather, Danny steeled himself to call Wendy. He hadn't seen her since that strange day at Rosie's house, and he had no idea how she was going to take this news.

"You're joking," Wendy said when Danny called and told her. "You've taken too much of something."

"This ain't just wishful thinking, Wendy. It's true. Will you come to the hospital with me so Ruby can meet her great-grandfather?"

"I'm not ready to take you back, Danny," warned Wendy. "Not yet. I need to see a change. A big change. I ain't seen it yet."

"I understand that. But this is for Ruby, Wend. Will you come? Please?"

"Fine," said Wendy after a moment. "Tomorrow afternoon at the hospital. I'll be there at two o'clock."

"I can give you a lift if you want," said Danny hopefully.

"We'll get there by ourselves. Don't be late."

At two o'clock, Danny waited anxiously outside the hospital for Wendy and Ruby to arrive. When he saw them turn the corner, he ran to meet them.

He wanted to hug Wendy and pick up his little girl and hold them close, but Ruby looked at him like a stranger and there was still a coldness in Wendy's eyes.

"Thanks for coming," he said awkwardly. "Can you believe this?" He smiled at Ruby, hoping she might warm to him. "Do you want to meet your great-grandad, Ruby?"

Ruby looked up to her mother for approval. "Grandad," she said. "Yes."

"Come on then," Danny said.

Wendy and Ruby followed Danny to Albert's ward. Ruby seemed fascinated by this new and strange place, waving to almost everyone she passed. Danny showed her which button to push in the lift, which pleased Ruby no end. Not quite a breakthrough, but a smile to Danny melted his heart.

"Oh my goodness," said Albert as they came into the ward. "How wonderful to see you, Wendy. And you, look at you, Ruby, you big girl!"

"Why is your leg up in the air?" asked Ruby.

"That is a very good question," said Albert. "The nice nurse said it would make it better."

"Oh, better," Ruby replied.

Albert looked at Wendy. "She's beautiful," he said. "You're doing a great job, Wendy, it can't be easy."

Danny flushed, but Wendy smiled.

"I got a new dolly called Pinky," Ruby announced.

"What a nice name," said Albert, returning his attention to the little girl. "Is pink your favourite colour?"

They chatted for a while about dolls and colours, animals and the weather and Albert's bandages. Danny watched, and wondered if he'd ever get to chat to Ruby that way again.

"Hope you'll be back on your feet soon, Albert," said Wendy at last, taking Ruby's hand. She glanced at Danny. "Bye then."

"Do you want me to show you the way out?" Danny asked.

"We'll find it," said Wendy.

Ruby looked back as they reached the door of the ward. Albert blew her a kiss, and she blew one back. Danny got a wave too. It was a start, he thought. Definitely a start.

Albert was slowly on the mend, uplifted by recent events, and Danny's visits were frequent and often. He loved hearing the stories of his late father's adventures as a scallawag in East London.

"Your father was fearless," Albert told him. "Him and his mate Charlie used to swim across the Thames trying to race the Woolwich Ferry. That was until he got a clip round the ear from a copper."

Danny fell quiet. "Do you know where Dad's buried?" he asked after a moment.

"In a war cemetery in France."

"Whereabouts in France?"

"A place called Brouay," Albert answered, "along with many others."

"Have you been there?"

"A long time ago," said Albert. "Just after the war, I went with the wife: your grandmother and the love of my life. I doubt if I'll see it again."

Danny smiled. "What was my nan's name?"

"Vera. And she was beautiful."

"Was my dad interested in boxing?"

Albert nodded. "He was, and he was a decent little fighter. But football was really his first love."

"Why did you lose contact with my mum?" Danny asked. "You knew she'd had me."

"These things happen," Albert said.

Hearing the pain in Albert's response, Danny put the question on the back burner.

When Danny told Rosie that Albert was his grandfather, the colour seemed to drain from her face.

"How do you know?" she asked faintly.

"The photo of Albert's son is the photo of Dad."

Rosie sat down. "Oh my gawd," she said.

"I should have worked it out quicker," said Danny. "His surname's Kemp, same as Dad's."

"I can't believe it," said Rosie. "I haven't seen Albert for what? Over twenty-five years."

"I know," said Danny. "He told me."

Rosie became defensive. "We didn't get on," she said.

"Why not?"

"I don't think he ever liked me," Rosie said. "He never thought I was good enough for his son, especially after..." She stopped.

"I know you went off with my step-dad soon after Dad was killed," Danny said. "Albert was upset about that."

"It was hard on me own," Rosie said plaintively. "And perhaps Albert was right. Perhaps I wasn't good enough." She leaned against the kitchen table, looking tired and sad. "Albert Kemp," she said, almost to herself. "Dear me."

"Perhaps you can meet up," Danny suggested. "Talk about Dad."

Rosie's face closed up. "Too much water under the bridge," she said. And Danny couldn't push her any further on the subject.

It wasn't long before Albert was up and hobbling impatiently around the hospital corridors with the aid of a crutch, dressed in a new pair of tartan pyjamas and some slippers with pom poms on that Wendy and Ruby had bought for him. He actually looked, for the first time, like a grandad.

He was ready to go now, more than ready to leave. He made his feelings known to nurses and doctors alike whenever one came by. After wearing the medical staff down to a ravelling, he was finally given the green light.

Hobbling and bobbling as fast as his plaster cast let him, down the familiar brown and cream corridor, he almost collided with a grumpy lady being wheeled along in a wheelchair on his way to the phone kiosk in reception.

"Clifton Garage," said Lenny, after what felt like an eternity.

"Hello, Lenny," said Albert. "I've got this broken-down wreck that needs picking up."

Lenny laughed. "So, you got me cake with the file in it that I sent you?"

"Yeah, it worked a treat," Albert replied, grinning. "I filed through the iron bars and I'm free. Do you reckon you could pick me up?"

"On my way," answered Lenny. "Tell that pretty Kingston girl Nurse Madeline that lover boy will be there soon."

"Tell her yourself, Casanova," Albert said. "Just bloody hurry up."

Danny had threatened to hold a little homecoming party for Albert at his house in Chigwell if Wendy agreed but, thankful as he was to be welcomed by his new family, Albert didn't need the fuss and told Danny not to bother. He was going home and that was that.

With a little help from Nurse Madeline, he packed his bits and pieces into his holdall and sat waiting for Lenny on the end of the bed, thinking about how things might have changed since he'd been away. Lenny had assured him he'd been feeding both Rocky and the ducks in the park, so that was one less thing to worry about. Danny, on the other hand… Danny, with his mood swings and temper, was a worry, that much was certain.

Albert was a lousy patient and had detested being immobile. The pain from the broken ribs he could cope with, but the plaster cast on his leg had to go. He had borrowed a knitting needle from a lady patient to scratch the itchy bits he couldn't reach, a valuable piece of kit that he made sure he packed in his bag. He thought about going back to work at the Live and Let Live, and about managing the stairs to his flat. He had been practising up and down some stairs in the hospital and had developed a nifty sideways action using the crutch as a lever, not unlike Long John Silver and with the same gusto. It was all going to be fine.

"You'll be home in time for the football," smiled Nurse Madeline, packing his final bits and pieces.

Albert was puzzled. He had been cut off from the outside world for weeks and had no idea what the nurse was talking about. "What football?" he said.

"The World Cup!" said Nurse Madeline. "Didn't you know, England is in the final?"

"No," Albert exclaimed. "Blimey, who they playing?"

"Germany, I think," said the nurse.

Albert's personal feelings about Germany still ran pretty high, even now in nineteen sixty-six. World War Two and the Blitz on East London had left scars, and a World Cup Final against the old enemy would feel like a re-run of the war.

Albert couldn't wait.

Lenny arrived, looking sharp in his cream suit and wearing a red carnation in his lapel.

"About time too," said Albert. "What you done up like an ice cream for?"

Lenny beamed at Nurse Madeline. "Nothing but the best for my Kingston girl," he said with his very best smile. "You're looking good, Nurse Madeline. I bet you're pleased to get rid of him."

The penny dropped. Lenny's suit was nothing to do with Albert's homecoming, and all to do with "the angel from home" as Lenny called her.

"No, we're gonna miss him," said Nurse Madeline. "I understand that nobody likes to be in hospital, though."

"Are we going or what?" said Albert, growing impatient with Lenny's flirting.

"Just give me a second," said Lenny as he guided Madeline out of Albert's earshot. A couple of minutes later he was back, a massive smile on his face and a twinkle in his eye.

"Right, champ," he said. "Let's get you out of here."

At the car, Lenny, the good Samaritan, tried to help Albert into the passenger seat, with limited success thanks to his unbendable leg in plaster.

"You're hurting me, you silly sod! Stick me in the back seat, there's more room, and put the passenger seat forward."

"Hey Albert," chuckled Lenny. "This is like one of those Laurel and Hardy films."

"Yeah, and I know who's getting a slap!" Albert retorted.

"Where to? Your flat?" Lenny asked as they finally set off.

"Did you feed Rocky this morning?"

"Yes I did. I did the ducks yesterday too."

Albert eased up on him. "Good man, I appreciate it," he said. "It's the World Cup match today, ain't it? The final, between us and the Jerries. Wembley would be good, but let's go to the pub and watch it on telly."

"The Live and Let Live it is."

It was about two-thirty when they reached the pub. After a few grunts and contortions Albert emerged from the back seat. Greeted like the returning prodigal son in the saloon bar, he acknowledged the warmth of the welcome with a wave of his good arm and did his best to avoid the fuss and concern.

Lenny grabbed a couple of seats from the willing locals and they sat down to watch the match.

Very few of the folks that packed the pub had televisions, so the pub's TV was a magnet: the next best thing to being at the game. There was palpable pride in the house as the traditional *Abide with Me* was sung by the packed stadium.

"A great occasion," said Albert.

"Yes indeed," agreed Lenny, even though it wasn't cricket.

They watched the teams line up for the respective National Anthems. Albert struggled to his feet and sang *God Save the Queen* at the top of his voice. Like most East Enders he was fiercely patriotic.

"Look at that, Lenny," said Albert as the camera panned across the teams. "Three West Ham players! Come on, you Irons!"

With the preliminaries done and dusted, the match kicked off with shouts of "Come on England!" from everyone in the pub. Wembley was jam-packed from the look of things, ninety-six thousand spectators roaring their teams on.

Too soon, English hearts were broken as in the twelfth minute Germany scored. It took the wind out of the sails of both the English supporters and the folks in the pub. But with so much time to go in the match, all was not lost.

"Plenty of time yet," said Albert optimistically.

In the seventeenth minute England struck back. A free kick was taken by West Ham and England captain Bobby

Moore, a beautifully weighted ball into the German penalty area. West Ham's Geoff Hurst managed to get on the end of it and powered in a fantastic header. One all.

As the ball hit the net, Albert shot to his feet, as did most of England. He would have gone flat on his face, hampered by the plaster cast, if it hadn't been for Lenny's quick reaction, grabbing him before he hit the deck. Albert recovered his balance and led a chorus of *I'm Forever Blowing Bubbles* to celebrate the goal made by West Ham.

The contest went on, accompanied by quite a lot of nail-biting and a few choice swear words. The match was pretty even, but Germany were looking dangerous. Half-time came and drinks were replenished in preparation for the second half.

"It's crazy!" said Maria as she helped pull the pints. "Italy should have been in the final."

The second half was tense and the folk in the bar were reasonably quiet as they were drawn deeper into the drama. Then, in the seventy-eighth minute, Geoff Hurst took a shot at goal which was partially blocked by a German defender, only to fall at the feet of another West Ham player. Martin Peters took the chance and walloped the ball into the German goal. Two one to England.

Delirium followed. The cheers of happiness rang out the length and breadth of England and beyond. The locals were hugging each other in the bar. Stranger or friend, it didn't matter. England were winning with just twelve more nerve-racking minutes to go.

In the ninetieth minute, just as the match was coming to an end and the Jules Verne World Cup trophy was practically in England's hands, Wolfgang Weber from Germany scored a heartbreaking, scrappy goal.

"That was hand ball!" came the verdict from the pub.

"Typical Germans, lucky bastards," muttered Albert.

Two goals each at full time meant extra time was to be played. If after thirty minutes the scores were still even, a replay would need to be arranged. No one wanted the anti-climax of a replay. Not against the Germans.

No one wanted it to go to penalties. Not against the Germans.

The players and spectators were exhausted after ninety minutes of high-energy drama. Drinks were taken by the teams and everyone in the pub several times over, and thirty more minutes of extra time kicked off.

"This could go either way," said Lenny as silence fell across the pub.

"Yeah," Albert agreed, biting his nails. "As long as it goes our way."

The Germans kept coming. Then, in the ninety-eighth minute of the match, high drama and controversy. Alan Ball, England's tireless winger, crossed the ball from the right to Geoff Hurst. With all the power Hurst could muster, he headed the ball goalwards, where the ball crashed off the crossbar and down past the German keeper.

"Goal!" Albert shouted.

"Goal!" bellowed the rest of the pub.

The English players and most of England appealed. Time seemed to stand still as the referee went to the Russian linesman for a decision.

England held its breath.

The linesman ruled that the ball had indeed crossed the line. Three two to England!

Watching the jubilation of the England supporters on TV, Albert felt proud and patriotic. Men, women and children, united in the collective happiness. Even Her Majesty was on her feet and applauding. Another rendition of *Bubbles* rang out in the pub.

The second half of extra time kicked off. Just fifteen minutes till the final whistle and an England victory. The German team threw everything they could at the tired but resolute English players. Minute by minute the clock ticked on, and it seemed like every minute was an hour as the nation waited for that final whistle.

The final minute. His chest almost bursting with his last effort of the game, Geoff Hurst received the ball in the German half just as some of the crowd thought that time was up and started celebrating. A few had already invaded the pitch.

"They think it's all over," remarked the commentator as the pub held its breath.

Hurst, exhausted and with his last ounce of energy, hammered the ball into the roof of the German net.

"It is now," said the commentator as the pub erupted.

They were words that would become part of English football history and folklore. The famous hat trick from Geoff Hurst, the only man in history to score three goals in a World Cup final, joined them. Four two to England and the celebrations of the nation were unleashed.

In the Live and Let Live, there were people dancing up on tables and hugging strangers. Everyone felt part of a history-making victory. It felt good to be English that day.

Albert was a bit tipsy as he made his way ecstatically from the pub to his flat, having told Lenny he could make it by himself. Strangers in the streets were united in their joy. Albert couldn't help feeling that the celebrations were not unlike that other victory against the same opposition, twenty-one years earlier.

He was looking forward to finally getting home. With just a few bumps and groans, he made the staircase and opened the door to his flat. The task was made a little more tricky as he was carrying the bag of home comforts Lenny had brought him, but he made it, and on a night to remember. All was reasonably right with Albert's world.

Rocky was so excited to see Albert she started doing back flips. Talking soothingly to her, Albert put the kettle on and unpacked his bag. As he took out Tommy's photograph, he reflected on finding his grandson and his new family. The photograph had been shrouded in sadness for so many years, but now it had a much happier tinge to it.

"Who would have thought, eh, Tommy boy?" Albert asked the photo as he placed it back on the sideboard. With a cup of tea and Rocky on his shoulder, he looked around. "It's good to be home," he said.

Rocky decided to relieve herself on Albert's shoulder.

"Thanks for the homecoming present, Rocky," said Albert with a smile.

CHAPTER TWENTY

WITHIN weeks the plaster casts were off and Albert was able to walk with just a stick.

Danny had picked him up and driven him over to the new house in Chigwell once or twice. Wendy was reasonably accommodating as far as Albert was concerned, because Ruby liked to see her new great-grandfather. Albert made Ruby laugh, and there was obviously a bond between them. Wendy had prepared the odd dinner with Albert's culinary favourite, a Sunday roast, which he was more than happy to have any day of the week.

Albert observed that Danny was still very much the outsider in the family. He wasn't living back in the house yet, and there was clearly work for him to do if Wendy was to take him back. Albert knew something was still very wrong, but as yet couldn't fathom what. He wished with all his heart that Danny could be back with Wendy and a father to Ruby.

For his part, Danny blew hot and cold. Albert grew used to a different Danny turning up almost every time he saw him. Talk of boxing and training had become almost taboo after the nightmare of the Livermore fight, and although

Albert regretted Danny's lack of commitment and interest, he thought it best to let time pass. Danny's wounded pride might recover in time. Nothing had been heard from Costa and Cohen since the fight, and it seemed that Danny's future was on hold.

After the recent wonderful revelations, Danny made a life-long wish for Albert come true. He organised a trip to France to visit Tommy's grave.

Albert was speechless when Danny surprised him with the tickets.

"I don't know how to thank you Dan," he stuttered. "This is a dream come true."

"For me too, Grandad," said Danny.

The trip to France was an adventure. Armed with their brand-new passports, Danny and Albert caught a ferry, then a train, to the small town of Broay. Danny liked France, finding it different, foreign and new. Although Albert was excited to be with his grandson and on the verge of making the journey to his beloved son's grave, he wasn't so keen on the place, and had packed some tea-bags just in case.

"The Frogs drink coffee," he told Danny darkly.

Unable to come to terms with the French francs, he let Danny deal with any money transactions. It seemed easy to be a millionaire here, with so many francs to a pound.

Getting into a taxi from the station, they were driven three or four miles to the cemetery. At the gates, Danny negotiated the francs and paid the rather bored-looking driver. Their emotions were raw as they walked through the gates and into the cemetery.

"So many graves," Danny said quietly as they looked at the endless rows of plain white headstones. "Hundreds."

"I've got the grave number here," said Albert. "I think it's near the chapel."

Checking names and numbers of the fallen, they searched for grave 229.

"There," said Albert, stopping. "Tommy's there."

They stood silent and looked at the headstone, two rows away. Slowly, they walked to the grave.

At the graveside Albert pointed to the headstone.

"They put Thomas Kemp," he said. "He hated the name Thomas. He was... he was Tommy."

Struggling to get the last words out, Albert fell to his knees, sobbing, as years of loss and emotion welled up and out. Danny rested his hand on Albert's shoulder, to try comfort him.

After a moment, Albert put out his hand to Danny to help him up. The two men hugged each other. Seeing Tommy's grave, both Albert and Danny felt at peace. Albert, because he thought he would never be able to see his son's grave again. Danny, because his thread to the red and silver box felt more complete.

Neither of them had yet talked about Costa and Cohen or Danny's future fight plans. It was as if they both sensed that it was still an open sore.

Danny drove Albert back after the trip. As he pulled up outside Simon's antique shop and Albert's flat, the evening summer rain dotted on the windscreen and twisted in the car's headlights. He switched off the engine and stared out of the car window at the dancing raindrops on the cobbled street. He seemed quiet, preoccupied, like there was something on his mind.

"You all right Danny?" asked Albert to break the silence. "You look like you've got the world on your shoulders."

"Just thinking," said Danny.

"Come on son, spit it out," said Albert.

Danny looked straight ahead, deep in his own world. A streak of lightning lit the dark grey sky, followed by a distant roll of thunder as he tapped his fingers on the steering wheel.

"It's sometimes good to talk," Albert said. "What do they say? 'A problem shared is a problem halved'? Something like that." He put his hand on Danny's to stop him tapping. "Talk to me, Danny."

There was a pause. Then the floodgates opened.

"I had good things, right Albert? A wife, a family, I've even got you now. But I get these black moods. The boxing's a mess, I'm a loser, I've got no money. Sometimes, I don't know what comes over me. Wendy won't take me back. I'm all over the place."

"People that taste success and money can change," said Albert after a moment. "They don't always find happiness the way they expect. Sometimes, I reckon, if you've got success and money, when you find out it's not the answer to all your worries like you thought it would be, it can leave you feeling lost and empty. Maybe you feel a bit like that. You need to show Wendy that you're still the Danny she loved and married."

Danny rubbed his face. "I try, Albert, I really try," he said. "But it's my temper. Little things get to me. Ruby is growing up and I'm missing it."

Albert watched him absently reach for the glove compartment, then pull his hand back.

"What's in there, son?" said Albert, looking at the glove box.

"Nothing," said Danny. "You getting out or what?"

"What you not telling me, Danny?"

Danny slammed his hands on the steering wheel. "Nothing, all right?"

It was all the proof Albert needed. He flipped open the glove box, stared at the bag of white pills inside.

He kept his voice gentle. "What are these?"

Danny's eyes darted from side to side. "Vitamins, food supplements, I dunno. Costa's been giving them to me in training. They're supposed to enhance your performance."

It was worse than Albert feared. "Believe me, son," he said quietly. "These ain't vitamins. How long you been taking them? What else you been taking?"

Danny swallowed. "Cocaine," he said. "Costa has loads of it."

"Jesus," said Albert in shock.

Danny laid his head on the steering wheel and broke down in tears. He looked like Tommy, Albert thought. The way Tommy had looked when he had hurt himself as a little boy, with tears rolling down his face.

"Oh Danny," he said, putting his arm round the boy. "You don't wanna do any of this stuff. If you're tested, you will lose everything you've worked for. You'll lose your reputation."

"Reputation?" said Danny. "I already blew it, Albert. I'm a laughing stock."

Albert struggled to process the fact that Costa and Cohen had turned Danny into a cheat and an addict. He clenched his fists. This was the boy he had nurtured. The son of his son.

Danny looked pleadingly at Albert. "I want you back in the team," he said. "Patsy is doing OK, but he's Costa and Cohen's man now. I don't think I can get through this without you."

Danny's face held that same look Albert had seen years before, the look that even then had reminded him of Tommy. He needed time to digest Danny's shattering confession. There was pride to swallow, and the shady Cohen and Costa to contend with. But Albert's desire to protect Danny was overriding these obstacles.

He decided to give Danny an ultimatum.

"Danny," he said. "If you want me involved, you'll have to stop taking this stuff they've been giving you. You go back to clean living and hard training, right? I reckon that will help heal things with Wendy too."

Danny nodded. "I will, I promise."

"Also, if you want me to straighten out Costa and Cohen, you will have to listen to my advice. You don't always have to take it, but at least listen, understand?"

"I understand," said Danny.

As if to seal the deal, he went to give Albert a hug, but

remembered the sore ribs just in time and shook Albert's hand instead.

"Well, quite a night," Albert remarked as they got out of the car. "Anything else on your mind?"

"Just a money thing," Danny said.

Albert frowned. "You've been doing all right, haven't you?"

"Yeah, at first. It's all gone now though. I fought that last fight, right? I know the place was a sell-out and held about five times more punters than the first fight. But after waiting for the purse for months, Costa and Cohen paid me less than for the first fight."

Rage swelled through Albert. Not only had they turned Danny into a cheat, *they* were cheating on *him*.

"That's not right," he said indignantly. "Did you ask 'em why?"

"They said it was the costs, the venue and advertising and that."

Albert snorted. "Well, I think you know what I think about those two gentlemen. Right. We start tomorrow. I'll see you at the gym eleven o'clock sharp, OK?"

Danny's face lit up. "You bet! See you tomorrow."

"Don't let me down or yourself down," warned Albert. "Get off that stuff and get your family back. But you gotta push through. You got an incentive now. You got your family to think of, and your boxing career. You're gonna pull through this, OK? You hear me?"

★

Albert's morning started with purpose. Something that had been missing in his life was back in place. Thoughts about this new beginning excited him, and he was determined to give it his best shot, despite the hindrance of his recent injuries. He managed his regular visit to the duck pond to issue rations, and then headed straight to the gym to meet Danny for training.

Danny was right on time.

"Morning Grandad," he said, and greeted Albert with a mock punch which Albert returned.

"Let's get cracking," said Albert.

Within half an hour, Albert had spotted a couple of chinks in Danny's armour. The boy had a tendency to lower his guard when backing off a fighter, and Albert thought his upper body movement could be better. The two began working, and working hard.

They were mid-session when Patsy came in.

"Hello boys," he said, clearly surprised to see Albert. "What's all this about?"

Danny took a break from punching the speed ball. "Albert's back in the team," he said happily. "I asked him and he said yes. Great, ain't it?"

"I see," said Patsy after a minute. "Yes, that's great. Do Cohen and Costa know?"

"They will," said Albert with menace. "Don't worry about that. I wanna talk to you, Patsy, in private. We'll be finishing soon. I'll pop into your office for a chat, shall I?"

Danny and Albert worked on through their routine. More of the boys started drifting into the gym to keep Patsy busy. Every now and again, Patsy shot a worried glance at Albert.

"Finish up with your warm-down," said Albert after another twenty minutes. "And we'll call it a day, Danny. Good work." He ruffled Danny's hair, then clicked his fingers at Patsy.

They went into the office. Albert shut the door.

"What the bloody 'ell do you think you're doing, Patsy?" Albert hissed, prodding Patsy in the chest. "Why d'ya let those scumbags give that stuff to Danny? You know it ain't right. The boy could lose everything. He pretty much *has* lost everything!"

Patsy was visibly shaken by the onslaught. "They were lining him up for a title fight and they wanted him to be at prime strength and fitness," he protested, raising his arms as if afraid Albert would hit him. "I'm sorry I went along with it, but they put me under a lot of pressure, Albert. They threatened to get rid of me!"

"It stops now," Albert ordered. "Danny will fight on clean, got it? You just focus on training a future champion, not a cheat."

Patsy sank into his chair with his head in his hands as Albert stalked out of the gym and headed downstairs to the bar, where Maria flashed him one of her rare smiles and set him to work.

It was good to be back.

If Danny was struggling to shake off his addiction, he hid it well. He made it to training a little pale at times, but he was always punctual. The incentive of putting his life back together was winning against the dark demons of his addiction. The old Danny was starting to shine through.

With Patsy and Danny now back on course, Albert started to think about wrestling control from Costa and Cohen. With Danny behind him, he now had the power.

"We need to arrange a meeting with them two clowns," Albert told Danny several weeks into the new regime. "Let's fix it up at the Bridge House pub in Canning Town. Let them come to us for a change. The mountain to Mohammed, sort of thing."

Danny arranged the meeting with Costa and Cohen as instructed. The men weren't happy with the venue, but agreed to come at one o'clock the following day after Danny stressed how important it was. Albert asked Patsy to attend, and he had nervously agreed.

On his usual mission to the duck pond, Albert went over the things he wanted to say and the points he planned to make. When he returned to his flat, instead of the usual suit, he put on a tailored black leather jacket that Danny had bought for him as a coming-home present. He looked sharp, and a bit tougher than usual.

Danny's car horn sounded from down in the street. With a last check in the cracked mirror in the bathroom, Albert grabbed his walking stick and made for the car.

"This meeting could get a bit bumpy, Danny," he warned as Danny drove them through the familiar streets. "Are you all right with that?"

Looking pale but focused, Danny nodded. "We need to

get some answers and straighten things out," he said. "I feel good about it."

It wasn't far to the Bridge House. After parking outside, Danny and Albert went in.

The pub was quiet at this time of day. Most of the pub's business was at night, enticed there by the strippers that regularly performed. It had a section of Victorian booths, ideal for a private meeting.

Already seated in a booth was Patsy, nervously tapping a beer mat on the dark mahogany table. Albert and Danny came to join him.

"Do you want a drink, Pat?" Albert asked,

"I think I might need one after this," Patsy muttered.

On cue, Cohen and Costa materialised.

"Gentlemen," said Cohen. His eyes rested on Albert for a moment.

"Drink, anyone?" offered Costa. "Jack Daniel's, Danny?"

"A couple of orange juices," Albert said firmly.

"Nice and healthy," said Costa with a grin. "Cheap too."

"Nice to see you, Albert," said Cohen, sitting down. "Danny told me the news. Grandad, eh? What a coincidence. Nice, very nice." His words were warm, but the way they were delivered was ice cold.

Costa came back with the drinks and sat down.

"So," Cohen said, "what's your grandad doing here, Danny?"

"Albert is back on the team," Danny replied. "I asked him."

"Is that wise?" Cohen asked.

Albert tightened his grip on his walking stick, but said nothing.

"It's my decision, Jack," said Danny.

Cohen snorted. "Back on the team? What does that even mean, back on the team?"

Albert lifted his walking stick and smashed it down on the table. Patsy flinched. Costa spilled his whisky down his expensive suit in surprise.

"I'll tell you what it means," Albert said, leaning close to Cohen. "It means you stop giving the boy drugs. If he's gonna fight, he's gonna fight clean."

"Whoa," said Costa, mopping down his suit. "We had a shot at the title lined up and was giving Danny a little help. That's all."

"You reckon?" said Albert. "You are teaching the boy to cheat."

Cohen turned to Danny, tipping his head at Albert. "What's his problem?"

"I think it's you," Danny replied.

"They was only amphetamines, Albert," complained Costa. "Just to help."

Albert crashed the stick back on the table, this time with even more force. "No more drugs," he repeated, "title fight or not. Got it? That's the way it's gonna be, right Danny?"

"That's the way it's gonna be," Danny forcefully agreed.

"Easy now, take it easy," Cohen soothed, switching on the charm. "We seem to have a clash of opinions."

"No," said Danny. "From now on there is only one opinion, and that's Albert's."

Cohen's expression hardened. "I see," he said. "I think we could fall out over this."

Albert was still on the attack. He pointed his stick at Cohen. "Pay Danny what he was owed for the last fight, or it may well be his last fight for you."

"Perhaps it *will* be his last fight," Cohen sneered. "After the fiasco of the Livermore fight, your boy was a shambles. We'll take another look at the accounts, but there were considerable costs."

"We can still work with you," said Albert. He shot a glance at Patsy, who had sunk down low in his seat. "But in the future, your take will be ten per cent and not fifty."

There was an almost theatrical intake of air from Costa.

Albert delivered his ultimatum. "We'll leave you to think it over," he said. "Give us an answer by the end of the week. Come on, Danny. We're leaving."

"That was impressive," said Danny as he and Albert walked to the car.

"They need you Danny," Albert said. "You can call the tune, believe me."

Danny rubbed his forehead. "I hope you're right," he said. "But what if they don't give me the money they owe me and they won't take a smaller cut? I don't want to give up boxing, do I? Then there's the contract I signed."

"Stop worrying," said Albert. "It's gonna be all right."

They reached Albert's flat. Danny switched off the engine. They sat in silence for a few moments.

"Thanks, Grandad," Danny said.

"Still can't get used to that," Albert remarked. "I'll see you tomorrow at eleven in the gym. And don't be late!"

Danny watched from the car as Albert negotiated his walking stick, key and front door. He thought about how strong Albert had been at the meeting, the opposite to the silent Patsy. It felt good to have him back on his side and fighting his corner. Costa and Cohen were the ones with the reputation, but Albert had put them in their place.

But as he drove home, doubts crept in again. It was true that Albert had stood his ground for all the right reasons, for Danny and his family's benefit, but it had thrown Danny's fight future into uncertainty. All Danny wanted to do was take care of his family and succeed in his chosen sport. The thought of complicating the situation worried him, not to mention the potential repercussions from the underworld that Costa and Cohen belonged to.

Serious training went on over the next few days, but there was an uncertainty in Danny's commitment. It was hard to train and focus not knowing if and when the next fight would take place.

The team, though, was upbeat, and confident that the outcome would be positive. Patsy had to some extent returned to the camp, and was back to putting Danny through his paces. When he could, Lenny would come by and watch Danny sparring. Just having Lenny and Albert around felt right to Danny, whatever the outcome.

After two weeks, Danny's state of limbo was beginning to take its toll.

He needed to talk to Costa and Cohen, but worried that it might be a sign of weakness.

The phone bell rang in the hall. Danny wiped the last bit of shaving foam off his cheek and went to answer it.

"Hello Danny," said Cohen. "How are you?"

Danny tried to gauge Cohen's mood. "All good," he said cautiously. "You?"

"Danny," said Cohen. "We have a problem. I think we should get together and have a chat."

"OK," said Danny. "I'll let Albert and Patsy know."

Cohen sighed. "I think it best that we meet without them," he said. "We don't want them muddying the waters."

"I don't know," said Danny. "I don't want to go behind Albert's back."

"You won't be. Just a friendly chat, that's all. How is eleven tomorrow at the office?"

Danny wanted to get this stuff resolved, but was suspicious at the same time. His impatience with the situation took precedence over his misgivings.

"OK," he said. "See you at eleven."

Putting the phone down, he couldn't help feeling he had betrayed Albert by not insisting that he came to the meeting too. It wasn't a good feeling, but his options were limited.

Danny heard a key in the door.

"Hello darling," Rosie said as she came in. "Was you on the phone to Wendy?"

If only, Danny thought. "Nah Mum," he said. "It was just about a meeting tomorrow to talk about the next fight."

Rosie took her coat off and headed for the kitchen. "I've got some nice boiled bacon for tea," she called from the kitchen.

"Lovely," answered Danny, relieved that she wasn't asking any more questions.

For the first time in weeks, Danny was missing the buzz the drugs had given him. He knew that if he had any, he would at this point take them. He rekindled his willpower and tried to put temptation out of his mind. So much depended on him being free from drugs and healthy. His reunion with Wendy and Ruby depended on it.

He just wanted to see what Jack and Tommy had to say. He could talk to Albert afterwards. Thinking about it this way helped him feel less like a traitor and more like a bridge between Costa and Cohen and Albert's principles. Comforted by the thought that he was doing the right thing, he would see what tomorrow would bring.

He called Albert at the Live and Let Live.

"I won't make it in for training till tomorrow afternoon, Grandad," he said. "I just need to see to a couple of things."

"Anything I can help with?" asked Albert.

"No, you're all right, no big deal. See you about three."

The feeling of guilt still surrounded Danny as he put the phone down, but he was optimistic. His actions would at least clarify the situation. He hated being in limbo, not knowing, and it was hard to train when he wasn't sure what the future held.

This meeting was necessary. Not only for Danny and his family, but for Albert too.

CHAPTER TWENTY-ONE

THE next morning, as Danny showered and shaved ready for the meeting, he felt sure that Costa and Cohen would see the sense of Albert's ultimatum. He looked forward to telling Albert the good news at the gym, later in the day.

There might need to be some kind of compromise, but he'd cross that bridge when he came to it.

Wearing a light brown suede jacket, white shirt and black trousers, Danny felt good. His need for the drugs was easing day by day. He remembered Wendy's words from way back, when she had said, *If you are going for a job, look like you don't need it and you will probably get it.* So looking sharp felt like the way to go.

Driving to Costa and Cohen's office had a feel of *High Noon* about it. Danny hoped no gun fight would ensue, just some straight talking.

Costa and Cohen were waiting for him in the reception. Their welcome was more matter of fact than normal. No big hug from Costa, no forced smile from Cohen. Just businesslike handshakes.

"Come through," said Cohen. "No telephone calls," he instructed Mavis the receptionist, and led the way along the corridor to his palatial office.

"Take a seat, Danny," said Cohen, seating himself behind his larger than necessary oak desk.

Danny sat down.

"You're looking good, Danny boy," said Costa.

"We wanted to talk to you because we care," said Cohen, "and we don't want you to make a mistake. Bringing Albert back on board is a mistake."

"That's right," said Costa. "Albert's a lovely man, but he's from another era. Faded glory, Danny. He doesn't understand today's fight game."

Danny said nothing.

"Let's look at the points Albert made," said Cohen. "The performance-enhancing pills we were giving you were for your own good, right? To help with your training and make you a better fighter."

"Patsy was all right with it, wasn't he?" said Costa.

Danny stayed silent. Cohen continued.

"Now, the fifty per cent management fee. Given your last performance, we feel it's more than fair."

"That ten per cent business is dear old Albert talking," said Costa. "He doesn't know about costs and advertising. It costs money to sell out a place like that."

"A lot of money," Cohen agreed. "It's only with our guidance that you could have a shot at a British title, Danny."

"You know who currently holds the belt, don't you?" Cohen asked.

"Billy Livermore," Costa said. "You remember that fight, don't you?"

Danny certainly did remember the Livermore fight.

"Yeah, you remember it," said Costa softly.

"You blew that one Danny, didn't ya?" said Cohen, standing up behind his desk. "Now Livermore has the title. It would have been yours if you hadn't fucked up, Danny. It would have been ours too."

"Yes Danny," said Costa.

"You fucked up big time, Danny boy," spat Cohen. "And we can't have that, can we Tommy?"

"No Jack," Costa agreed. "It ain't right."

There was a tangible menace in the room. Danny felt frozen as Cohen opened the drawer to his desk and took out some papers.

"See this?" he said, shaking the papers in Danny's face. "This is your contract. You know what we're gonna do? Me and Mr Costa? We're gonna tear it up."

He ripped the contract to pieces and threw the remains into a nearby wastepaper bin.

"Good shot," said Costa.

"Good riddance," said Cohen.

And for the first time, Danny heard Jack Cohen laugh.

Cohen pushed his intercom as Danny tried to process what had just happened. The receptionist came in.

"Show Mr Watson out, Mavis," said Cohen. "Goodbye Danny."

Speechless, Danny followed Mavis out to the street.

★

"I can't believe you did that," said Costa.

"The boy's a loser," said Cohen. "And that silly old git Albert's a nuisance. I've had enough of that fucked-up junkie. He's dead meat."

"Dead meat?" said Costa.

"Yeah, Tommy. Dead meat."

Danny was in shock as he walked to his car. This was not what he had expected. He knew Cohen was angry at his lack of performance and preparation for the last fight, but Danny had always hoped there was a future. But now, nothing.

The realisation that Costa and Cohen would not compromise and had torn up his future was devastating. He had gone to the meeting full of optimism, but had left with an impossible situation. He drove to the gym on automatic pilot, his head full of questions that were hard to answer.

Lenny was just coming out of the public bar as Danny parked outside the Live and Let Live.

"Albert told me you and him have sorted that Costa and Cohen," Lenny said with a satisfied smile. "Good thing."

"Yeah," said Danny, squirming inside.

"I'll drop by later," Lenny said. "Albert tells me you're as sharp as a tack now."

Danny forced a smile. "What does he know?"

It was a good question, Danny thought to himself as he headed inside the pub. What did Albert really know? Danny needed to think, and quickly. He'd gone behind Albert's back with the secret meeting and now he had to admit to Albert that Cohen and Costa had dropped him. This wasn't going to be easy.

Albert was sat on the edge of the boxing ring reading a newspaper.

"Wotcha Danny," he said, upbeat as ever.

After Danny's uncomfortable meeting, seeing Lenny, Albert and the familiar surroundings of the gym was soothing. These were his people. Straight and with none of the innuendoes of Cohen and Costa, their clever manipulation or false charms.

He began his regular training regime under the watchful eye of Albert.

As he dutifully went through the motions, he couldn't help being distracted by the guilt he was still feeling.

"Mind elsewhere, Danny?" said Albert. "You seem a little absent today."

Danny needed to tell Albert what had happened. He needed a way out of the worry weighing down on him. Taking his boxing gloves off, he took a deep breath.

"I went to see Costa and Cohen this morning," he said sheepishly.

Albert's eyebrows rose. "Oh yeah?"

"Yeah," said Danny.

Albert was looking unimpressed. "What happened?"

This was difficult to answer.

"They tore up my contract," Danny said.

Saying the words out loud made Danny realise what had actually happened. It was over. The end. Through the hammering in his head, he wondered how Albert would react to the news.

"Blimey," said Albert after a moment.

"They said they wouldn't move on their percentage," Danny said in desperation. "And the money from the last fight? Because of their expenses, they said it was right."

"That's bollocks," said Albert angrily. "We need to see their accounts for ourselves. And fifty per cent from a fighter is criminal. Fuck 'em, I say."

Danny could see the anger in Albert's eyes. He'd never heard his grandfather swear before.

"You know what?" said Albert, slamming his hand on the canvas of the ring. "We'll promote the fight ourselves. I still know people in the fight game."

Danny felt energised by Albert's reaction. He was going to take over Danny's career and keep it in the family. It felt good.

"They told me Livermore was up for another fight," he said. "It would be for the title this time."

"Then we don't have a problem," said Albert emphatically. "I'll get cracking and make some calls. Now, it's gonna be a tough fight. Are you gonna get your mind back to winning?"

He tossed Danny's gloves back to him with an enquiring look.

"You bet," said Danny thankfully.

With Albert barking instructions even more loudly than before, Danny let himself go, hitting the punch bag with a clear mind and renewed commitment. Everything was working out.

*

The moment Danny left for home after the session, Albert started to contact faces he knew who could help put this title fight together.

First, he called his old friend and past foe, Harry Baldock.

"Harry mate. My boy Danny has parted company with those crooks Costa and Cohen. We're gonna promote his next fight ourselves. What do you reckon?"

Harry's reaction was positive. "Getting rid of those two shysters is the best day's work you've ever done, Albert. I know Livermore's manager, I'll give him a call."

Putting the phone down, Albert reflected on the task ahead. In many ways it was uncharted waters, but he was confident that with a little help, it would work. The thought of a career for his grandson without the involvement of Costa and Cohen was like a dream come true. Albert was determined to get it right, to get Danny the title he deserved and the financial security and respect he was owed.

There was a flipside of course. Knowing their taste for violence and their unsavoury protection-money contacts, Albert fully expected repercussions from Costa and Cohen. So thinking ahead, he made a couple of calls to some tasty contacts gleaned from Harry Baldock's circle of East End wide boys, to put the frighteners on them.

Just as an insurance policy.

CHAPTER TWENTY-TWO

AS the weeks went on, Albert made good progress. He confirmed the fight with Livermore's representative, and dates and a venue were pencilled in. As a makeshift Cupid, he was making progress too. He caught the bus to Wendy's regularly, both to see Ruby and to build bridges between Wendy and Danny.

"Danny has changed for the better, you know," he told Wendy over a cup of tea. "He's like his old self. Maybe you should give him a chance."

"I want him in our lives but only if he's the Danny I knew and loved," was Wendy's response.

Albert instructed Danny to call Wendy and keep in touch. Slowly, Danny's visits to Chigwell increased. Bit by bit, Danny and Wendy were moving back emotionally to where they had once been: in love. Ruby and Danny were getting on like father and daughter were supposed to now, and Danny could do no wrong in her pink little world.

Everything was going smoothly until Costa and Cohen decided to pay Danny a personal visit at the gym. They walked in, unannounced, as Patsy was putting Danny through his paces. Danny stopped punching the pads and Patsy seemed to disappear into the shadows. The room fell silent.

"Good afternoon gentlemen," said Costa.

"Just thought we would drop by and see how it's going," said Cohen.

"Did you get my messages from your lovely wife, Danny boy? I've called you a couple of times but you never called back."

"Naughty naughty," said Costa.

Cohen picked at his nails. "What's this silly rumour going round that you and old Albert are putting together the Livermore fight?"

"I think you'll find that's our job," said Costa, cracking his knuckles.

"Not any more."

Albert stepped out from the shadows, fixing the unwanted visitors with a glare.

"You still here Albert?" said Cohen, lifting his eyebrows. "Why don't you go and collect a few empty glasses? We are talking to Danny."

"Well I don't want to talk to you," Danny burst out. "It's like Albert said. You don't work with me no more, remember? You tore up my contract. We don't need you."

Cohen raised his hands. "Look," he said, "we don't want to throw any spanners in the works. We just want you to be happy, Danny. We want to help promote the fight, be involved."

"I am happy," said Danny. "Happy with you two out of my life."

"Off you go," said Albert, ushering Costa and Cohen towards the door. "If you ask nicely, I'll see if I can get you a couple of tickets for the fight."

Costa shot out a fist and grabbed Albert by his shirt collar. Danny moved forward to help, but Albert just smiled and sniffed the air.

"You been eating garlic, Tommy?" he asked.

"Come on Tommy," said Cohen sourly. "Let's get out of this dump."

"As my mum always said," Albert observed as the promoters left the room, "good riddance to bad rubbish."

Over the coming weeks, arrangements were firmed and the date and venue for the big fight was set. It would take place on October the first at the Wembley Arena: a big venue for a much-anticipated fight.

Harry Baldock had been worth his weight in gold and opened many doors for Albert. Albert had put him on a promise for a handsome back-hander for all his help and, of course, a couple of ringside tickets for the fight.

After weeks of hard training and many press interviews Danny was ready. Tickets had gone even better than expected, ensuring a very big turn-out on the night.

Towards the end of September, there were queues in the streets around Wembley Arena as fight fans waited to witness the historic rematch weigh-in. Danny and his team drove carefully to the venue through crowds of well wishers and not-so-well wishers. Livermore's following was stronger than ever since winning the title, and plenty of fans believed that he was going to retain the title without any problems.

"Looks like the whole world knows about this fight," Danny remarked nervously, gazing out of the car window at the throng.

"Just concentrate Danny, and make sure you retain your dignity if you're provoked," Albert advised.

Lenny made it through the crowds and drove Danny and his team round to the back of the venue. Standing at the open door, flanked by security, were two familiar faces.

"What are Costa and Cohen doing here?" said Danny warily.

"I don't know," growled Albert, getting out of the car. "But I intend to find out."

Danny, Lenny and Patsy waited and watched as Albert strode up to the two promoters. Hostile gestures and words were exchanged. After a few minutes, Albert returned to the car, fighting through a gaggle of fans looking for Danny's autograph.

"You will never believe it," he said. "They've only gone and muscled their way in to Livermore's camp!"

"Are you serious?" Lenny demanded.

Albert nodded. "And, I quote, they said: 'We thought we would just say hello to Danny before he goes to intensive care after the fight.' Cheeky bastards."

Danny felt a strange mixture of anger and relief. He had been concerned for Albert's welfare, alone in his flat with two formidable enemies in the shape of Costa and Cohen, worrying that he'd started a vicious vendetta. But it looked like his worries were unfounded. Costa and Cohen appeared to have jumped ship, and wanted revenge in a more civilised manner. They wanted Livermore to knock Danny into kingdom come on their behalf. If Danny needed any more motivation for the fight, he certainly had it now.

"So," Albert continued, "not only can you beat Livermore, but you can now beat those two tosspots at the same time!"

"Happy days," murmured Lenny.

Harry Baldock was waiting outside Danny's allocated room. With a swift spot of shadow-boxing he greeted the team.

"Albert," Harry said in a voice like a street-market trader as he slapped Albert on the back. "How about you and me getting on the card and showing 'em how it's done?"

"I don't think I can remember how it's done," Albert said humorously. "Listen Harry, thanks for your help. I appreciate it."

"No problem," Harry replied. He winked at Danny. "As long as you win, son. I've put a few bob on it."

Danny laughed. "How can I lose with this lot in tow?"

He stripped down to his claret and blue shorts in the changing room. As Albert handed Danny his dressing gown, they could hear the excited buzz of the crowd in the hall.

"Here you are son," said Albert. "Put this round your neck."

In a slightly ceremonial moment, Albert hung Tommy's medal for bravery around Danny's neck. "There you go," he said, his voice charged with emotion. "Now you're invincible."

They made their way to the stage in a relatively low-key way as cheers and jeers echoed through the hall. Livermore's entrance was anything but low key, and accompanied by the earsplitting James Brown number *I Got You (I Feel Good)*. Livermore was flanked by a dozen or so security men, trainers, cut men and, walking by his side, Costa and Cohen. All and sundry were doing their best to out-physique Danny and his team.

"Look at them, bathing in Livermore's reflected glory," Albert muttered, clenching his fists as the hall went wild. "I could punch their lights out."

"That would only lower us to their level," Danny pointed out. "Self-control, Albert, remember? It's all about self-control."

Danny met Livermore in the centre of the ring. The fighter's attitude seemed to have changed since they'd last met. Previously, there'd been a dignity and sportsman-like quality to the man that Danny had warmed to. Now he seemed full of himself, arrogant and hostile. If looks could kill, Danny and his team were already dead.

The officials began the weigh-in. As the challenger, Danny was summoned first. Taking off his dressing gown and his father's cherished medal, he handed them to Albert.

"I'm gonna show 'em, Albert," he said.

Walking to the scales, he could feel the hostile stares from Costa and Cohen burning through him. He made the weight limit with only a pound to spare.

Livermore made the weight with two pounds to spare. To everybody's surprise, he took the microphone from the Master of Ceremonies.

"This clown is not worthy of even being in the ring with

me," Livermore shouted, spittle flying. "He got lucky last time: I didn't kill him. But this time I will show no mercy!"

"You're going down!" shouted Costa as the hall erupted.

Without taking his eyes off Danny, Cohen lifted Livermore's arm. "You might as well throw the towel in now, Albert, you joker," Cohen taunted. "This champ is a different class."

"Say goodbye to your family, tosser!" Costa shouted. "You won't be seeing them after Saturday!"

Mention of his family made Danny see red. This time it was Albert who stepped in, turning Danny's head away from the three tormentors.

"Danny, listen to me," he said. "It's like you said. We can't sink to their level. The truth is, we're bigger than them and they're frightened of you. This is just a front 'cos they're scared of ya. Don't rise to it."

"Bastards," Danny raged, trying to twist away from Albert's grip.

Albert held him firmly. "Smile," he said.

"What?"

"Just smile. It'll spook them."

Danny forced a smile. Albert smiled too. Cohen and Costa looked taken aback. As for the crowd, they loved it. The ones that had been talking big were suddenly looking small.

More senseless rantings accompanied Danny and his team as they made their way off stage. Danny started enjoying himself, smiling back and waving.

"Thank you, Wembley Arena!" Albert shouted, blowing kisses. "We love you!"

Danny sensed the crowd sliding his way. All the fans who had been neutral before the weigh-in started shouting his name. Reaching the changing room, they could still hear the chants of "Danny! Danny!" echoing around the hall.

"I think we won that one, don't you Danny?" said Albert.

Danny grinned at him. "I think we did Albert, I think we did."

"Roll on Saturday," said Albert.

"Can't wait," said Danny.

CHAPTER TWENTY-THREE

FOR the night before the fight, Albert suggested that they stay at a hotel near the venue in Wembley. A good night's sleep for Danny would be better served away from his mum's. So Lenny, along with their overnight bags, dropped Albert and Danny at the hotel.

Albert's hotel room looked and felt like a palace. It even had a TV. He especially like the electric teamaker and trouser press. Sitting back in a modern comfortable chair and looking around, he thought how different the room was to his little flat. Albert had never had money and was suspicious of luxury and wealth, but sitting there, in the lap of luxury, he thought he could get used to it.

He turned on the television. Pictures flashed past his eyes, but he had no interest in what he was watching. His mind was on the fight. Livermore was a dangerous fighter, and having Costa and Cohen in his corner made him doubly so.

Albert wondered what tricks they were going to pull. No doubt they had plied their new boy with pills and whatever else they could conjure up, filling his head with hatred.

They had turned this from a boxing match into a vendetta. He felt nervous thinking about it, the identical feeling he used to feel before he went into box back in his glory days. Back then, he'd been able to do something about it. He'd been the fighter after all, in control of his destiny. Now, Danny was the fighter and Albert was on the sidelines. Destiny lay in his grandson's hands and Albert could only watch.

He thought about Tommy for a while, and how he used to get nervous watching him playing football for the school. The nerves came second only to the pride Albert had felt whenever Tommy did something special or scored a goal. This was a lot bigger. It felt like Tommy was in this fight too, right alongside his son.

With a head full of thoughts, Albert went to bed and tried to sleep.

Unlike Albert, Danny hadn't taken much notice of his swanky surroundings. The first thing he'd done was call Wendy to check that all was well.

"How are you feeling?" Wendy asked. "Have you got those butterflies you get?"

They felt more like fruit bats batting their wings than butterflies, Danny thought. "No, I'm feeling good," he lied. "It's a nice hotel. Is Ruby all right?"

"She's fine. She's still up, actually. Do you want to talk to her?"

"Hello Daddy," Ruby piped down the receiver. "When are you coming to see me?"

These innocent words choked Danny up. Ruby didn't know about the fight, Wendy hadn't told her.

"As soon as I can," he said gently.

"Bye bye," said Ruby.

"Sorry, Danny," said Wendy. "She's had enough, she wants to get down. We'll be thinking of you. Night."

"I love you," said Danny.

"We love you too," said Wendy.

Danny put down the phone and sat on the edge of the bed, feeling comforted. It had been a painful journey to convince Wendy that he was the old Danny again, the man she'd loved and married, but he'd done it, kicking the drugs and getting his life back with his family. He remembered Costa shouting "Say goodbye to your family!" at the weigh-in. He was never going to let them go again.

His resolve hardened. He was ready. Ready and able for whatever Livermore planned to throw at him.

He went to bed and turned off the light.

Fire bells were ringing. Danny woke up with a start. He could hear a voice in the corridor shouting: "Please leave your rooms immediately and make your way to the car park! Do not use the lifts!" over and over in a chilling machine-like voice.

Grabbing his dressing gown, Danny made his way out through the panic, to the rain-drenched hotel car park. He was confronted by women in curlers, overweight men in underpants, shivering children and Albert fully dressed.

"What's this all about?" Danny said, yawning. "I was asleep."

"Bloody fire alarms went off," Albert replied.

"You got dressed," said Danny, noticing.

"Fire or no fire, I'm not standing out here in me Y-fronts," said a defiant Albert. "I've got your dad's medal."

Danny rubbed his eyes. "Right. Good. Thanks."

The manager minced out of reception, huddled under an umbrella.

"My apologies, ladies and gentlemen," he said. "The fire brigade have now checked the building and it is safe to go back to your rooms. It appears to have been a false alarm. It seems we have some jokers in our midst."

There was a communal groan.

"It's three o'clock in the morning!" grumbled a guest. "Some joke."

"I bet I know who did this," said Albert as they walked back to their rooms.

"Livermore's lot?" Danny guessed.

"Costa and bloody Cohen," said Albert. "Try to get some sleep, Danny, and call me when you wake up. Night. Or morning, I should say."

In spite of the rude awakening Danny did get some sleep. All those interrupted early nights with Ruby in the early days had taught him to fall back to sleep at the drop of a hat. Waking up at ten-thirty, he gave Albert a call.

"They've finished doing breakfast," Albert told him, "but

you can order something from room service. Have steak and eggs. Good for ya."

"I'll see what they've got. What time we meeting up?"

"I've got us a late check-out. After last night's bleedin' fiasco, they should let us stay for free! Let's meet in the reception about four, then we can get to the hall in good time to warm up and get sorted."

Danny was struck by Albert's professionalism. "OK boss. See you at four," he confirmed.

Danny did as Albert said and ordered steak and eggs with some fruit salad to follow.

Though Danny seemed reasonably relaxed, Albert wasn't. He had not slept at all and had spent a good deal of the night sitting in his damp clothes on a chair in his room, his mind full of those strange thoughts that seem to overtake you in the early hours when you feel that you are the only one awake in the entire world, and small problems seem so much bigger.

Memories of Tommy before he had gone into the army floated by with a clarity they had not had for years. Albert had buried them in his subconscious, but because of the gravity of his grandson's impending battle, they had resurfaced.

He thought about Tommy's escapades and adventures. There had been that time when Tommy had nicked his tobacco, smoked it all and finished up a shade of green; the time he'd borrowed Albert's James Captain motorbike without permission aged just fourteen, and been stopped by a copper for speeding on the A13. Albert remembered picking him up from Barking Police Station and giving him a clip round the ear, all the time knowing that he probably would have done the same thing if his dad had had a motorbike.

He remembered Tommy bringing Danny's mother Rosie home for the first time: his first and only girlfriend. Albert hadn't been sure she was right for Tommy even then, but had kept his mouth shut. He remembered too how proud he'd been when he first saw Tommy dressed in his army uniform, and the deadening pain he'd felt when he was told of Tommy's death; the hurt, when the pregnant Rosie had betrayed Tommy and his memory.

Then, in his mind, from the blackest of places, a light broke through. Albert thought of his newly found grandson and great-granddaughter and how destiny had brought them together. Like an angel, Ruby helped calm the storm in his mind, like a rainbow after a downpour.

Albert had an early breakfast and walked around the nearby streets. Time was dragging, and Albert was flagging too. Not only was he tired from a restless night, but the aches and pains from the accident were playing up. Looking for a sit-down and a rest, he came across a park gate, then a park, and finally a bench overlooking a boating lake. Laying his walking stick by his side, he sat down.

How strange that everything here was nice and tranquil, and still would be tonight whilst Danny and Livermore did battle in front of thousands of spectators baying for blood. Looking at the lake took him back to meeting young

Danny in those early days. He wondered how fate could be so cruel and yet so kind, taking his son but giving him his grandson instead. He thought about the emotional journey they had been on together. The climax could be just hours away.

Albert believed there was something – a power, a God – although he hadn't formed a firm opinion. He never prayed; he'd stopped doing that when Tommy was killed. But here on the park bench, he prayed.

"Dear God. I know we don't talk much, but I wanted to thank you for finding my Danny. Thank you for everything, for little Ruby, for all of it. Please, dear God, take care of Danny tonight, keep him safe. Thank you. Amen."

Back at the hotel, Danny had started pacing up and down in his room. He looked out of his bedroom window at the majestic Wembley Stadium standing so stately in the distance, the scene of so many sporting triumphs and defeats: a theatre of dreams and nightmares.

He could glimpse the arena beside the stadium. Already there were early spectators and a few ticket touts outside, no doubt flogging their tickets at inflated prices. What would tonight bring, triumph or defeat?

"Don't even think about losing," Albert had said.

Danny checked his watch for the tenth time. Ten minutes to go before they had to leave. His bag was packed and sitting by the door. It had been ready for hours. So had Danny.

He needed to stop thinking of what might be and what

might not. It was time to get going. Time to get this battle on. He had prepared for months, and this was his moment.

Along with Albert, Patsy and Lenny, Danny had studied endless films of Livermore. He knew what he was facing and how tough it was going to be.

He left his room and walked through the hotel corridor to the lift. More of Albert's words came into his head. *Just believe you're the best, and there's a good chance you will be the best.*

Patsy and Lenny were already waiting at reception.

Putting his arm around Danny's shoulder, Patsy said: "Can we have a word?"

Danny let the big Irishman lead him to a quieter corner.

"Danny," Patsy began. "I want you to know how pleased I am that Albert is back. I want to apologise if my loyalty to you and Albert has ever been in question. My priority has always been to see you reach your potential, and cosying up to Costa and Cohen was wrong. I'm sorry."

There was truth and real regret in Patsy's eyes. For Patsy, this was a big step. To show any emotion at all was unusual.

Danny shook Patsy's hand. "Water under the bridge, Patsy," he said. "Let's get this fight on, eh?"

Patsy looked to be on the verge of tears. "You bet," he said. "And you know what? You're gonna win."

"How can you charge people top whack for a night's kip when a fire alarm wakes 'em up and you herd everyone into a car park in the pissing rain for half the night?"

Danny and Patsy both looked round at the hotel reception desk. Albert was arguing his case for a reduction to the bill. The hotel manager was looking nervous and awkward as Albert's voice rose in volume.

"And don't give me any of that bollocks about company policy, you hear?"

"We're terribly sorry sir," said the manager. "In the circumstances, and after due consideration, we would be prepared to offer you a discount."

Danny watched as money changed hands. Deal done, Albert headed their way, looking pleased with himself.

"It's the principle of the thing," he said with a sharp nod. "Now, let's go and knock this Livermore bloke out."

With purpose and a collective energy, Danny and his team made their way to the venue. Dropping their bags in their allocated room, they decided to take a look at the battleground while it was still empty.

Danny whistled, looking around the cavernous space. "Look at the size of this place!" he said.

"It's big," Albert agreed with a smile. "And every ticket sold out. In just a few hours, the place will be packed."

They stood around for a while and watched the Wembley Arena staff place chairs and vacuum with a vengeance.

"Right," said Patsy at last. "Let's go back to the room and do some warming up. Time to get focused, and then relax."

Back in the changing room, Danny hit some pads and did some gentle skipping to loosen up while Albert listened to the radio for the football results. In the nineteen sixty-seven season, West Ham were in their usual mid-table position. As Danny lay on the massage table being pummelled by Patsy, Albert leaped to his feet.

"Yes!" he cried, waving his walking stick and doing a jig that resembled something out of *Mary Poppins*. "Five nil to the Cockney boys! What about that, Danny boy? West Ham five, Newcastle nil! Now that's a good omen if ever there was one."

Danny tried to smile, wincing at Patsy's less than gentle massage and managing a strangled: "Come on you Irons."

Albert grinned. "I'm just gonna take a look at how it's going in the hall."

Albert walked into the hall and stood by the ringside, looking up at row upon row of empty seats.

"The calm before the storm," he said to himself. "Come on Danny."

Three men stood in a huddle on the far side of the room, having a whispered conversation. Moving a bit closer, Albert saw it was Costa and Cohen and the referee for the night, Stan Webster.

Knowing Costa and Cohen and their history of dirty tricks, it seemed obvious to Albert that Webster was looking a little too friendly with the two promoters. Albert had always thought that Webster was a straight and honest referee, but now he wasn't so sure. He thought about confronting them, but decided against it.

A trickle of fight fans was beginning to take their seats. Albert headed back to the changing room, where Danny was recovering from Patsy's over-zealous pummelling.

"How's it looking, Albert?" he asked.

Albert pushed the image of Costa, Cohen and Webster to the back of his mind. Mentioning it to Danny might dent the boy's confidence. "All good mate," he replied. "They're just starting the support bouts. I reckon we've got about an hour and a half to the fight."

"Right, good," said Danny. "I just wanna get going."

"Yeah, I know. Won't be long now. How you feeling?"

"Really nervous," Danny admitted.

Albert could see the child in his grandson's eyes. The look reminded him of Tommy, whenever Tommy had been scared of being told off by his dad.

"That's all right," Albert soothed. "Nerves ain't a bad thing. You don't wanna be too cocky. Nerves can put you on your guard."

He sat down next to Danny. "You have every right to that title. You have worked for it. You came out of a dark place, and you deserve it. Just do what we have worked on a thousand times, and you will be the new British title holder, I promise."

Danny nodded. "I'm glad you're here," he said.

Albert put his arm round his grandson. It was a special moment.

"I love you Danny," he said.

"I love you too, Grandad."

Patsy and Lenny came back in the room.

"They reckon about half an hour, then it's us," said Patsy.

"That Livermore must be quaking in his boots," said Lenny, ever the optimist.

Harry Baldock put his head round the door.

"Go well tonight, son," he shouted to Danny. Then nodding at Albert, "Albert, can I have a quick word?"

Albert followed Harry outside. Looking around to make sure he was not overheard, Harry spoke in whispers.

"Albert, I thought I better tell you that I think Costa and Cohen have got to one of the judges, given him a backhander."

"How d'ya know?"

"A friend of mine, a bookie, told me."

Albert wasn't surprised by Harry's tip-off.

"I think they've got the ref in their pocket too, the bastards," he said with feeling.

Harry nodded. "Just thought I'd tell ya. But whatever happens, the boy's gonna make good money tonight. It's packed out there."

"Thanks for letting me know, Harry," said Albert, rubbing his chin. "I appreciate it."

Back into the room, Patsy was bandaging Danny's hands.

"What did Harry want?" said Danny, looking round.

Albert thought on his feet. "He was just saying how well the tickets have gone and that."

"You got Dad's medal?"

"Here in my pocket Danny," said Albert. "Safe and sound."

"Ready when you are," said someone in a bow tie and dinner suit who had poked his head round the door.

Patsy firmly tied Danny's boxing gloves. Albert draped an English flag over Danny's shoulders and hung Danny's father's medal around his neck. To the music of *Land of Hope and Glory*, Danny and his team entered the auditorium.

The noise from the crowd almost lifted the roof off the arena. Shadow-boxing his way to the waiting ring, Danny already felt like a champion.

Albert eyed up the referee and looked over at the three judges. Which one of them had Harry tipped him off about? Which one of them was in Costa and Cohen's pocket?

The crowd hit another crescendo as Livermore and his entourage made their entrance. Danny watched the procession enter. There seemed to be fifteen or so of them, and right in the heart of the throng of the Livermore mob were Costa and Cohen.

The anticipation in the arena had grown to fever pitch as the two fighters were summoned by the referee to the centre of the ring.

"Ten four-minute rounds, no holding, break when I say break," the referee barked.

Danny and Livermore stared at each other, searching for weakness, looking for fear. There was nothing child-like in Danny's eyes now. Just pure determination.

Livermore looked at the medal around Danny's neck and laughed.

"Putting your trust in a dead man?" he mocked.

Danny lunged at him, but Webster the referee stepped in.

"Back to your corners, gentlemen," he ordered.

Danny was seething as Albert took off the medal and Patsy handed over his gum shield.

"He's trying to wind you up," Albert warned. "Just keep cool and box. Don't get into a street fight. Box clever and keep your distance."

"Seconds out!"

Amid the roar of the expectant crowd, the bell sounded for round one.

The two fighters moved around the ring just as they had at their previous meeting. A few punches were thrown. Both fighters were feeling each other out, sizing one another up. As the bell went for the end of the round, Danny sat down in his corner. He had hardly broken sweat.

"That's good," said Patsy. "Let's see if we can step it up this round."

"Jab and move," advised Albert. "Keep him guessing."

The bell rang out for round two as the crowd roared, looking for more action this time. They got it.

Danny was putting some very good combinations together. He jabbed and followed up with some powerful body shots. Livermore's technique wasn't as strong as Danny's, but he was a stronger puncher, proved by how many of his wins had been knock-outs.

Danny got one of those big punches towards the end of the round. Livermore landed a brutal left hook to the side of Danny's head that weakened Danny's legs, but Danny managed to retreat, dance his way out of trouble and recover.

"Lucky punch Danny, that's all," Albert told him at the

end of the round. "Keep your distance. You won that round on points, same again."

Round three began. The crowd were on their feet, anticipating a knock-out from the reigning champion. But Danny back-pedalled and kept his distance, frustrating Livermore into throwing venomous punches which, as they flew by Danny's head, were heartily cheered by the crowd. Livermore hissed insults as Danny parried his blows. At the end of the round, Danny headed back to his corner, full of purpose.

"That's it," Patsy encouraged, giving Danny water. "Now you keep that going. Frustrate him!"

Danny spat the water into a waiting bowl and turned to Albert.

"How am I doing, Grandad? He's taking the piss, he's calling me Daddy's boy."

"You're doing just great, Danny," Albert said. "Ignore him, you're going well."

The bell went for round four. In a quick exchange of punches, Livermore's head clearly butted Danny.

"Ref!" Albert shouted.

"Cheat!" shouted eight thousand spectators.

Danny looked to Webster, but was ignored.

The round went on. Livermore targeted Danny's face, hitting that area whenever he could, attacking a cut that was beginning to open on Danny's forehead with a vengeance. Through the blood, Danny glimpsed Costa and Cohen sitting at the ringside. Costa gave him a knowing smile. The smile of a stitch-up.

Danny was now struggling to see. Albert jumped in the

338

ring at the end of the round and led him back to his corner, where Patsy frantically patched Danny up.

Webster came over. "Still up for the fight?"

Through the fog in his head, Danny got the impression the referee wanted to end the fight.

"He's all right," said Albert coolly. "Just a small cut."

"You heard the man," said Patsy.

"What's going on with him?" asked Danny groggily as Webster backed off. He was struggling to stay focused.

Albert slapped his face. "Listen to me," he said, holding Danny's chin. "I'm gonna tell you something important."

"Yeah?" Danny slurred.

"The odds here are against you. You need to go out there in this round and knock him out. Spark out. Got it?"

Something sharpened in Danny's head. The referee, Costa and Cohen. He looked at Albert, took his father's medal hanging round Albert's neck and kissed it.

The bell for round five rang out.

Danny was first to his feet. His change of tactics clearly unsettled Livermore. From being the aggressor, the title holder was now being pushed back as Danny came forward. In a flurry of punches that got the crowd not only to their feet but standing on their chairs, Danny had Livermore cornered and in serious trouble.

"Break!" Webster called.

No one had been holding. Most of the crowd began booing, sensing either bad decisions or something more sinister.

Moving back to the centre of the ring, Livermore came at

Danny like a demented windmill. With a nifty piece of footwork, Danny sidestepped him and hit him with a massive right upper cut to the side of his head. The punch had so much force that it not only hurt Danny's wrist, but sent the defending champion to the canvas.

The place exploded.

Livermore stayed down for a count of seven. Getting back to his feet, he was helped by the over-fussy "Wipe your gloves!" instruction from referee Webster, which helped delay proceedings. Livermore charged at Danny, right into a combination of punches that lifted him into the air and brought him crashing down on the bloodied canvas once again.

Before the count could begin, the bell went for the end of round five.

There was more booing from the crowd. Livermore's team got him back to his corner and were doing their best to revive him.

Back in his own corner, Danny's wrist was agony.

"Good boy," enthused Albert. "Leave nothing to chance."

"My right wrist is hurting bad," Danny mumbled.

"Nearly there," said Patsy.

"He's on his knees," said Albert. "Do it early."

The bell rang for round six as the fighters came out. Webster took Livermore back to his corner to attend to a stray bandage from one of his gloves. Danny sensed another delaying tactic to give Livermore a chance to recover. The crowd sensed the same thing, to judge by the boos and jeers.

Livermore came out again. He seemed to have renewed

energy, and attempted to put Danny under pressure. His illegal, below-the-belt punches were ignored by Webster, but Danny was given a public warning for holding.

The boos were growing louder. This seem to pump up Livermore, who came at Danny with renewed force. The flurry of his desperate punches was short-lived. Fighting through the pain of his wrist, Danny unleashed another barrage of punches that sent Livermore's gum shield into the crowd and Livermore down to his knees. This time, he was definitely out.

Webster had no alternative but to count.

"... seven, eight, nine... ten!"

Livermore still lay flat on the floor. It was over.

There was mayhem. Albert almost somersaulted into the ring, hugging Danny and lifting him up.

"You did it!" he wept. "You did it, boy! Here, take your dad's medal... take it. Your dad would be so proud. Well done, Danny!"

His face bloodied and bruised, Danny looked deep into Albert's eyes as his grandfather draped his dad's medal around his neck.

"We did it, Grandad," he said in wonder, feeling as if he and Albert were the only two people in a crowded hall. "You, me and Dad. We did it."

Lenny had watched the fight from the ringside, living every punch. He was beside himself with joy. A barrage of security men attempted to calm him down, but nobody was going to stop Lenny celebrating this wonderful moment.

"This is my family!" he shouted. "This is their night! This is *my* night! Hallelujah!"

He and a jubilant Patsy lifted the new British champion on to their shoulders and paraded Danny around the ring.

"Hallelujah!" Lenny shouted again, tears pouring down his face.

Albert couldn't help a sarcastic smile and a wave of his walking stick at Costa and Cohen, standing motionless by the ringside. Tumultuous cheers rang out on all sides. Cameras flashed. History had been made.

Albert's faded glory had been restored to a shining glory.

As Lenny and Patsy paraded Danny shoulder-high around the ring, Albert looked up to the sky. With tears of joy in his eyes, he whispered: "I know you're looking down, Tommy. He did it, Tommy son. Your boy's a champion. A British champion."

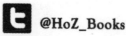